J. J. Davies

History and Business Directory of Madison County, Iowa

Containing a complete history of the county - together with a description of its

natural resources, and sketches of its public buildings, schools, churches,

prominent citizens

J. J. Davies

History and Business Directory of Madison County, Iowa
Containing a complete history of the county - together with a description of its natural resources, and sketches of its public buildings, schools, churches, prominent citizens

ISBN/EAN: 9783337264093

Printed in Europe, USA, Canada, Australia, Japan

Cover: Foto ©Andreas Hilbeck / pixelio.de

More available books at **www.hansebooks.com**

MADISON COUNTY COURT HOUSE, WINTERSET, IOWA.

HISTORY

AND

Business Directory

OF

MADISON COUNTY,

IOWA.

CONTAINING

A COMPLETE HISTORY OF THE COUNTY;

TOGETHER WITH A DESCRIPTION OF ITS NATURAL RESOURCES, AND
SKETCHES OF ITS PUBLIC BUILDINGS, SCHOOLS, CHURCHES,
PROMINENT CITIZENS, &c., &c., &c.

BY J. J. DAVIES.

DES MOINES:
MILLS & CO. PRINTERS AND PUBLISHERS, "REGISTER BUILDING."
1869.

PREFACE.

We lay the present book before our patrons, believing that our first efforts to produce a History and Business Directory of Madison County will prove to be a valuable advertising medium for the county, and will be fully appreciated by those who have the best interests of the County at heart.

The Historical and Descriptive sketches of the County and the several Townships, will, no doubt, be read with interest; containing as they do, plain, simple facts, which neither time nor labor have been spared in procuring. In this connection we are under many obligations to friends and old settlers in the county, for the information and assistance they have given us.

We have endeavored to show the natural advantages and resources of the County just as they are, and believe we have given a faithful description of the soil, the stone, the streams, the timber and the natural wealth of the County; and we have also endeavored to give a correct description of the towns, villages, churches, schools, public buildings, and, in brief, a full report of what Madison County is at the present time—making it a useful book to persons abroad who may desire information about this portion of Iowa.

We have tried to perform our work accurately and well; but if errors should appear they are such as our foresight could not have prevented. The old settlers, of whom we obtained most of the historical facts and data, gave them mostly from memory; errors are, therefore, liable to occur, but in the main, the history, descriptions and items are reliable and true, as published.

We point with considerable pride to the work itself, and to the matter contained therein; also with satisfaction to its general appearance. There are, perhaps, some omissions and other faults, which we hope our patrons will pass graciously by, believing that we have endeavored to do ample justice to the County and her citizens.

To the advertising patrons of the book, we return our best wishes; we feel satisfied that the benefit that will ultimately accrue to each will richly repay them many times its cost by an increase in trade.

We trust that our efforts to please our patrons and the public will be kindly received and appreciated. To our obliging friends we tender our warmest thanks, for the assistance, respect and kindness shown us.

Respectfully,

J. J. DAVIES.

IOWA HISTORY.

The History of Iowa has never been written, with the exception of sketches which have appeared from time to time in the *Iowa Annals*. What a bright field and golden opportunity is presented here for the future historian. The past, present and future of the great State of Iowa, with her round million of intelligent, energetic, liberty-loving and God-fearing people; her thirty-five million acres of prairies, forests, hills and valleys; her mighty rivers and rich fertile soil; her inexhaustible stone quarries, coal, lead and iron mines, and other mineral wealth; and her great natural and acquired advantages,—all combine in themselves a theme which would require the pen of a Bancroft or Macauley to honor. It is hoped that some historian equal to the task, may soon be found, who will write a complete and faithful history of the "Gallant Young Hawkeye State."

In a work like this, purposing to contain a history of a county, a brief history of the State would, very naturally, be appropriate. We have found it difficult to obtain material from which to glean much of the early history of Iowa; but we will try and make good use of such information as may be at our command. For the following historical memoranda we are indebted to the reports of state officers:

The territory embraced in the State of Iowa was originally a part of the Louisiana purchase. Previous to the year 1763, and at the close of the "Old French War," the entire continent of North America was owned by France, Great Britain, Spain and Russia. In 1763 France parted with her share of the continent, and Spain obtained by cession the territory west of the Mississippi; and Great Britain retained possession of the Canadas and the region to the northward, which she had conquered during the war. On the 1st of October, 1800, by treaty of St. Idlefonso, Spain ceded back to France the territory of Louisiana. By treaty of April 30, 1803, France ceded it to the United States, in consideration of the sum of $11,250,000, and the liquidation of certain claims held by citizens of the United States against France, not exceeding in amount $3,750,000. By act of Congress approved March 31st, 1803, the President was authorized to take possession of the territory and provide for it a temporary government. By act of Congress approved

March 26, 1804, the newly acquired country was divided October 1st, 1804, into the Territory of "Orleans," (south of the thirty-third parallel north latitude) and the "District of Louisiana." The latter being placed under the authority of the officers of Indiana Territory. On the 4th of July, 1805, under act of Congress approved March 3, 1805, the "District of Louisiana" was organized into a territory of the same name, and it so remained until 1812. On the 30th of April, 1812, the Territory of Orleans became a State of the Union, under the name of "Louisiana," and on the first Monday in December, by virtue of an act approved June 4th, 1812, the Territory of Louisiana was re-organized, and called the "Territory of Missouri." By act of Congress approved March 2, 1819, and taking effect July 4th, the same year, "Arkansas Territory" was formed, comprising the present State of Arkansas and the territory to the westward. By a joint resolution, approved March 2d, 1821, the "State of Missouri" being a part of the territory of that name, was admitted into the Union. By act of Congress approved June 28, 1834, the territory "bounded on the east by the Mississippi River, on the south by the State of Missouri," &c, was made a part of the territory of Michigan. On the 3d day of July, 1836, "Wisconsin Territory" embracing within its limits the present States of Iowa, Minnesota and Wisconsin, was taken from that of Michigan, and given a separate government. *On the 3d day of July*, 1838, by virtue of an act of Congress, approved June 12, 1838, *the territory of Iowa was constituted*; including, in addition to the present State, the greater part of what is now Minnesota, and extending northward to the British line.

By act of Congress, approved March 3d, 1845, provision was made for the admission of Iowa into the Union, with boundaries extending on the north to the parallel of latitude passing through the mouth of the Mankato or Blue Earth river, and on the west only to 17° 30′ west from Washington, corresponding very nearly to the existing line between Ringgold and Union counties on the one hand, and Taylor and Adams on the other. The Constitutional Convention of 1844 had adopted much more extensive boundaries even than those of the present State, the northwestern line extending from the mouth of the Big Sioux or Calumet river direct to the St. Peter's river where the Watonwan river enters the same; thence down the main channel of said river to the main channel of the Mississippi river, and thence down the Mississippi, embracing within its parallel limits some of the richest portions of the present State of Minnesota. The reduction of these boundaries being quite distasteful to the people, the whole plan was rejected at a popular election.

In 1846 Congress proposed new boundary lines, which were

embodied in the Constitution adopted that year ; the State retaining
the Missouri slope, but submitting to a material reduction of its
pretensions on the north, its western line, however, being extended in
that direction to the Big Sioux river. The Constitution, with these
modified boundaries having been accepted by the people, the *State of
Iowa* was formally *admitted into the Union on the 28th day of December*,
1846, as the twenty-ninth State in the Confederacy.

For some of the following interesting items concerning the State,
we are indebted to our excellent Governor (Merrill) :

The State is settled mainly from Ohio, Indiana and Pennsylvania,
with a large admixture from New England. About one-sixth of the
entire population came from foreign countries. A people loving
liberty and order, and respecting and prizing the political, religious
and educational privileges of our State, is the natural result of the
aggregation of such material.

The first permanent settlement in the State was made in Lee
county, in the south-eastern part of the State, less than forty years
ago.

In 1836 the population of the State was   10,531.
"   1838   "   "   22,859.
"   1846   "   "   97,588.
"   1856   "   "   519,055.
"   1867   "   "   902,040.
And it is now estimated at   1,200,000.

And yet much more than two-thirds of the State is just as it came
from the hands of nature. From twenty to twenty-five millions of
prairie land have not been touched by the plow.

The soil of the State is of surpassing richness and affords an
abundant supply of all the necessaries and luxuries of life. The
character of the soil is thus described by that eminent Geologist,
Dr. James Hall, of New York :

" Upon the great prairies in Central Iowa, one may frequently
travel over a large extent of surface without seeing a single stone, not
even so much as the smallest pebble. In the swales and in some of
the bottom lands, especially in the southern part of the State, the rich
black vegetable mould is very deep, but on the prairie it is usually
from one to two feet. The subsoil is almost invariably a quite
argilaceous loam, and there is a gradual passage downward into a
material which, though containing sandy portions and occasional
pebbles, the argillaceous element greatly preponderates. "

The State is situated centrally in the Union, bounded east and west
by the two great rivers of North America. In extent, it is about 300
miles east and west, and a little more than 200 miles north and south ;

and its parallel of latitude is designated as 40° 31′ on the south, and
43° 30′ on the north. Its area is 55,045 square miles, nearly as great as
all England, much greater than that of Ireland, and nearly twice
as large as Scotland. Its surface is over 90 per cent prairie, nearly
all "rolling" or undulating, only a small part being what is
denominated "flat prairie;" and while there are no mountains
there is a constant succession of gentle elevations and depressions,
and along the Mississippi and Missouri rivers bold eminences and
picturesque valleys heighten the beauty of the scenery. The table
lands between the waters of the two great rivers attain, in the
northern part of the State, according to our State Geologian's
survey, an altitude of 1,400 feet above the level of the sea.

Among the many fine streams of the State are the Des Moines
river (only three hundred miles long); the Iowa, the Cedar, and
others, flow into the Mississippi; while numerous tributaries of
the Missouri drain the western counties. These streams are almost
invariably skirted with timber, some of them heavily wooded.
The timber consists of elm, black walnut, oak, linden, cottonwood,
blackberry, sycamore, poplar, ash and other varieties of forest
trees.

Coal is found in many parts of the State; it is being rapidly
developed and is a source of vast wealth. In 1866 our State census
shows there were 99,320 tons taken out, against 66,664 in 1864. Peat
has also been discovered within a few years in many parts of the
State in quantities which promise an abundant supply of fuel.

A few statistics of the crops of 1866 and other years will give
some idea of the resources of the State:

Wheat is grown in every county in the State, and no part seems
unfavorable to its production in generous quantities. Spring wheat
is the variety mostly raised. As early as 1850, Iowa was the
fifteenth of the States of the Union, in the production of this
valuable cereal, and in 1860 it stood eighth; while in the former
it was the twenty-fifth in the number of acres improved, and
in 1860 was fifteenth. The following are the figures of the production
of wheat for a series of years:

1864	15,021,149	bushels.
1866	14,635,520	bushels.
1867 (estimated)	20,000,000	bushels.
1868	25,000,000	bushels.

The next federal census (1870) will probably show a yield in
the State of at least 35,000,000 bushels of wheat. Such is the
opinion of intelligent agriculturists.

In 1849 Iowa stood eighteenth in the States in the production of corn, coming next to the old State of New Jersey at that early day. In 1869 it was the seventh, raising about 5 per cent of all the corn raised in the country, and now ranking next to Tennessee; the other States standing above her being in their order Illinois, Missouri, Ohio, Indiana and Kentucky. The census of 1870 will probably place Iowa *third* in the order of the States in the production of this grain. We give the figures for a series of years:

1864..	48,471,123 bushels.
1866..	56,928,938 bushels.
1867......(estimated)	74,000,000 bushels.
1868..	90,000,000 bushels.

It is estimated that in 1870 the yield will exceed one hundred and twenty million bushels. The following table gives the figures of other crops for the years 1862, 1864 and 1866:

	1862	1864	1866
Oats, bushels...	7,582,060	15,928,777	15,860,449
Rye, bushels..	474,675	662,388	492,841
Barley, bushels..	385,067	959,696	1,197,729
Potatoes, bushels...	2,362,918	2,760,811	2,666,678
Sweet potatoes, bushels.................................	37,498	26,222	5,380
Onions, no report...		207,638	213,285
Sorghum, gallons...	3,012,393	1,443,605	2,004,507
Hay, tons..	1,632,553	1,002,166	1,409,851
Butter, pounds...	15,675,500	14,538,216	19,192,727
Cheese, pounds..	902,701	1,000,738	1,403,864
Grapes, pounds..	291,755	399,499	549,179

Stock-raising and wool-growing are profitable pursuits, and all kinds of live stock thrive finely in all parts of the State, no contagious or epidemic diseases having ever prevailed.

The following are the statistics of live stock for several years:

	1863	1865	1867
Horses	275,697	316,702	425,055
Mules and Asses..	12,022	14,302	22,687
Milch cows..	292,025	310,187	326,559
Work oxen..	56,596	37,707	27,246
Sheep...	599,369	1,450,787	1,708,958
Swine...	1,743,865	1,037,117	1,629,089
Other cattle	548,629	553,977	692,564
Pounds wool shorn...	1,429,209	2,813,020	5,323,385

According to the last report of the Department of Agriculture, giving the average yield per acre of the principal crops of the United States for 1868, it would seem that nature has decided that Iowa should be *the* Corn State of the Union,—the figures prove it. On corn, the average yield per bushel in Iowa—the highest in the list—was 37 bushels per acre; Illinois was 34,2; and in Indiana it was 34. This speaks volumes, and is a great honor to the raw, unmanured prairies of Iowa. Let the millions who are looking for new homes, consider this fact; and let them also bear in mind that Iowa is yet but a young State, and when her bounteous soil is cultivated to a higher degree, she will wear the envied crown of "the best Agricultural State in the Union."

In wheat, the average yield of Iowa is reported at 14 bushels; an average excelled only by Vermont, Nebraska, Minnesota and Kansas, —Vermont leading at 16.

On potatoes, Iowa is averaged at 96 bushels per acre. On sorghum, the yield is placed at 117 gallons per acre. On other crops, the State is also highly complimented by the official figures.

The State of Iowa has received and now controls, for the purpose of aiding the common schools of the State, an aggregate of 1,548,487.97 acres of land, besides a fund already acquired from sales of land and other sources, the magnificent sum of $2,557,107.10; which places our Common School system on a grander scale than even that of Massachusetts; 208,430,30 acres of land have also been appropriated for the benefit of the Agricultural College; and 92,030,37 acres toward a State University fund. For railroad purposes, 3,270,702 acres have already been certified, while the estimated amounts inuring to the State for the different roads under the laws of 1856, 1862 and 1864, will increase the amount by as much more.

There are no less than five great railroad routes across the State. They are as follows: The Northwestern railroad, extending from Clinton across the State to Council Bluffs; already completed. The Chicago, Rock Island and Pacific railroad from Davenport to Council Bluffs; this road was completed through in May, 1869. The Dubuque & Sioux City railroad, extending from Dubuque to Sioux City, will be completed through in 1870. The Des Moines Valley railroad, from Keokuk to Sioux City, and the Burlington and Missouri River railroad from Burlington to Council Bluffs, will be completed through in September, 1869. There are various other roads in process of construction, constructed and projected. Over 1,500 miles of road are already completed, and six hundred miles are under contract, and the number of miles in contemplation will bring the inhabitants of almost every county within reasonable distance of railway communication.

Among the benevolent institutions which the State has liberally provided for, are the Hospital for the Insane, at Mt. Pleasant, which, for extent and completeness, is said to be second to none in the United States. The Blind Asylum, at Vinton, is also a magnificent edifice and is said to be the best managed of any institution of the kind in the west. The Asylum for the Deaf and Dumb will be erected at Council Bluffs during the year 1869.

And another Hospital for the Insane is already in process of erection at Independence, Buchanan county. The State has also made bountiful provision for the orphans of soldiers who died in defense of their country during the late war; and three Orphans' Homes have been established, and are located respectively at Davenport, Glenwood, Mills county, and at Cedar Falls. The State Prison is located at Fort Madison. The Agricultural College is located in Story county, and has connected with it a Model Farm in successful operation. The State University is located at Iowa City. A Reform School for juvenile offenders, has been established at Salem in Henry county. There are other benevolent institutions amply provided for by the State; but sufficient has been cited to show that the State is not behind her sister States in her liberal provisions for her educational and charitable institutions.

Centrally situated as the State is, midway between the Atlantic and Pacific oceans, bounded by the two mighty rivers of the continent, traversed by the great Pacific railroad, and destined to become the very garden spot from whence the teeming millions of non-producing inhabitants—who are bound sooner or later to develope the mineral resources of Colorado, Montana, Idaho, Utah, and the vast mineral regions of the Rocky Mountain country—must obtain their food; and they must rely mainly upon this garden for their cereals and for their vegetables. And the cattle which are fattened upon our prairies; and the cloth made by our manufacturies from the wool shorn from our sheep; and the flour made by our mills from the wheat grown in our rich soil; and our agricultural products of every kind, will find in those unproductive plains the best market the world ever saw. The hay from our prairies will also be bundled up into bales and sent there; and stone from our inexhaustible quarries will be transplanted to build their ranches, villages and cities. Who then can estimate the future wealth and greatness of this favored State?

There is no State in the Union which can offer the emigrant so many advantages, such liberal inducements, alluring attractions or brighter prospects than the "Hawkeye State." It offers health, wealth and happiness. It has everything to offer that the heart of man could wish or fancy dictate. It is a land literally flowing with milk and honey. It is blessed with millions of acres of the most fertile land; with a salubrious climate; with a live, intelligent population; with many institutions of learning and a good system of popular education; abounding with many churches and Sabbath Schools; with a liberty-loving people, where freedom in all its broadest sense and glory reigns; where every man feels that he is made in the image of his God, as free and independent as the pure air he breathes, occupying as his own a portion of God's footstool, where he can, with his beloved wife and children, worship his Maker under his own vine and fig-tree, with none to molest or make afraid.

The State is out of debt and has a large amount of funds in its treasury. It has prospered with rapid strides from a wilderness to a magnificent garden, and from barbarism to the most advanced civilization.

TERRITORIAL GOVERNORS.

Robert Lucas, appointed 1848.
John Chambers, appointed 1841.
James Clark, appointed November 1845.

TERRITORIAL LEGISLATURE.

The first Territorial Legislature was convened at Burlington, Nov. 12, 1838. Burlington remained the seat of government until 1841, when it was changed to Iowa City.

December 6th, 1841, the Territorial Legislature convened at Iowa City, which remained the seat of Government until 1858, in which year Des Moines was made the capital of the State.

GOVERNORS OF THE STATE.

Ansel Briggs, Jackson county; elected October 26, 1846; oath of office administered December 3d, by Chief Justice Martin.

Stephen Hempstead, Dubuque county; elected August 5, 1850; oath of office administered December 4, by Chief Justice Williams.

James W. Grimes, Des Moines county; elected August 3, 1854; oath of office administered December 9, 1854, by Maturin L. Fisher, President of the Joint Convention.

Ralph P. Lowe, Lee county; elected October 13, 1857; oath of office administered January 14, 1858, by Chief Justice Wright.

Samuel J. Kirkwood, Johnson county; elected October 11, 1859; oath of office administered January 11, 1860, by Chief Justice Wright.

Samuel J. Kirkwood, Johnson county; re-elected October 8, 1861; oath of office administered January 15th, 1862, by Chief Justice Baldwin.

William M. Stone, Marion county; elected October 13, 1864, by Chief Justice Wright.

William M. Stone, Marion county; re-elected October 10, 1865;

oath of office administered January 11, 1860, by Lieutenant-Governor Eastman.

Samuel Merrill, Clayton county; elected October 8, 1867.

SENATORS FROM IOWA.

'James Harlan, Mt. Pleasant; term expires March 4, 1873.
James W. Grimes, Burlington; term expires March 4, 1871.

REPRESENTATIVES FROM IOWA, 1869.

James F. Wilson, Fairfield, 1st District.
Hiram Price, Davenport, 2d District.
William B. Allison, Dubuque, 3d District.
William Loughridge, Oskaloosa, 4th District.
Grenville M. Dodge, Council Bluffs, 5th District.
Asahel W. Hubbard, Sioux City, 6th District.

U. S. ASSESSORS.

Of this (5th district) Cole Noel, Adel, Iowa.
C. S. Wilson, Winterset, Iowa, is the Deputy Assessor for Madison County.

U. S. COLLECTORS.

Of this (5th Collector's District) Sampson P. Shannon, of Des Moines.
A. B. Smith, Winterset, Iowa, is the Deputy Collector for Madison County.

U. S. PENSION AGENT.

For this part of the State, Stewart Goodrell, of Des Moines.

STATE OFFICERS, 1869.

Samuel Merrell, Governor.
William H. Fleming, Private Secretary to the Governor.
John Scott, Lieutenant-Governor, P. O., Nevada.
Nathaniel B. Baker, Adjutant and Inspector-General, and Acting Quartermaster-General.
Frank Sutton, Clerk to the Adjutant-General.
George W. Bourne, Clerk to the Quartermaster-General.
John C. Merrill, State Librarian.
Amos N. Currier, Superintendent of Weights and Measures, P. O., Iowa City.
Ed Wright, Secretary of State.
G. A. Warner, Deputy Secretary of State.
John A. Elliott, Auditor of State.

Samuel A. Ayres, Deputy Auditor of State.

Samuel E. Rankin, Treasurer of State.

Isaac Brandt, Deputy Treasurer of State.

Cyrus C. Carpenter, Register of the State Land Office.

John M. Davis, Deputy Register State Land Office.

Henry O'Connor, Attorney-General, P. O., Muscatine.

Abraham S. Kissell, Superintendent of Public Instruction.

Lewis I. Coulter, Deputy Superintendent of Public Instruction.

Frank M. Mills, State Printer.

James S. Carter, State Binder.

Charles A. White, State Geologist, P. O., Iowa City.

O. H. St. John, Assistant State Geologist, P. O., Waterloo.

Josiah A. Harvey, Commissioner of Land Claims at Washington, D. C., P. O., Sidney.

John N. Dewey, Commissioner of War Claims at Washington, D. C.

SUPREME COURT.

John F. Dillon, Chief Justice, Davenport, Scott County. Term expires December 31, 1869.

Chester C. Cole, Judge, Des Moines, Polk County. Term expires December 31, 1870.

George G. Wright, Judge, P. O., Des Moines. Term expires December 31, 1871.

Joseph M. Beck, Judge, Fort Madison, Lee County. Term expires December 31, 1873.

Charles Linderman, Clerk, P. O., Des Moines. Term expires January 1, 1871.

Edward H. Stiles, Reporter, Ottumwa, Wapello County. Term expires January 1, 1871.

CIRCUIT JUDGE.

Frederick Mott, Circuit Judge, 2d Circuit, 5th District, Winterset, Madison County.

MADISON COUNTY.

Madison county was marked out and its boundaries defined by act of the Territorial Legislature, approved January 13th 1846 ; but it was not organized until April, 1850. It is situated on 40° 30ʹ north parallel of latitude, and its location in the state is south-west, being but three tiers of counties from its southern and three from its western boundaries. It is bounded on the east by Warren county, on the west by Adair, on the north by Dallas, and on the south equally by Clark and Union It contains an area of twenty-four square miles, equal to 368,640, acres and is divided up into seventeen townships, as follows: Penn, Madison, Jefferson, Lee, Jackson, Douglas, Center, Union, Crawford, Webster, Lincoln, Scott, South, Grand River, Monroe, Walnut and Ohio. The altitude of the county is high and dry ; being over five hundred feet above the low water mark of the Mississippi River at Burlington ; a portion of the county, the south-western portion, lying directly upon the dividing ridge between the watersheds of the Mississippi and Missouri Rivers, and a part of the water falling within its limits flows to the Mississippi River and a part to the Missouri.

It is claimed by the sages of Europe that a high mountainous country is inimitable to Freedom, and that Liberty can find a healthy and free scope only among the mountain gorges and lofty peaks which concert among the stars, where the heart of man expands like a summer's cloud, prompting thoughts of noble aspirations, and filling the heart with purity and love. If all this be true, what then shall we say of the people of this favored land who dwell many thousand feet above the level of the sea, as high as their mountain peaks, and in close proximity to the stars.

FIRST SETTLEMENT OF THE COUNTY.

Previous to the year 1845, the Fox, Sac and Winnebago Indians held possession of this part of the state. In that year they gave quiet possession of the country to the Government and by stipulation of treaty removed to Kansas. The land thus conveyed to the Government, was soon after thrown into market, and hundreds and thousands of persons in Missouri, Indiana, Ohio and elsewhere who had been anxiously await-ing this event, that they might seek in this land of beauty and plenty a home for themselves and their families, where all that heart could de-sire, would spring up like magic to the wand of industry; they had rightfully pictured in their imaginations all the bright and cheerful comforts of a future happy home for themselves, their wives and chil-dren, and were willing to endure all the privations and hardships of the first few years of pioneer life. They were invariably poor but brave and noble-hearted people.

About the first of May, 1845, a lonely traveler came winding his way across the country from the southward, reviewing with admiring gaze, and examining with a critic eye the wide expanse of green prairie, and the clear streams and beautiful woodlands, with the determination to select for himself the choice of his fancy for his home. His only com-panions were his team and his faithful dog ; he stopped at last in Craw-ford township, and located on the place now known as the old Cason farm. Here, all alone, many weary miles from the residence of any white man, HIRAM HURST, *the first white settler in Madison County*, staked out his "claim," plowed the ground and planted his corn. He came from Andrew County, Missouri. He remained all summer ; built a cabin, raised a crop, and then went back for his family.

On the 3rd day of May, 1846, a few days after the arrival of Hiram Hurst, a lonely, weary train might have been seen wending its way along the lovely hills and dales on the divide between Middle and South rivers, until they arrived on the banks of a pebbly stream in the south-east part of Madison county, not far from the present town site of St. Charles. The company consisted of Joel Clanton, Isaac Clanton, Charles Clanton, and Caleb Clark, with their wives and children and all their worldly goods.

Joel Clanton lives on the same farm that he staked out for himself the same day that he came. And the family of Isaac Clanton are also living on the same farm. He has now been deceased several years. Charles sold out some years ago, and now resides in Oregon. The Clanton family are a quiet, honest and industrious people. By common consent, the Creek they settled upon has taken the name of Clanton, and will perpetuate their names more permanently than can be done by the pen of history.

Caleb Clark "squatted" on a claim near the Clanton's. He now resides near Winterset, just south-west of town. His daughter, now the wife of Andrew Tusha, was the first white child born in Madison county.

Some time in April, 1846, Samuel Guye, his wife, and his sons James, George, Francis and Houston, left Nodaway County, Missouri, to search for himself and family a new and more congenial home in Iowa. They reached this county on the 3d day of May following, and on the same day that the Clanton's arrived here. On that lovely May morning they came up the beautiful district between Middle and North Rivers. Their hearts were overflowing with joy and thankfulness that they had found a country so bountifully blessed by nature. A grand panorama of beautiful sights met their admiring gaze as they wended their way. And after meandering along that beautiful divide, never before traveled by wagon or team; the rank, green grass untrampled or disturbed, save occasionally by the moccasin of the Indian or the hoof of the buffalo, the elk and the deer, and the feet of wild animals, dotted with millions of flowers of every possible form and hue—the rarest gems in the vegetable kingdom—waving and sparkling in the sunbeams, skirted with clear sparkling stream-lets, and with beautiful groves of forest timber, with all nature glowing and smiling just as it came from the hand of Him whose wisdom and whose power can alone create such a scene and such a country; combining so many elements of the beautiful, the sublime and the practical, is the fair land where Samuel Guye and his family found a home.

They located on North River, near where the family now reside. In two days after their arrival, they finished their log cabin and moved into it. This was the *first house* built in Madison county. The family—with the exception of Francis, who has gone to Oregon—still reside around the old home selected for them by their father. The family are remarkable for their large physical proportions, and for their urbanity and kindness of heart. Their industry and quiet virtue all would do well to imitate.

When they first settled in their new home, although all out-door creation was as pleasant and lovely as the heart of man could wish for, yet the family were sometimes quite lonesome; and they were exceedingly anxious that the day should soon come when other settlers would stake their "claims" near them. For, like Adam, who yearned in the garden of Eden for a companion, so they desired for company in this Garden of Iowa—their wants were soon gratified. One morning, before the sun had peeped from the horizon, they were aroused from the drowsy god's couch by the glad sound of a tinkling cow-bell. Its "soul enlivening lays" thrilled every nerve. The cry of "land ahead" to the sailor who has been long from home, a wanderer on the ocean's wave, could not have been more pleasing to their ears than was the tinkling of that cow-bell to the Guye family. Breakfast was forgotten, the labors of the day were driven from the mind, and haste was made in the direction of the sounding bell. After traveling three or four miles, a camp-fire loomed up to view ; and upon nearing it, they found a settler named John Evans, who had selected a home south of Cedar Creek, and two miles north of Winterset. The place he improved is now the farm of William Pitzer, and is unsurpassed for beauty or fertility in Madison County.

The next day after the Clanton colony and the Guye family arrived in the County, Crosby B. Jones and Seth Adamson settled on Middle River, where the Huglin Mill now stands, three miles north of St. Charles.

P. M. Boyles was the next settler in the county. He came from Andrew county, Missouri, and located on the farm he now lives on, one half-mile east of town, the 11th day of November, 1846. The first work he done after arriving was to build him a *palace*. He was his own carpenter and architect. He hauled a load of poles, fastened them together with wooden pins, and then covered them with bass-wood bark. Its dimensions were six by ten feet. In this house he and his little family resided six months. For the first few years Philip had to endure many privations and hardships. But he is now comfortably fixed; is the owner of a farm situated as lovely as the heart could wish for, and he has beautified his place, and is surrounded with every comfort and convenience. At one time he was so hard up for money that he walked to Saylorville, in Polk county, and worked two weeks at the rate of fifty cents per day, to get a little money to buy seed-corn with. The first three years he was without a horse, for want of means to buy one. And he endured all the privations of the early settlers, of which we will mention in another place. He was elected Clerk of the Court of County Commissioners at the first election of the county, which office he filled with honor to himself and the county. Phillip is a jovial, good-feeling man, a pleasant neighbor, a good citizen, and a kinder-hearted man cannot be found.

Among the early settlers who came about the same time, May, 1846, are the following: Irwin Baum, who is still residing on the claim he first selected, Martin Baum, Jacob Combs, John Butler, Lemuel Thornbrugh, J. R. Bedell, Wm. Combs and Wm. Butler.

William Butler settled on the farm now owned by Theodore Cox, two miles south-east of town.

William Combs was one of the active, stirring politicians, in the

early days of the county ; he was one of the first County Commissioners, and was elected to the office of Sheriff at one time. It is
related of him that he polled the only Whig vote that was cast at the
first election after the organization of the county. The man that cast
that vote is a hero and is deserving of a gold medal ; and history
should bear record of it so long as Madison county is recognized as one
of the prominent counties of the State.

Among those who settled in the summer and fall of that year, (1846)
are the following individuals : Alfred D. Jones, E. Bilderback,
Bowman McDonald, David Bishop, Enos Bishop, Joseph Bishop,
C. J. Casebier, P. Casebier, David Cracraft, J. T. Carson, Josh
Casebier, Robert Deshaser, John Deshaser, J. K. Evans, John Esley,
W. J. Esley, Louisa Fiddler, William Gentry, D. D. Henry, Wm.
Harman, A. Hart, C. Jones, P. T. Jones, C. Mendenhall, G. Michael,
D. McKenzie, G. W. McKenzie, Clayborn Pitzer, A. Q. Rice, C.
Randall, J. B. Sturman, Sheckle, T. Stewart, J. Thornburgh, J.
Vanhouten, Michael Whilhit, John Wilkinson, B. Wagoner and
E. Ward.

Among the names of those who came the following season, are :
E. R. Guiberson, J. C. Hempstead, Enos Berger, A. Snyder,
Samuel Snyder, Dr. M. F. Turner, and others.

Among the names of those who came as early as 1848, 1849 and 1850,
are the following : M. L. McPherson, John Heaten, Otho Davis,
Israel Guiberson, T. D. Jones, Alexander Blair, Joseph Brinson,
Mathew Watson, Jonathan Myers, John Rodgers, John A. Pitzer,
Dr. L. M. Tidrick, Dr. G. H. Gaff, William Compton, N. S.
Allcock, Acquila Smith, Reuben Hannah, Wm. Stinson, Sherwood
Howerton, Jacob Fry, George Fry, R. P. Bruce, Robert Evans,
Charles Wright, Bassil Pursell, John Brinson.

E. R. Guiberson was one of the prominent men of the county.
He was the first Representative of the county after its organiza-
tion, being elected to that office in the year 1857. He represented
at that time, together with Lysander Babbitt, the counties of
Marion, Polk, Dallas, Jasper, Marshall, Story, Boone, Warren and
Madison. And in 1858 he was again elected as Representative of
Madison county. He has also held the offices of School Fund Com-
missioner and County Judge. He has now been deceased several years.

William Compton was the first man who sold groceries in Madison
county. He commenced business in a little log hut, on the southeast
corner of the public square, where Stone & Sturman's hardware store
now stands. In those days it was not considered out of place or
disreputable for a grocery keeper or merchant to traffic in "sod-corn."

Mr. Compton afterward bought of Hart & Hinkly their mill-site, on Middle River, where they had been running a "corn-cracker." He built on this fine mill-site the first grist mill erected in Madison county. This mill has been a great blessing to the county and a source of great pecuniary benefit to Mr. Compton. He is now grown quite wealthy, and has built around his mill the town of Buffalo, quite a little village. He has also been an industrious, energetic man and a good citizen and well deserves the success he has acquired.

Bassil Pursell bought and improved a farm near the Guye settlement, and he lived there in peace and plenty until a few years ago, when he sold out and moved to town. He is now quite aged, but his friendship and social hospitality is as fresh and young as ever. All honor and respect Uncle Bas.

Dr. J. H. Gaff was the first physician who settled in the county. He was a gentleman of a high order of intellect and an accomplished and well read physician. He was called to his heavenly home several years ago. His son, Francis M., who died about a year ago near Denver City, was the first boy born in Madison county.

Doctor L. M. Tidrick came in the fall of 1850. He has practiced medicine longer than any other man in the county. Although his health has been somewhat impaired by his long and severe practice, he is still engaged in the practice of medicine in this county. Always being a great student in his profession, he is a well read and thoroughly posted physician. He is a graduate of some Eastern school of medicine and has attended several courses of scientific medical lectures held by the Medical Faculty in St. Louis, Philadelphia, and other cities. He has always been identified with the public interests of this county and was for a number of years Treasurer and Recorder of the county. He is, in all respects, a number one citizen.

Many of these early settlers are still residents of the county, living monuments of the permanent character of the inhabitants of this county, having remained from the first settlement, on their choice, and made good comfortables homes for themselves and their families, living in quiet contentment and in peace with all mankind.

William Gentry was one of the first County Commissioners and he settled on the farm now owned by Amos De Cou, located one-half mile east of town.

Enos Berger was the first settler in Winterset, and he built the first house. It was located on the lot now occupied by the residence of J. J. Hutchings, Esq. This house still remains on the lot, in the rear of Hutchings' large two-story house. It is now covered with side-boards, and used for a wood-shed. Of this house we shall have occasion to speak again, for it bears a very conspicuous place in the history of this county. Berger afterwards settled on the west half of the town plat of Winterset, and built the house where V. Hawkins now resides. He is now a resident of Rock Bluffs, Nebraska. Mr. Berger was Recorder from 1853 to 1855, and he was a whole-souled, hard-working, and persevering man. He was also the first Postmaster of Winterset. A little anecdote is related of him, which we give as it was told us, as near as may be: In those early days there was no bank or safe place for the deposit of money, and at one time Berger had more of the county funds than he could conveniently carry in his pocket, so he placed it in his wife's blue stocking, and stowed it away under the bed. A neighbor observing how he kept the money, remarked to him that perhaps that was rather a loose way to keep the county funds. Berger replied, "Tut, tut, man, *there is no vault in America safer than my wife's stocking.*"

Another anecdote is also related of Berger. At the time the town of Winterset was being located, the surveyors wanted a flag to sight by in marking off the town plat. They asked Berger if he could supply them with a flag of some red material, so they could see it across the location. Berger began to look around, but goods of so flashy a kind were scarce in those early days. However, he was not to be discomfitted, when a county seat was coming so close to the door of his cabin, so he stepped aside and tore off *a piece of his red flannel shirt*, and stuck it on the sighting pole ; let all then, who enjoy the straight streets and square lots of Winterset, remember that they are greatly indebted for them to Berger's red under-garment.

Henry McKinzie settled on the farm on Hoosier Prairie, now owned by our fellow townsmen, W. W. McKnight, and he held the office of county commissioner at the second election of the county.

N. S. Allcock settled on the north side of Clanton Creek, where he now resides. He held the office of county commissioner, at the second election of the county's organization. He is in every sense a very worthy man, a gentleman and a christian.

ALF. D. JONES.

In the early history of this county, perhaps no man has borne so conspicuous a part as Alf. D. Jones. Of him it may be said he "run the whole machinery of county affairs." He settled on the " Narrows," four miles east of Winterset, on the Fort Des Moines road, where the road enters the timber, and where John Orman now resides. Here he erected two log-houses ; one he used for a dwelling, the other he used for a store house. This was the first store, and he was the first merchant in Madison County. The first post-office was also kept here, and it was called Mt. Pelier. Mr. Jones was the Postmaster. A. Snyder, a brother to Samuel and Hardety Snyder, was the mail carrier, and carried the mail semi-occasionally from the soldiers garrison, at the Raccoon Forks, now the capital of the state.

When the county seat was located and surveyed, Mr. Jones moved his store and family to Winterset. He was the first lawyer in and first prosecuting attorney of the county. He was the first county surveyor, and he surveyed the town of Winterset at the time the county seat was located. And he, together with E. Bilderback, the organizing sheriff, organized Madison county. Jones was the Deputy, and did the work. Perhaps a brief sketch of his life would not be inappropriate here. He was originally a plasterer by trade. Educated himself at the Marrietta and Farmers' College, O. Emigrated to the West, where he has held nearly every office within the gift of the people, from school Director to Speaker of the House of Representatives; studied and practiced law; was the M. W. G. Master of the I. O. O. F. of his state, and was elected Grand Representative to the Grand Lodge of the United States. He was a practical surveyor and civil engineer, and in the early days of the new settlements of the West, was familiarly known as the "Pioneer Land Hunter and Town Builder." He is now a successful retired merchant and land speculator, and resides at Omaha, Neb., in a magnificent mansion, and is said to be worth not less than one hundred thousand dollars.

JOHN A. PITZER

Is one of the early and prominent settlers of Madison county. He came in 1849, and during that year he surveyed and laid out into sections the north half of the county. Enoch Eastman surveyed, at the same time, the south half. Mr. Pitzer, soon afterwards, started a store in Winterset, and he was the first merchant that ever sold goods in Winterset. He is to-day one of the most prominent merchants of the place, and he has continued in the same business ever since he first commenced, with the exception of the time during which he was paymaster in the army. He is one of our most honorable and substantial citizens; a man in whose integrity the people of the county have placed the most implicit confidence, and they bestowed upon him the highest office within the county in 1851, and upon the expiration of his term of office in 1855, they re-elected him, and again in 1857. He proved himself worthy in all respects, of the trust bestowed on him. It is related of him that during the hard times of 1855 and

1856, that he gave away to destitute families over five hundred sacks of flour, and that he trusted almost the entire people of the county, who were destitute, for provisions, groceries and the necessaries of life. As times improved and the people became able, a large portion of them came forward and paid the Judge for what he had trusted them. But the Judge has laid out in this way many thousands of dollars which have never been returned to him. There is no man in the county more honored and respected—especially by the old settlers —than is Judge Pitzer to-day. No man in the county has made so many substantial improvements and done so much for the building-up of the county, as Judge Pitzer. All honor to the Judge! May he live long to enjoy the good he has done!

JOHN EVANS was the first preacher in the county. He was of the denomination known as the Hardshell Baptist, and he used to preach at John Butler's place, now known as James' Farm, and at other private residences. In the fall of 1849, two Methodist ministers used to come up from Fort Des Moines, as often as once in two weeks, and would preach at the house of Amos Case and Claiborn Pitzer.

EARLY INCIDENTS AND REMINISCENCES.

In 1850 and 1851, and even later, "new comers" came into the county so fast, that provender was often very scarce, and it was very difficult for many, especially those who came too late to cut hay, to obtain provender sufficient to keep the stock which they had brought with them alive over winter, and their cattle were only kept alive by driving them daily into the bottoms along the streams, and cutting down small trees for them to browse on. The trees were mostly linn and elm, and the cattle subsisted on the buds and twigs.

In the early days of the county, the settlers had to go a long distance to mill; often as far as Oskaloosa and Ottumwa, and they sometimes went to St. Joseph, Mo., to get their groceries and necessaries.

They were often without meal, (flour was out of the question) to make bread with, and they often subsisted for weeks at a time on grated corn and potatoes. They would often, however, manufacture a " sort of meal " in this wise: They would dig a hole in the top of a stump of a tree, which answered very well for a mortar; and they made a pestal by fastening an iron wedge to the end of a stick. With this machine, they would pound boiled corn and make *meal*. They ground buckwheat in coffee mills; and many a tempting " flap-jack " made from flour thus ground, has been eaten with relish, and hunger was well appeased. As late as 1850 flour would bring in Winterset as high as eight and ten dollars per hundred weight, and could seldom be had at that ; and wheat was always reserved for "company," or for great occasions.

If bread was *dear*, meat was *cheap*. The early settlers always had plenty of the choicest meats—enough to make the most fastidious epicure smack his lips with delight. There were plenty of deer, turkeys, and all the various wild game common to this country. One old settler informed us that in the winter of 1853, he purchased three two-horse wagon loads of hams, jerked, or Indian smoked, for two and a half cents per pound.

In 1848 and 1849, the great California emigration passed through the county. Corn sold readily at that time at two dollars per bushel. It is said that Claiborn Pitzer and others were frequently known to stand at their corn cribs and measure out corn all day to California emigrants at these figures. Those were golden days for our farmers. One bushel of corn would buy two calico dresses for " the goode wife," and a frock for the baby, to boot ; for calico was only eight and twelve and a half cents per yard at that time.

In the early days of the county the merchants used to have their goods hauled from Burlington and Keokuk by ox teams, for which they paid teamsters only from $1,50 to $2,00 per cwt. P. M. Boyles hauled the first goods that ever came to Madison county, from Keokuk, for A. D. Jones. No roads were worked or bridges built at that early day, and the poor oxen had to swim creeks and have a hard time of it, generally.

Before the california emigration commenced, money was very scarce so much so that it became a general saying that the Old Oxen was the sole *circulating* medium.   •

The old settlers endured all their privations heroically, and never complained. They knew they had a good country, and waited with patience the better day, which by diligence and perseverance on their part must surely come. They always " put the best foot forward ;" and so patient and cheerful were the people, that the casual observer passing through the country, could not observe by their actions, but that they were blessed with all the comforts and necessaries that could be desired. An early settler illustrates this by a little incident which he relates with great glee : A mail carrier who was returning from his first trip west, complained that at the station where he had stopped to get his meals, they had treated him niggardly, and remarked with much feeling they had *grated corn* for the "Dutchman to eat;" he being a German, was impressed with the belief that they would not treat any one so but a foreigner. But it was the best they could do, even at a public house.

THE GREAT SNAKE HUNT.

Previous to the organization of the county, the county was full of rattlesnakes, rendering life precarious. They were especially a great
source of anxiety to the woman folks. The rattle of the snake was often heard on every hand, sometimes causing the strongest nerves to
fear. And men would sometimes wear leggings as a safety against the
snakes. A farmer named McKinsey, who lived on the farm on Hoosier Prairie now owned by W. W. McKnight, used to remark that he
had rattlesnakes enough on his farm to fence it, and then have enough
left to make a respectable snake hunt. One day Irwin Baum and Wm.
Combs thought they would go down to North River, near where they
reside, on a "little frolic", and see how many rattlesnakes they could kill.
The result of their "frolic," was ninety slayed rattlesnakes in one hour
and a half's time. Geo. Guye once killed thirty-five rattlesnakes, which
were rolled up together, like a round ball.

The settlers deeming that some vigorous measures should be resorted
to, to rid the county of the venomous reptiles, called a meeting for the
purpose of adopting some measure for that purpose. After due consideration, it was consided necessary to form a company and wage a war of
extermination upon the reptiles; so a company was duly formed, each
member to pay two bushels of corn as a fee or bonus. The company
was divided equally, Middle River making the dividing line, beyond
which neither party were to hunt the "varmints;" and the victorious
party was to take all the corn as a "reward of merit." Captains were
duly elected, who made choice of their comrades for their snakish
bravery and perseverance. The parties were instructed to go forth
with a steady and determined purpose to obtain the desired victory, and
rid the county of the enemy of progress. The result of the hunt was to
be made known on the 4th day of July, 1849. Preparations had also
been made for a Grand Barbecue and 4th of July Celebration, on that
day, at Guye's Grove; where the whole county assembled to hear the result, and to enjoy the first Fourth of July Celebration ever held in Madison county. While dinner was preparing, the rattles were counted,
and they numbered *three thousand seven hundred and fifty*; and it was
said to be a poor year for rattlesnakes, too!

The speakers and orators, at this celebration, were Lysander W.
Babbitt, who was at that time the Democratic candidate for Representative of this part of the State, and Dr. Baugh, his opponent, an independent candidate who resided on Middle River, in the then unorgan-
ized county of Warren, together with Alfred D. Jones. Mr. Jones was
also the reader of the Declaration of Independence.

Among the volunteer toasts given was one something like the following, offered by Alfred D. Jones:

" To the Captain and Company of the victorious Snaking Party— May their names be handed down to the future generations of Madison, for their snakish bravery and for compelling their opponents this day to *acknowledge the corn.* "

This celebration was a gay day to the people of Madison county. All were cheerful and happy. They danced, sang and cheered, and mirth and jollity were unrestrained. At the close of that gala day, the happy people returned to their quiet and pleasant homes well contented that they had obtained so great a victory over their wily foe. Thus ended the great " Snake Hunt. " Since that eventful Spring snakes are scarce in Madison county.

The corn was to be delivered at Casebiers' mill, for the relief of a poor widow woman residing in that neighborhood. But history records that the committee appointed, got into a muss while under the influence of "sod-corn," and quarrelled, and the subject was never afterwards broached.

THE GOLD EXCITEMENT.

In the summer of 1858 small particles of gold were discovered in some of the black sand on our streams. As usual, the discovery of gold produced great excitement, and wild and extravagant stories soon spread abroad of the rich beds and mines that had been discovered in Madison county. John Taylor and others found a few small particles of dust and left them on exhibition at the banking house of A. West & Co. Rev. Thos. Evans found on his farm a lump worth ninety cents; and a report circulated far and near that one man had found a two hundred dollar lump near the Union county line. A steamboat arrived at Des Moines, carrying quite a number of gold hunters who came to seek their fortunes in this new Eldorado. Fred. Somers, an eminent jeweler of Winterset at that time, advertised that he had established an " Assay Office, " and that he was fully prepared to assay, smelt, or examine specimens of gold, &c. But the gold " diggins " soon played out, and we are sorry to add that nobody was the richer for it. Fine particles of gold dust, however, were found; and it can be found at any time along our streams, but not in quantities sufficient to pay for the trouble.

FIRST MARRIAGES.

The first marriages in the county were as follows :

License No. 1, was issued to David S. Smith and Jane Cason, April 17, 1849, by one George W. McClellan, Clerk Dist. Court, M. C. Iowa.

—(Mem.) It is very natural that an official should get "M. C." mixed in with his first official acts; for all men who run for office aspire to this.

The certificate in this case shows that the ceremony was performed on the 19th of April, 1849, by *Seth Adamson, J. P.* Also that the blushing bride was of tender years—viz: 15.

License No. 2, showeth that the tender heart of Sarah Evans was made harder than iron, by virtue of its uniting with Casteel—christened Meshack. This terrible deed was enacted by another J. P. of those days—Joshua C. Casebier, on the 13th day of August, 1849.

License No. 3—Lewis Baum to Barbara Wolverton, by Alfred Rice—another J. P.

The record shows up to this date that, between J. P's and Ministers, the former were in the ascendant.

THE FIRST ENTRIES OF LAND MADE IN MADISON COUNTY.

Below we give the names of those who first entered land in the several townships of the county, together with the description of the lands and their date of entry.

Ohio Township—John Hinkle and George D. Hartman were the first to enter land in Ohio Township. Hinkle entered the S. E. qr. of the S. W. qr. of sec. 27, and Hartman entered the N. E. qr. of the S. E. qr. of sec. 23. They both entered the same day, Nov. 8, 1850.

Scott Township—David Fleener entered the N. W. qr. of the N. E. qr. of sec. 3, Nov. 8, 1850.

Lincoln Township—Elijah Perkins entered the south half of the N. W. qr. of the north half of the S. W. qr. of section 13.

Grand River Township—A. J. Hasty entered the N. E. qr. of the S. E. qr. of the S. W. qr. of section 8, November 9, 1852; and on the same day J. C. Barker entered the S. W. qr. of section 9 and the N. E. qr. of section 27; and L. B. Barker entered the N. W. qr. of the N. E. qr. and the S. E. qr. of the N. E. qr. of section 17, also, on the same day.

Webster Township—F. Howard entered the north half of the N. W. qr. of section 16, July 8, 1850.

Crawford Township—John Carroll entered the N. E. qr. of the S. E. qr. of section 25, October 24, 1850.

Lee Township—John Hoge entered the N. W. qr. of the N. E. qr. of section 5, Oct. 25, 1850.

Union Township—George W. Guye entered the S. W. qr. of section 5, Jan. 21, 1850. This was the first piece of land entered in Madison county.

Douglas Township—Quite a number of entries were made February 4, 1850, by John A. Pitzer, Claiborn Pitzer, and others.

Madison Township—Henry Groseclose entered the S. W. qr. of section 22, February 4, 1850; and Robert G. H. Hannah entered the S. E. qr. of section 35, on the same day.

Jackson Township—R. L. Tidrick entered the west half of the S. E. qr. and the east half of the S. W. qr. of section 11, October 25, 1850.

Penn Township—W. M. Mendenhall entered the N. W. qr. N. E. of section 1, October 3, 1858.

Monroe Township—J. C. P. Malone entered the first piece of land in this township, June 12, 1851.

The first transfer of land made in the county was a piece of land in Douglas township, sold by **J. A. Pitzer** to John Wilhoit, February 7, 1850.

STONE.

Madison county is famous far and near for her excellent stone. It exists in inexhaustible supplies in all parts of the county, excepting only the north-east part. It would not be exaggeration to state that all the State could be supplied with lime made from the stone of her quarries, and that all the roads of the county could be macadamized and the farms fenced with stone fences, without any apparent diminution of the quantity remaining in store in her quarries.

Geologically, the rock belongs to the coal formation, and consists of sand-stone, fire clay, slate, shale and lime-stone. The sand-stone, which is the lowest formation, is generally too soft for practical purposes, but occasionally quarries of fine texture are met with, out of which good building stones and grindstones are procured. Above this lie beds of very pure limestone, composed entirely of fossil shells, and forming a rich mine to the geologist, rare and beautiful specimens being continually met with. The limestone lays in beds from two to twelve inches in thickness, growing heavier as the quarries are wrought into the bluffs. It generally breaks with a glossy fracture and spawls well. It makes excellent lime, and is a strong and durable building material, too hard to be crushed by any weight and is not subject to

---

NOTE.—In the early days of the county the records were kept on loose sheets of paper, and some deeds have no doubt been lost. By act of the Legislature, approved January 19, 1855, I. D. Guiberson was appointed to gather up and record all deeds and mortgages. The papers which he gathered and transcribed filled a large blank book of 260 pages. Now the total number of pages recorded in the Recorder's office, is 13,801; 6,326 pages have been transcribed since the time that our present Recorder—O. A. Moser—came into office in 1855; showing that the transactions in real estate in this county, of late years, is immense.

disintegration or decay in the building. It exists in the greatest abundance, all the bluffs along the streams being composed of it, and it is generally easily quarried. In the west and south-east part of the county, on the top of the highest bluffs, above the common limestone, is found several layers of Oalitic limestone. This is much softer than the common limestone and makes a good stone for cutting purposes. It is of a rich cream color,—the true "stone color," as seen in the paleons of architects—sometimes nearly pure white, sometimes nearly yellow. It takes a good finish with the tool and hammer, but is not fitted for polishing. It retains its color well; the buildings constructed out of it twelve years ago looking as bright after a shower as when first erected. It makes an excellent building stone, and is probably the best or among the best stone for cutting purposes found in the State. It is not nearly so abundant as the common limestone, but there is enough of it to supply a large demand for several years.

When the quarries are first opened, the stone is small as "ripple stone," but soon grow into ledges, and when fairly opened, they are about eight feet in thickness of this stone, generally capped by a "bustard" stone, about one and a half feet thick, which is unfit for cutting purposes, while the floor of the quarry, which is generally a perfect level, is composed of the common limestone, and it continues downward for about fifty feet further, when beds of shale, slate and fire clay are met with, while the whole is underlaid with the "drift" formation, composed of the plutonic rocks, granite, parphy, conglomerate, etc. It is probably from this formation that the specimens of lead, iron, copper and gold ore, which have been found in the county, have been derived. The slate shales contain an oil resembling, if not identical with petroleum, the oozing out of which, in the Spring, led some unfortunate individuals to invest in oil wells, and the finding of black sand in the sloughs led others to invest in the search for gold, resulting very unsatisfactorily.

It is not probable that Madison county will ever be celebrated for its mineral wealth, but the abundance and quality of her stone, with the nearly total destitution of the surrounding counties, point to a large and continually increasing revenue for her people from this source alone. And her citizens have already realized, in their public buildings, their magnificent stone mansions, farm houses, barns and fences, that it is a very handy thing to live in a county blessed with an abundance of limestone. Large quantities of Madison county lime and stone have been carried off to Des Moines and other places.

Among the most noted quarries in the immediate vicinity of Winterset, we will mention those owned by David Harris, W. P. Cassidy and Elias Stafford.

TIMBER.

Early settlers inform us that when they first came into the county, more than one-fourth of the entire county was composed of timber lands. And it is now so abundant along the streams as to make it desirable to check rather than encourage its encroachments upon the prairie. It is of excellent growth and quality. The numerous saw mills in Madison county will abundantly testify as to the quantity and quality of her timber. The different varieties of timber are as follows : White and red oak, cottonwood, elm, hickory, black and white ash, linden, black walnut, white walnut, willow, wild cherry, hackberry, crab-apple, wild plum, white maple, sugar maple, white birch, black locust, sarvis, and other varieties. Along the bluffs of North and Cedar rivers, are found considerable growths of cedar, hawthorn and kinekanick. Many trees not indigenous to the soil of Madison county, are also cultivated with considerable success.

COAL.

The coal veins of Madison county have not, as yet, been developed to any considerable extent. The abundant supply of wood for ordinary fuel, and for running steam machinery, have greatly retarded the development of the coal beds of the county. There are mines, however, that are worked to some extent, in the north part and also in the southern half of the county. The veins now tapped in the county, range from nine inches in thickness to three feet. The cheapness of wood has prevented the outlay of capital in opening veins, except to obtain surface coal. Prof. White, the state Geologist, when he visited this county, gave it as his opinion that abundance of coal could be reached by sinking shafts from one hundred to two hundred feet in the valleys of the streams. It is the opinion of others, capable of forming a sound judgement on such matters, that there is an abundant supply of coal within the county, and that it but needs to be developed.

WILD FRUIT.

The early settlers found in the timber and along the streams, an abundance of wild fruit, such as plums, grapes, crab apple, wild cherry, wild currants, gooseberries, blackberries, strawberries, raspberries, sarvisberries, black and red haws, etc. Butternuts, walnuts, hickory-nuts and hazel-nuts also abounded in great profusion. The plums are of three varieties,—and the large yellow, sometimes measuring three and a half inches in diameter, is as luscious as any Damask or Yellow plums that ever grew in gardens. Some of the crab apples are also of the large variety, about the size of common hen's eggs. The wild fruit is still grown in great abundance along the river bottoms. Where nature has done so well for wild fruits, it certainly will do equally well for tame, or grafted fruits, of equal hardihood.

CROPS.

Corn, wheat, oats and potatoes are the principal crops of Madison county, though rye, barley, sorghum, and the principal grasses are raised very extensively.

Corn in this county will generally average about sixty bushels per acre. The varieties mostly raised are the "White" and "Yellow," without any particular name ; though all varieties are raised. Sometimes enormous yields of corn are produced. We remember that at the County Fair of 1865, Jonathan Cox brought proof that he had measured one acre of his corn crop, and that it had yielded him one hundred and seven and a half bushels per acre. J. W. Cooper had raised one hundred and four bushels per acre, and Wm. R. Shriver had raised sixty-five bushels on one half acre of ground. These are only a few of the many instances where the corn crop has yielded over one hundred bushels per acre.

The wheat crop of the county will average from fifteen to twenty bushels per acre. The Spring varieties are mostly raised.

The oat crop of the county generally averages about thirty-five bushels to the acre.

The potato crop is very extensively cultivated and with great profit, the crops sometimes yielding as high as three and four hundred bushels per acre.

Grasses are now being cultivated to a considerable extent, especially in the more thickly settled portions of the county, where the range has been fenced in ; but in the more sparsely settled neighborhoods the prairie grass furnishes as good hay as is desired. Timothy and Blue Grass are the standard cultivated grasses.

Sorghum thrives exceedingly well and for a number of years past Madison county has made its own molasses, none worth mentioning being imported.

Hedging with the osage orange in Madison county has been tried by many farmers, with great success. We are informed by reliable nurserymen that there is at the present time, over two hundred miles of osage orange fence in the county.

SOIL.

According to the report of our State Geologist, sustained by the actual experiments of our farmers and the yearly yield of grain, the quality of the soil of Madison county is not surpassed anywhere. It is a black loam and is as rich as can be. It is, on an average, two feet deep all over the prairie, and it is almost impossible to distinguish between the soil and the sub-soil. For several feet down it is of the richest lime, and partakes of the argillaceous nature. In the south part of the county sand enters as a constituent more largely than in other parts of the county. The soil in all parts of the county, however, is so light and porous and the general surface of the country being so well drained that it dries soon after a heavy rain ; one day's sunshine is sufficient to dry the roads completely. All the vegetables and cereals common to the temperate zone grow luxuriantly in this fertile soil. On the prairie is a solid formation of clay, which gives the soil the power of retaining moisture a remarkable length of time, so that drouth does not affect this section of country to any considerable extent. Consequently an entire failure of crops has never been known.

WELLS AND SPRINGS.

Abundance of good pure, limestone water, clear and sparkling as crystal, is found in almost all parts of the county, by digging from ten to thirty feet.

There are thousands of beautiful springs scattered all over the county, in every direction. Many of them never dry, in the dryest seasons, or freeze over in the coldest winters. One large spring, near the Madison Woolen Mills furnishes sufficient water for the use of that steam factory and for small villages which has sprung up around it.

CLIMATE AND HEALTH.

The health of Madison county is as good as that of any county in the state, and will compare favorably with that of any other state in the Union. There is but little rain or mud in the winter season, the roads generally being dry all winter. It is not common to have more than six inches of snow, although it drifts to a considerable extent. High winds prevail to some extent in the winter, and the climate is somewhat rigorous, but not any more so than in the same latitude in the Eastern states. The summer and autumn are most delightful. During the enchanting seasons of summer and autumn, everybody is impressed with a sense that Iowa is the most delightful country on the face of the globe. Fever and ague, and other disorders which result from miasmatic influences, are scarcely known in Madison county. The climatic conditions of this part of Iowa are such that it cannot help but being healthy.

STREAMS.

Madison County is within the limits of the "Three River country." It was thus designated, because of the three rivers, nearly of the same

size, but a few miles apart, and running parallel to each other, in a
direction slightly north-east, directly through the county, emptying into
the Des Moines River. These streams were early designated according
to their respective positions. North River rises in Guthrie county,
runs through the north-east corner of Adair county, and enters Madison some six miles south of the north-west corner, and in running through
it from west to east, passes through seven different congressional townships. It affords sufficient water power for manufacturing and milling
purposes, during the year, except in extremely dry seasons, when it is
necessary to economise in the use of the water. It has two principal
branches. North Branch and Cedar Creek. North Branch is north of
North River, and heads near the Adair county line, nearly at the
north-west corner of Madison, and runs in a direction slightly south-
east through the three westerly townships, of Penn, Madison, and Jackson of the north tier in the county, before emptying into North River.
This branch is also large enough to afford water power for ordinary
purposes. Cedar Creek is a smaller stream than North Branch, and
rises near the center of the west part of the county, and flows slightly
north of east, through three townships, Douglas, Union and Crawford,
before reaching North River. It received its name from the fact that
quite a large growth of cedar trees extend along its banks. Middle
River likewise heads in Guthrie county, and passing through Adair,
enters Madison near the center of the west line, and in flowing in the
general direction from west to east through the county, waters five
different congressional townships.

It furnishes water-power sufficient for ordinary purposes, during the
year, except in very dry seasons, when it is considerably weakened.

Clanton Fork of Middle River, waters the three westerly townships
—Grand River, Monroe and Walnut—of the southern tier in the
county, by flowing from west to east, and thence running southeast,
and furnishing water for the southern townships of the eastern tier, and
passes out of the county near the centre of the east line. This stream
is also large enough before leaving the county to furnish water power
during a portion of the year for milling purposes. It received its
name from the fact that the Clanton brothers were the first settlers who
located on its banks.

Jones' Creek is a goodly sized stream, north of Clanton, and furnishes
water for the three easterly townships, of the second tier from the
south line of the county. It empties into Clanton some three and a
half miles west of the east line of the county.

South River, the last of the triple rivers, flows from the south-west
to the north-east, traversing a distance of some six or seven miles

across the south-east corner of the country. It is, like North and Middle River, sufficiently large to furnish good water-power.

Grand River is west of the Middle, on the " Slope. " It flows from the north-west, slightly east of south, through the south-western corner of the county, over a distance of some ten or twelve miles, furnishing water for the two southerly townships,—Grand River and Webster—of the western tier. It is large enough to furnish water for milling purposes. It is said to have received its name from the size it attains in Missouri, before emptying into the Missouri river. In comparison with the pretty streams on either side of it, flowing from the same general direction; being the largest, it was considered a grand river, and hence took the name of Grand.

Badger Creek rises near the center of the north tier of townships and flows through the center of the two easterly townships—Jefferson and Lee—of the tier to the county line on the east. It is a goodly sized stream, furnishing water for stock and other purposes, during the year. It is said to have taken its name from the animals bearing the same, which at one time were quite numerous along its banks.

The principal streams of the county have now all been mentioned ; but there are still others large enough to furnish sufficient water for stock and farm purposes, and there are numerous springs in different parts of the county which yield bountiful supplies of water for the entire year.

The streams are so favorably situated and flow in such directions as not to leave a single township of the seventeen without plenty of stock water ; and at least ten of them, and perhaps twelve, have water sufficient for milling and manufacturing purposes.

APPLE ORCHARDS.

In the early days of the county a prevailing opinion existed among the settlers that fruit would not succeed well in this climate, and they regarded it as a useless expense to lay out money for the purchase of fruit trees. But experience has long since taught them that they were mistaken, and that this is, on the contrary, a favorable climate for hardy varieties of fruit. A few of the early settlers, however, more venturesome than the rest, planted fine orchards. Among them, we might mention the following: James Harris, N. S. Alcock, Alexander Blair, James Butler, Bassil Pursell, Albert Getchel, T. D. Jones, Aaron Howell, Otho Davis, P. M. Boyles, and others. Their orchards are all doing well, and they bear magnificent fruit. For size, beauty and flavor, the apples grown in Madison county are not, perhaps, surpassed by any grown in the West. At the State Horticultural Society Fair, held at Des Moines last fall, A. A. Getchel, of this county, took the premium for the largest and best variety of apples. And it is a common remark that the apples displayed yearly at the Madison County Fair, are "the finest apples ever seen anywhere." T. D. Jones reports that one of his Pearmain apple trees bore eighteen bushels of apples, in one season, ten years after it had been planted out. For hardy varieties of apples, this portion of Iowa will compare favorably with the best fruit growing sections of the West.

We copy the following in regard to the cultivation of the apple, from the pen of our fellow-townsman, Jeff. T. Seevers, Esq:

"Any variety of apple, by constant propagation, will so much partake of the seedling stock on which it may be grafted, that the fruit will deteriorate until it becomes nearly worthless. The yellow Bellflower has grown so much into decline that it is almost discarded. The White Winter Pearmain is not now in Iowa what it was ten years ago. The apples are small and not so well flavored as formerly. This deficiency could be avoided by raising trees from their own roots.

"The following varieties would be a good and certain list for an orchard of five hundred apple trees, or less. New York Pippin or Ben Davis, White Winter Pearmain, Wine Sap, Wilton, Jonathan, Janette, Oskaloosa Apple, and Nonsuch, for Winter varieties. The Maiden's Blush,—(a little tender)—Dominie, and the Dutchess of Oldenburgh, for fall varieties. For summer, the Early Pennock, Red June, Sweet June, Red Astrachan, and Keswick Codlin.

"One and two year old trees are best to transplant. When trees are planted in the Spring, always put some simple mulch, such as straw or hay, for several feet around the roots. If you plant large trees cut off some top. If the tree does not bear by the middle of May, cut off some more. Never plant large trees if you can get small ones. The best location for an orchard is on the east, north-east or north location. South, or south-west, or west, should always be avoided. Trees require no manure in our soil; the richest soil is not the best for the apple. Let trees top near the ground, not higher than one or two feet. Look out for borers all the time. The trees need a general going over each fall and Spring to clean off all worms; and a washing with soap-suds will be found very beneficial.

"Canada Fink; one of our fruit farmers, who is, perhaps, one of the best posted fruit men in the West, gives us the following items in regard to apples: "Apples are peculiarly adapted to this country. Whenever the wind blows on an apple tree so that it stands to the north-east, it will not be long until the worms eat it up, unless it receives frequent attention. This is one of the reasons why there are frequent vacancies in many of the orchards of this country. All apple trees, whether large or small, must be diligently watched to rid them of all worms. By a little attention, apples will thrive exceedingly well in this climate."

There are many thriving young orchards in the county; almost every farmer deeming a good orchard indispensible. It is estimated by our nurserymen that over two hundred thousand apple trees have been planted in Madison county during the past four years. The county already raises almost enough apples for home consumption. In a few years it will have largely in excess what may be needed for home use.

STRAWBERRIES.

Strawberries are indigenous to this county, and they grow in the greatest profusion in many portions of the county. This excellent fruit, when cultivated, thrives exceedingly well, and yields more bountifully here than we have ever known it to do elsewhere. Its cultivation requires but little attention, and when grown for marketable purposes, it is, perhaps, the most profitable of all fruits; a small bed in a garden, say twenty feet square, is generally sufficient to supply the wants of an ordinary family.

In regard to the cultivation of the strawberry, Canada Fink gives the following advice: It is the universal recommendation to plant for a new bed in August; but this will not do in this county, unless it is a wet August, which seldom happens in this country. It is also generally recommended to confine the plants to one hill, and cut the runners. This will not do in this county, as far as my experience goes, because a vine thus treated will form a large bulb, out of which the fibres strike. The best time to plant is early in the Fall or in the Spring. The surest plan to raise strawberries is to keep them clean, and in a good season they will cover the ground.

RAILROADS.

As early as 1853, General Curtis, the prime mover in the great Pacific Railroad enterprise, and who was honored with the title of " Father of the Great Pacific Railroad," made a speech on the subject of the Pacific Railroad, in the "Old Log Court-House" in Winterset. He afterwards, in the year 1858, delivered a speech on the railroad in the east front of the St. Nicholas Hotel, then known as the Pitzer House. His speech was one of the most masterly orations ever delivered on the subject of railroads in the West; he also pictured in the most vivid and eloquent manner the importance of that road. He pictured in glowing terms the magnificent perspective of a line of new States that would grow up across the continent—of a commercial stream diverting the commerce of the world from its accustomed channels—withdrawing the teas, silks, spices and the great trade of China and the Asiatic Empires across the Pacific to San Francisco, and thence across the Pacific Railroad to New York, from whence they would be distributed to Europe in half the time now required in their transit. He also spoke of how it would develop the great natural wealth of the Rocky Mountains, and seemed to grasp the importance of the great enterprise in all its bearings. The town was full of people at the time he made this speech, and the writer well remembers—for he was present at the time—with what eagerness the crowd listened to his prophetic remarks. Half doubting the success of so great an undertaking, yet they could not help being filled with visions of the wealth, the greatness and grandeur that would necessarily result from an enterprise of that kind, But eleven years have now elapsed since Col. Curtis made that prophetic speech, and his predictions are being rapidly fulfilled.

In 1852 or '53, Alf. D. Jones surveyed the route of the Philadelphia, Ft. Wayne & Platte River Air Line Railroad, through the State from New Boston, on the Mississippi River to Council Bluffs. The route of this road passed directly through Winterset, and depot grounds were marked out for it in the north east part of town.

To aid in the construction of this Air Line Railroad, Judge Pitzer, in compliance with the petition and request of a portion of the people of Madison county, called a special election for the purpose of deciding the question, "Will the people of Madison county subscribe one hundred thousand dollars stock in the Philadelphia, Ft. Wayne & Platte River Railroad." The election was held on the 24th day of December, 1853. and the election resulted as follows: one hundred and eighty-three votes were cast in favor of the loan, and ninety-four against it. For the payment of this sum it was provided that the county should issue bonds payable at such time as was deemed advisable by the County Judge, in not less than ten or more than twenty years from the time of their date, to bear interest not exceeding eight per cent per annum. To liquidate these bonds, the County Judge was authorized to levy such annual tax, not exeeding one per cent, nor less than two mills on the dollar, of the county valuation, as may be necessary therefor. This loan still stands in full force and effect on our statute books. A route through the state along this line must yet be built, it being on a direct air line continuation of the Pacific Railroad, from Omaha to Philadelphia and the East, and the nearest and most natural route for the road. It will be built in time, and will be the main thoroughfare of the great Pacific Railroad.

The Chicago, Rock Island & Pacific Railroad passes through the north line of Madison county. It was completed through to Council Bluffs last May. This road has developed the country along the line of its route, with the most astonishing rapidity. Of the towns located along its line in, and contiguous to Madison county, we will mention elsewhere in this book.

The Bedford, Winterset & Des Moines Railroad is an organization which has in contemplation the building of a railroad from Des Moines via Winterset and Bedford, to St. Joseph, Missouri. The Iowa division of this company is officered as follows:

William Compton, President; L. M. McPherson, Secretary; John A. Pitzer, Treasurer, and F. W. Palmer, Theodore Cox, Eli Cox, W. W. McKnight and D. P. Kenyon, Board of Directors.

The State of Missouri has granted this road a subsidy of ten thousand dollars a mile from St. Joseph to the Iowa state line, *provided*, the road is completed to the State line by the first of December, 1869. The road will be completed so far, within the time specified. The road will also be completed as far as Bedford, in Taylor county, Iowa, by the first of January, 1870.

The citizens of Madison county have raised by taxation and subscription, about seventy-five thousand dollars to aid in the construction of this road. But the late decision of the Supreme Judge of the State declaring taxation for railroad purposes illegal, has compelled the citizens to drop the plan of raising money for that purpose by taxation. Efforts are now being made to raise the amount required of this county, one hundred and fifty thousand dollars, by donations and subscriptions of stock. There is no doubt that the road will soon be built clear through.

TEACHERS' INSTITUTE.

The Madison County Teachers' Institute was organized at Winterset in October, 1858, by J. H. L. Scott, an eminent educational man, who resided at that time at Osceola. The organization has held its annual meetings from its commencement down to the present time; and it has been the means of accomplishing a vast amount of good for the cause of education in Madison county. The teachers of the entire county attend its meetings and all take an active part in the various exercises of the Institute. And many citizens of the county who are not teachers often take an active part in the exercises. Its meetings are always interesting and instructive and they are very largely attended. The citizens of the county take a great deal of pride in the Institute, for it is doing much to advance the cause of education in the county.

SCHOOL STATISTICS OF MADISON COUNTY.

The following is a list of the Sub-Districts, the number of Sub-Districts, the number of schools, the number of persons between five and twenty-one years of age, the number of school-houses and of what materials constructed, for the year 1868:

Sub Districts.	No. of School Districts	No. of Males	No. of Females	No. of Schools.	Log School Houses	Frame School Houses.	Stone School Houses.
Crawford	6	144	128	6	1	5	3
Douglas	5	128	131	5		2	
Grand River	6	114	98	5		5	
Jackson	5	93	74	5		5	1
Jefferson	6	86	91	5		4	1
Lincoln	6	131	103	5		3	
Lee	5	71	58	2		3	
Monroe	4	84	57	4	1	3	1
Madison	8	138	131	5	1	3	
Ohio	4	99	94	2		4	
Penn	4	56	49	6		4	5
Scott	6	230	231	5		1	
South	7	188	198	5	1	4	1
Union	5	194	176	5		4	2
Walnut	6	156	124	6		2	1
Webster	4	67	56	4		4	
Independent District of Winterset	1	269	263			2	1
Independent District of Brooklyn	1	49	60	1			
Independent District of Lincoln	1	54	51				
Total	92	2,345	2,187	84	4	59	15

H. W. Hardy, our excellent County Superintendent, has visited all the schools during the past winter, (1868 and 1869) and reports them all in a flourishing condition. Every exertion is being made to advance and improve the schools, and the standard of qualifications of teachers is being raised.

THE WINTERSET PUBLIC SCHOOL-HOUSE.

Winterset has a magnificent public school-house, one of the best, perhaps, in the State. It was finished in the fall of 1868. It is located on a very beautiful eminence—overlooking most of the city, and very beautiful scenery to the south and southeast—about three blocks from the Public Square. The lot on which it is located contains just two acres of ground, and is the most beautiful location in the city. The grounds slope off gradually in every direction, and they are fenced in with a good substantial fence. And the grounds will be beautifully ornamented with trees and shrubbery.

The house is a two-story building and built of native stone, strong and durable, and cost $30,000. Its dimensions are 65½ x 81½ feet, with a front projection of 6 x 19 feet. It contains eight rooms 30 x 30 feet each; two rooms 16 x 25 feet; two halls—one up stairs and one down—16 x 40 feet, and a large cellar, or basement, in which the coal and wood is stored away. A well proportioned cupola or belfry sets off the building in fine style. The bell inside the belfry is a clear sounding one and weighs 420 pounds.

The several school-rooms are all well seated and furnished with all necessary furniture, books and school apparatus. The seats are all of the latest improved patterns.

The school-house was commenced, managed and completed under the charge of the following Board of Directors: M. R. Tidrick, President; I. G. Houk, Vice-President; W. H. Lewis, Secretary; and H. J. B. Cummings, Fred. Mott, J. T. White and W. W. McKnight, Directors. They deserve great credit and the thanks of the community for the faithful manner in which they have discharged their duties.

Mr. C. C. Chamberlin is the Principal and Superintendent, and is a teacher of long experience, in every respect eminently qualified to fill the duties of his position. He is also assisted by an able and experienced corps of teachers.

The public schools opened in the new school building October 5th, 1868. C. C. Chamberlin, A. M., having been chosen Superintendent of the schools and teacher of the High School Department, with the following Assistants:

Mary L. Adams, for the Grammar Department.

Ella Cassidy, for A, Intermediate Grade.

Helen Arnold, for B, Intermediate Grade.

Annie McCaughan, for A, Primary Grade.

Florence Parker, for B, Primary Grade.

And the second week of the term: Sarah A. DeCou for B, Grammar Grade.

The schools commenced with 270 pupils and the number rapidly increased.

From the Superintendent's first quarterly report we gather the following items:

Enrollment for the term, 464; average number belonging, 364; average daily attendance, 325; average age of pupils in High School 17.4 years; A, Grammar, 15.5 years; B, Grammar, 12.3 years; A, Intermediate, 10.9 years; B, Intermediate, 9.2 years; A, Primary, 8 years; B, Primary, 6.7 years.

At the close of the fall term Sarah A. DeCou and Ella Cassidy resigned their places in the school, and Etta Mayo and Mrs. H. C. Weston were appointed to fill the vacancies.

An additional school was also provided, in charge of Mrs. L. Patterson.

HISTORY OF M. E. CHURCH, MADISON COUNTY.

BY REV. H. H. ONEAL.

The first Society of the M. E. Church in Madison county was organized in Winterset in the Summer of 1849. At that time all of the State

of Iowa was included in one Conference, and Winterset formed a part
of the Three Rivers Mission, Iowa City District, Iowa Conference. Rev.
Andrew Coleman was Presiding Elder of the District and Rev. G. W.
Teas, Preacher in charge of the Mission. Three Rivers Mission inclu-
ded the following appointments, located in Madison, Warren and Polk
counties, viz: Linden's, Laverty's, Allcock's, Smith's, Fleming's,
Winterset and Linn Grove. The records of the first Quarterly Confer-
ence of this year are lost, but at the third, Felter's appointment and
Indianola had been added to the Mission. In September, 1850, Rev.
David Worthington, now gone to his reward, was appointed Presiding
Elder of the District, and the pastoral charge of the Mission was supplied by Rev. V. P. Fink, a Local Preacher belonging to the Mission.
During this year the first Quarterly Meeting in Madison county was
held in Winterset, July 12th and 13th.

At the session of the Iowa Conference in 1851, Rev. James Hayden
was appointed Presiding Elder of Ft. Des Moines District, and Rev. D.
T. Sweem, Pastor of Three Rivers Mission.

The history of Madison county Methodism properly commences in
the year 1852. From this year it was no longer lost in the wide field
embraced in the Mission. It was recognized by the Annual Conference
of this year as Winterset Mission, including all of Madison County.
Henceforth it has a name, an individuality, a history, all its own.

STATISTICS OF M. E. CHURCH IN MADISON COUNTY.

Year	Station or Circuit	Name of Pastor	Name of P. E.	No. of Members.	Value of Ch. Prp'ty.	No. of S. S. Sch'lrs.	No. of Vol'ms in Libr'ry
				Unknown.	None.	None.	None.
1849	Three Rivers Mission	George W. Teas	Andrew Coleman	311			
1850	Three Rivers Mission	V. P. Fink	D. Worthington				
1851	Three Rivers Mission	D. S. Sweem	John Hayden				
1852	Winterset Mission	R. G. Hann	John Hayden				
1853	Winterset Mission	R. Swearingen	John Hayden				
1854	Winterset Mission	R. Swearingen	John Hayden				
1855	Winterset Mission	Leonard Parker	J. B. Hardy				
1856	Winterset Mission	Samuel Weeks	J. B. Hardy				
1857	Winterset Mission	James Haynes	J. B. Hardy	311	$2200	155	399
1858	Winterset Circuit	S. M. Goodfellow	J. B. Hardy	393	200	200	500
1858	Brooklyn	J. B. Rawls	R. S. Robinson				
1859	New Virginia	J. W. Anderson	R. S. Robinson				
1859	Winterset Circuit	W. S. Peterson	J. F. Stewrt				
1860	Brooklyn	J. B. Rawls	R. S. Robinson	208	1000	160	350
1860	New Virginia	J. W. Anderson	R. S. Robinson	192	800	28	200
1860	Winterset Circuit	U. P. Golliday	Sanford Haines	50			
1861	Brooklyn	J. M. Baker	Sanford Haines	230	1500	388	350
1861	New Virginia	Enoch Wood	Sanford Haines	220	1500	100	300
1861	Winterset Circuit	J. F. Goolman, D. Thompson	Sanford Haines	65			
1862	Brooklyn	M. Sheetz	Sanford Haines	286	1500	367	544
1861	New Virginia	S. Jones	Sanford Haines	210	1500	140	200
1862	Brooklyn	R. S. Robinson	Sanford Haines	65			
1862	New Virginia	M. Sheetz	Sanford Haines	291	1800	356	800
1863	Brooklyn	S. Jones	Sanford Haines	393	1500	140	200
1863	New Virginia	G. Jay Nixon	E. H. Winans	70	600		
1863	Brooklyn	Charles Woolsey	E. H. Winans	311	2000	571	471
1863	New Virginia	J. Knotts	E. H. Winans	374	1000	350	450
1864	Winterset Circuit	C. C. Mabee	P. F. Brese	80			
1864	Brooklyn	W. Abraham	P. F. Brese	198	1000	190	350
1864	New Virginia	J. Knotts	P. F. Brese	282	300	290	600
1865	Winterset Station	C. C. Mabee	P. F. Brese	245	2200	285	550
1865	Winterset Circuit	I. W. Adair	P. F. Brese	155	480		
1865	Brooklyn	W. Abraham	P. F. Brese	134	2000	150	350
1866	Winterset Station	W. F. Smith	D. Thompson	279	650	550	600
1866	Winterset Circuit	J. W. Adair	D. Thompson	198	2200	175	100
1866	Brooklyn	I. Mershon	D. Thompson	160	800		
1866	New Virginia	J. Hestwood	D. Thompson	228	1000	250	500
1867	Winterset Station	H. H. Oneal	D. Thompson	322	160	200	600
1867	Winterset Circuit	J. Hestwood	D. Thompson	291	220	200	468
1867	Ohio Circuit	A. A. Powell	D. Thompson	100	800		
1867	New Virginia	M. Sheetz	D. Thompson				

STATISTICS OF M. E. CHURCH IN MADISON COUNTY.—CONTINUED.

Year.	Station or Circuit.	Name of Pastor.	Name of P. E.	No. of Members	Value of Ch. Prp'ty.	No. of S. S. Sch'rs.	Vol'ms in Libr'y
1868	Winterset Station	H. H. Oneal	Not yet Reported.				
1868	Winterset Circuit	John Hestwood					
1868	Ohio Circuit	A. A. Power					
1868	De Soto	J. E. Darby					
	Aggregate of Statistics for the year, commencing September, 1868,			941	$6600 00	820	968

For the names of the ministers who have labored in Madison county since this year, the reader is referred to the statistical table, which forms a part of this sketch. The growth of the church was rapid, keeping pace with the steady increase of wealth, population and enterprise in the county. The labors of many of the ministers have been remarkably successful. Societies are formed in almost every neighborhood in the county. In 1856 the mission became self-sustaining and Winterset circuit was formed. It was the same field as before, but no longer assisted by the missionary society. In 1858, Winterset circuit was divided, the work having grown beyond the ability of one man to supply. Brooklyn circuit was formed, with Rev. J. B. Rawls as Pastor. Brother Rawls and one of his successors, the venerable Charles Wolsey, died on this circuit and now lie buried near Ebeneezer Church. New Virginia Circuit, a part of which was in this county, was also formed the same year. In 1865 Winterset Station was formed, since which, Winterset has had the exclusive service of one man.

The following names I find prominent upon the records of the church, and my sketch would be incomplete without at least a passing notice of these:

James Spinlock, Cyrus Spinlock, Wesley Spinlock, J. W. Guiberson, I. D. Guiberson, W. B. Ruby, J. F. Brock, Jacob Hyskell, Claiborn Pitzer, Wm. S. Goe, G. N. Elliott, and Martin Ruby.

Many others there are of whom worthy mention might be made, but not having access to the records, I can give only the above.

The preceding table will give a view of the measure and extent of the progress the church has made. While the Madison county Methodists are divided into five distict pastoral charges, they still feel that they are a unit in the great work of evangelization.

THE WINTERSET BABTIST CHURCH,

A large and substantial stone edifice, is located on the north-east corner of the public square. Organized January, 1856, with seventeen members. House of worship built, 1862. First Pastor, Rev. J. Elledge ; served one-half year. Second Pastor, Rev. A. W. Russell ; served three years. Third Pastor, Rev. W. A. Eggleston ; served four years. The fourth, and present Pastor, Rev. O. T. Conger, settled with the church, October 12th, 1867.

Within the past year and a half its growth has been remarkable, having received within the time over two hundred and sixty accessions —one hundred and eighty of them within the last six or seven months. The present membership is three hundred and eighty-six. Membership of Sabbath School over two hundred.

Deacons—Richard Bell, C. P. Lee, Israel Moody.

Clerk—Dr. A. J. Morris.

Sabbath School Superintendent—W. C. Newlon.

Preaching every Sabbath at 11 A. M., and at night. Sabbath School every Sabbath at 2½ o'clock P. M.   O. T. CONGER.

THE FIRST PRESBYTERIAN CHURCH

of Winterset, Iowa, was organized October 10, 1854, with eight members.

The following have served the church as Ministers or as ruling Elders :

Ministers—Rev. J. C. Ewing, stated supply, served from 1854 to 1863 ; Rev. A. M. Heiser, stated supply, served from 1864 to 1868 ; Rev. Edward Dickinson, stated supply, served from 1868, (the present Minister).

Ruling Elders—Dr. J. H. Gaff and Mr. David Lamb, ordained and elected October 1854 ; J. M. Selfridge and James Shepherd, ordained and elected February, 1856 ; J. S. Gaff and J. I. Denman, ordained and elected July 1859 ; Mr. J. T. White, ordained and elected January 1863 ; Dr. David Hutchinson, ordained and elected March 1864 ; Dr. Wm. L. Leonard, Mr. A. G. Welch and J. D. Jenks, Elders of the Presbyterian Church, (O. S.) received with that church.

By a harmonious and unanimous action on the part of both churches, the Presbyterian Church (O. S.) made application and was received as an organization by the Presbyterian Church, (N. S.), December 16, 1867, the officers of the former retaining their official position in the united church.

The present membership of the church, including some who have removed, is one hundred and sixty-six.

The Sabbath School, of which Maj. T. C. Gilpin is Superintendent, numbers about one hundred and fifty.

The present ruling Elders are Dr. Wm. L. Leonard, Dr. David Hutchinson, Mr. A. G. Welch and Mr. J. T. White.

Brief Notice of Ministers.

Rev. J. C. Ewing, who organized the church and was its acting Pastor for nine years, died at Winterset, December 16, 1868, in the 66th year of his age. He was born in the town of Marysville, Blount County, Tennessee, in the year 1803. In 1832 he graduated at the Collegiate and Theological Institute at Marysville, and was licensed, and in 1834 received ordination. After eleven years, following his ordination, of labor in his native State as Missionary at Large, Pastor and Teacher, he removed in 1845 to Davis county, Iowa, where he was engaged for eight years in pastoral work in connection with the

Presbyterian churches at Troy and Shunem. He has been a resident of Winterset fourteen years; in every relation in life a christian, upright, genial and faithful, universally respected and beloved.

Rev. A. M. Heiser, now settled as stated supply of the Presbyterian Church, (N. S.) at Montana, Iowa, was born at Kossuth, Des Moines County, Iowa. In 1861 he graduated at the college at Yellow Springs, Iowa, and in 1864 at the Theological Seminary at Auburn, New York. After spending a brief season in Colorado he took charge of the Presbyterian Church at Winterset, which he served for a little more than three years, with great energy, fidelity and success, since which time he has been upon his present field of labor.

The present acting Pastor, Edward Dickinson, was born at Avon, New York, in 1832; graduated at the University of Michigan in 1861, and at the Theological Seminary at Auburn, New York, in 1864. He took charge of the Presbyterian Church at Fenton, Genesee County, Michigan, continuing there three years and a half. Having received a call from the Presbyterian church at Winterset, he entered upon his present field of labor at the beginning of the year 1868.

The North River Presbyterian Church was organized by Rev. A. M. Heiser with a membership of five. Mr. J. M. Stewart was elected and ordained a ruling Elder. Its present membership is eighteen.

Brief Synopsis of Doctrines Received by the Presbyterian Church, as Taught in the Holy Scriptures.

I. That there is only one living and true *God*, infinite, eternal and unchangeable in every attribute and perfection, and existing in the equal persons of the Father, the Son, and the Holy Spirit, and are alone worthy of religious worship.

2. That the scriptures of the Old and New Testament are given by inspiration of God and are the *only perfect* rule of faith and practice.

3. That *God* is the creator and upholder of all things and in a sovereign manner so governs the whole as to secure His eternal purposes in Providence and Redemption.

4. That God created our first parents in His image, holy and happy; but that they fell by disobedience, and in consequence of their apostacy their posterity are corrupted, destitute of true holiness, enemies to God and under the condemnation of His law.

5. That God in His infinite and sovereign mercy has provided a Savior, Jesus Christ, who being God and Man in one person, as mediator has made a complete atonement for sin by His sufferings and death for the sins of the world, so that God can now be just and yet pardon every penitent believer.

6. That salvation provided *for* all is freely offered *to* all, but that all are so prone to sin and so averse to God and holiness that none do truly repent and believe but such as are called by the special and renewing influences of the Holy Spirit "according to the purpose of God which he purposed in Christ Jesus before the world began," and that all such will persevere in faith and holiness being "kept by the power of God through faith and salvation."

7. That Christ has always had a church in the world, but first established it in visible form in the family of Abraham ; that the visible church under the gospel dispensation is composed of all that profess faith in Christ and submit to the laws of His kingdom and that its sacraments are Baptism and the Lord's Supper ; the latter to be administered to professing believers and the former to them and to their households.

8. That the first day of the week is the christian Sabbath, to be kept holy unto the Lord, agreeably to the Fourth Commandment.

9. That at the end of the world there will be a resurrection of the *bodies* of all mankind, when Christ the Judge will sentence the wicked to endless punishment and receive the righteous to life everlasting.

Ministers of the Presbyterian Church, (O. S.)

Rev. Walter Lowrie Lyon, graduated at Jefferson College, Cannonsburg, Pennsylvania, and at the Allegheny Theological Seminary, Pennsylvania. He was the first stated supply of the Presbyterian Church (O. S.) and served the church for two years in that relation, viz: from 1857 to 1859.

Rev. Thomas Jefferson Taylor was born in Indiana, Indiana county, Pennsylvania, September 23, 1828. He graduated at Washington College, in 1852, and at the Allegheny Theological Seminary in 1855. After one year spent at Coshocton, Ohio, he removed in 1856 to Montezuma, Iowa where he remained three years. From 1859 to 1862 he had charge of the Presbyterian Church, (O. S). He then became Chaplain of the 39th Iowa Infantry, H. J. B. Cummings, Colonel. His health failing, he resigned in June 1863. He then removed to Tolono, Illinois, and took charge of the United Old and New School Presbyterian Churches, until 1865, on the first day of the first month of which he died, in the 37th year of his age.

The Presbyterian Church (O. S.) was organized in 1856 by Rev. Mr. Jacobs, of Knoxville, Iowa, with eleven members, and Messrs. J. R. McCall and James Jenks as ruling Elders. The number of members at the time of the union with the Presbyterian Church (N. S.) was fourteen.

UNITED PRESBYTERIAN CHURCH.

In the year 1855 the Associate Presbyterian Church and the Associate Reformed Presbyterian Church both effected small organizations in Winterset, the former having six and the latter seventeen members. The Associate was organized by Rev. Messrs. Vance and Tate, and the Associate Reformed by Rev. Fee, acting by authority of their respective presbyteries. The Lorimers, Campbells, Camerons, Newlons and Hindmans, so well known in the county, were among the first members of these congregations. They maintained their separate organizations until the year 1858, when the two bodies with which they were connected, after many years of negotiation, came together and formed " The United Presbyterian Church of North America. "

From this time until the year 1865, the united church, in Winterset, as each separately had done before, continued to receive such supplies of preaching as could be sent to them. Rev. James Shearer and Rev. A. Pattison each labored near two years among them. The Rev. John Graham, also, who had located on his farm, three miles east of town, some time before the union, frequently preached to them, and took a deep interest in the welfare of the congregation, as he still does, though now seldom able to meet with them.

In April, 1865, Rev. C. T. McCaughan became pastor of the congregation. At this time the communicants, living in different parts of the country, and many of them quite distant from Winterset, numbered about seventy-five, and the congregation was still without a house of worship. Two years after this, they entered a comfortable church building of their own. One year later they dismissed thirty members, who were organized as the congregation of Mt. Pelier.

The growth of the congregation has been steady, gradual, and healthy. It now has about one hundred and forty members ; and it is expected during the present year to organize two new congregations, of about forty members each, within its present territory of the North and West.

The fundamental principle of this church is, that the word of God is the only infallible rule of faith and practice ; and its views of the leading principles and duties enjoined in this word, are embodied in the Confession of Faith, drawn up by the Westminister Assembly of Divines.

For near half a century this church and its predecessors have excluded slaveholders from its communion. It regards oath-bound secret societies as unscriptural and of dangerous tendency. It believes that the only psalms, hymns, and spiritual songs, divinely authorized to be used in the celebration of God's praise, are those contained in

His holy word. And it believes that while the christian church
remains in its present divided and unnatural state, good order and
edification are best promoted by members, under all ordinary circumstances, observing the Lord's supper only in that denomination to
whose government they profess subjection. It earnestly invites a calm,
deliberate and prayerful investigation of its principles.

C. T. McCAUGHAN.

THE FIRST CHRISTIAN CHURCH

Of Winterset was organized by Elder A. D. Kellison, July 20th, 1853,
with the following members: John Brinson, Elizabeth Brinson,
David Bishop, Ersula Bishop, Peter Moore, Thomas Moore, Thomas
Dryden, Mrs. Dryden, and Samuel Smith. Elder Kellison remained
in charge of the church eleven years. In 1855 its church building—
which is a large stone edifice—was built. During Elder Killison's
administration the membership grew to three hundred and eighty-two
persons. Elders Fleming, Scott, and N. Summerbell had charge of the
church for a short time each after the resignation of Elder Kellison.
Then Elder Kellison again took the charge of the church, and continued to be its pastor about one year. Elder A. Bradfield was the
next pastor, and the church continued under his administration two
years, and he then resigned. Elder N. C. Stoors was the next pastor
and remained eighteen months, when he resigned his pastoral duties.
After the resignation of Elder Stoors, Elder J. G. Bishop was the
pastor for two years, and then resigned because of ill health. Elder J.
Ellis was the next pastor and remained one year. Elder P. W. Jellison is the present pastor of the church.

The present membership of the First Christian Church is one hundred
and seventy-four. The number of volumes in the Sabbath School
Library is one hundred and fifty.

The church has four organizations in the county, with good church
buildings at Peru, St. Charles, in Scott township, and at Winterset.

The organization at Union Chapel, in Scott township, is in a flourishing
condition and has a membership of about seventy-five persons. The
pulpit is supplied at the present time by Elder Henry Surber. The
church at Peru has a membership of about one hundred persons, but its
pulpit is unsupplied at the present time.

A Statement of Doctrine of the First Christian Church.

1. That the Holy Scriptures of the Old and New Testament do
contain the revealed will of God to his creature, man, and are alone
sufficient for everything relating to faith and practice of the Christian,
and they were given by the inspiration of God.

2. That the Holy Scriptures are addressed to the reason of man and may be understood by him, and that every person has the inalienable right to the reading, and to the exercising of his own judgment with regard to their true import and meaning.

In regard to the doctrine they contain, with all defference to others, the Christians hold,

I. That there is but one living and true God—the Father Almighty, who is unoriginated, infinite and eternal: the Creator and preserver of all things visible and invisible; and this God is one Spiritual intelligence, one infinite mind, ever the same and unchanging.

II. That this one God is the moral governor of the world, the absolute source of all blessings of nature, providence and grace; in whose infinite wisdom, goodness and benevolence, have originated all moral dispensations to man.

III. That man is a free agent, never being impelled by any absolute necessitating influence either to good or evil, but has it continually in his power to choose the life or death set before him; on which ground he is a responsible being, and is answerable for all his actions; and on this ground alone he is a proper subject of rewards and punishments.

IV. That all men in every age and country, and condition of society, sin and come short of the glory of God.

V. That Jesus Christ is the Son of God, the promised Messiah and Savior of the world; that there is Salvation in no other name, and that he is able to save unto the uttermost all that come to God by him.

VI. That Jesus Christ, in pursuance of the glorious plan of Salvation, and for the benefit of mankind, without distinction, submitted to the painful and ignominious death of the Cross; by which death the New Covenant was sealed, ratified and confirmed, so that, henceforth, His blood is the blood of the everlasting Covenant, and the Gospel is the New Covenant in His blood; and that, on the third day after His Crucifixion he was raised from the dead by the power of God.

VII. That pardon of sin is communicated through the mediation of Jesus Christ, through His sufferings and death, and is received by repentance toward God and faith in our Lord Jesus Christ.

VIII. That God freely forgives sin, on the ground of His own rich mercy, and not on any account of merit or worthiness in man; so that we are justified freely by His grace.

IX. That the Holy Spirit is the power and energy of God—that holy influence of God, by whose agency, in the use of means, the wicked are regenerated, sanctified and converted to a holy and virtuous life; and that the Saints, in the use of means, are comforted, strengthened, and led in the path of duty by this Spirit.

X. That the souls of all truly penitent believers may be cleansed from all the defilements of sin, and be brought into a state of holiness and purity with God, and, by continued obedience, live in a justified state before God.

XI. That the whole period of human life is a state of probation, in every part of which a sinner may repent and turn to God, and also in every part of which a believer may relapse into sin, and fall from the grace of God; and that this possibility of rising and liability of falling are essential to a state of probation.

XII. That all the promises and threatenings of the Gospel are conditional, as they regard man with reference to his well being, here and hereafter; and on this ground alone, can the sacred writings be consistently interpreted, or rightly understood.

XIII. That Jesus Christ has ordained two institutions to be perpetually observed—baptism and the Lord's Supper—which are commemorative of His sufferings and death for the sins of the world.

XIV. That there will be a resurrection of the dead, both of the just and unjust.

XV. That there will be a day of judgment, after which all will be rewarded according to the deeds done in the body.

This summary, it is believed, contains all the essential principles of Christian doctrine that come under the rule of faith.

Very Respectfully,

P. W. JELLISON.

Winterset, Iowa.

DISCIPLES' CHURCH.

The Disciples' religious denomination has three church organizations in Madison county, to wit: one at Winterset, one at St. Charles, and one at Smith's Mill. The church at Winterset numbers about one hundred and fifty members; the one at St. Charles about seventy-five members, and the one at Smith's Mill about eighty members.

The Rev. J. P. Roach, who now resides at St. Charles, is the only regular minister that the church has in the county.

As a religious body they discard all human creeds, confessions and disciplines. They profess to take the Bible alone as their rule of faith and practice, maintaining that what cannot be learned from the Bible is no part of Christianity.

J. P. ROACH.

CITY OF WINTERSET.

The city of Winterset was located in July, 1849. William Combs, David Bishop, and William Gentry were the locating Commissioners. The town was surveyed, platted and laid out on the 18th day of July,

1849, by Alfred D. Jones, assisted by P. M. Boyles and Enos Berger. The original town site, comprising one hundred and seventy-five acres of ground, was deeded to the county by John Guiberson for the sum of one hundred and ninety-four dollars and fifty cents. The plat was divided off into lots one hundred and thirty-two feet in length north and south, and sixty feet in width, east and west. The public square was located in the center, and it is four chains in width, east and west, and four chains and a quarter, north and south, and contains one acre and seven-tenths of ground. The lots were appraised and sold at from three to fifty dollars each.

The town obtained its name in this wise: The Commissioners had been busy all day assisting the surveyors, and the day was quite cold and blustry for that time of the year, and they were quite chilly and tired. They met in Enos Berger's house—located where J. G. Hutchings' residence now stands—for the purpose of giving the new town a name. Independence, and a score of other names were suggested. One of the Commisioners suggested the name of Somerset, when William Combs, who had been nodding his head, almost asleep, and partly under the influence of " sod corn, " immediately jumped up and remarked, " I think we'd better a darned sight call her Winter-(hic)-set !" The rest of the Commissioners laughed very heartily over this, but it struck them as a very favorable name. Alfred D. Jones, who was a very good scribe, took a pen and wrote " Winterset " in large, bold letters, and held it up to the window, where it could receive all the benefits of the light. It looked well and pleased them, and by the consent of all, they named the town Winterset, and will bear that name so long as the town exists. There is no other town of the same name in the world, and the people of Madison county have always been well pleased with the name of Winterset. In honor of this name, A. D. Jones offered the following toast at a subsequent Fourth of July celebration : " By the scrutiny of a Combs, the perseverance of a Gentry and the candor of a Bishop, Winterset was prevented from taking a Summerset. "

The first house built in the town has already been mentioned. John A. Pitzer built the first store house, immediately after the location of the county. It was a log-house, located on the west side of the square. The same building is now occupied by Mr. Baily, for a jewelry shop. It is so covered now, however, that the casual observer would not notice that it is a log-house.

Soon after Mr. Pitzer's store house was built, Alfred D. Jones erected a log store-house, where Kenyon's hardware store now stands. About the same time a man named Roberts came up from Missouri, and built a store house on the north side of the square, on the lot now occupied by Hatch's grocery. The same log-house is now used by Hatch as a ware room for his grocery.

Soon after this, Enos Berger built a hotel, on the east side of the square, on the south corner lot. It was a story and a half log-house, and the largest house in the county at the time it was built, and has long been known as the " Old Goe House." It was destroyed by fire about a year ago. This house was long the principal hotel in this part of the State. It had been a resting place for many a weary sojourner, and a gathering place for many a kindred social heart ; and many a harmless joke has been cracked in its cheerful bar-room. *Peace to its ashes.*

About this time—in the summer and fall of 1849—A. D. Jones also built a private residence, (log) on the place now owned by T. D. Jones, known as " Park Wild. " E. R. Guiberson was the planner and Jacob Fry the builder. The log-house still stands there, but is covered with side-boards. E. R. Guiberson also put up a log-house in that same neighborhood the same season. Other houses were also soon erected, but we have not room to mention them all. Suffice it to say, it was a town of log-houses, roomy front yards, and happy hearts. No " pent-up Utica" to distress the minds of the people in those times.

In 1850 John A. Pitzer erected the first frame-house in the county. It is the building north of the St. Nicholas Hotel, now occupied by Hugh Cassidy. It is yet a good substantial building and was, at the time it was built, the largest house in the county.

In 1856, Mr. Pitzer built the " Pitzer House, " now known as the " St. Nicholas Hotel. " It is a large three-story stone house, and was, at the time it was built, the largest hotel in southwestern Iowa. It cost twelve thousand dollars.

At about the same time the Pitzer House was erected, quite a number of fine buildings and costly mansions were erected ; and the town kept up with the improvements of older settled portions of the State ; and, to use an old settler's phrase, it " sprung up like a weed." Among the various magnificent edifices erected about that time we might mention the large two-story stone store house, erected on the south side of the square by J. G. Vawter, who was for many years one of the most popular and thriving merchants in this section of the State. This building is now occupied by the large Dry Goods store of W. H. H. Dunkle, Esq. Mr. Vawter also built the large two-story and a half stone mansion, now the private residence of W. W. McKnight, Esq. This is the finest dwelling-house in Madison county.

Dr. J. H. Gaff erected the large two-story stone house, now used by Judge Pitzer for his private dwelling.

The large two-story brick mansion on the hill, just south of town, was erected by C. D. Bevington, President of the National Bank of Winterset, and is now occupied by him as his private residence.

James Hornback erected the three-story brick building on the west side of the square, now occupied by the dry goods store of J. A. Pitzer & Sons. This building cost seven thousand dollars, and it was built expressly for the dry goods business. Mr. H. together with his father and his brother George, were flourishing merchants at that time, but we are sorry to add that the hard times immediately following proved disastrous to them. They are worthy men and deserving of a goodly share of this world's goods.

Among the other good class of buildings erected in 1854, 1855 and 1856, are the private residences of Dr. David Hutchinson, built by L. N. Sprague ; the residence of Derrick Bennett, built by himself ; the residence of J. J. Hutchings, built by Judge Pitzer ; the " Winterset House " and the " Madison House ;" the two-story brick dwelling of L. M. Tidrick ; and several fine church edifices, among them the New School Presbyterian, the Old School Presbyterian, the Disciples, and the Methodist church ; all large and commodious frame buildings ; and the Christian Church, a large stone edifice.

Among the fine class of buildings erected in late years, are the following : The private residences of A. Crawford, M. J. Pitzer, Wm. R. Shriver, and M. R. Tidrick,—all large stone buildings ; the residences of Thomas Garlinger, built by E. W. Evans ; and the residences of S. G. Ruby, Wm. C. Newlon, D. P. Kenyon, and others, large and commodious frame buildings ; the fine brick residences of I. L. Tidrick, J. H. Barker and David Reese. Among the fine substantial business houses are the two-story stone store-house, built by E. W. Evans, now occupied by Messrs. Munger & White ; the National Bank, a two-story stone building, and the new school-house, of which we give full particulars elsewhere, in this book.

THE COURT-HOUSE.

Madison County commenced the erection of a magnificent Court House building in the Spring of 1868. At the time of writing, the foundations have been laid, and the walls finished above the water tables. It is expected to be finished within three years from the time it was first commenced. When completed, it will be the finest Court-House building in the State. [See engraving in the front part of the book.] The description of the building is as follows :

The form of the building will be a Greek Cross, each arm of the Cross presenting a front, and each front exactly alike. Over each front will be a fine piazza, with stone columns for its support. This will stand eight feet above the natural level of the ground, and four flight of stone steps, fifty feet wide will lead to it, supported on either side by stone balustrades. The dimensions of the building, not including the piazzas, will be from end to end of opposite arms of the cross one hundred feet, and the width of each arm will be fifty feet.

The basement will extend, as we have said, eight feet above the level of the ground, and will be graded up three feet. That above ground, will be cut stone. This basement will be floored with concrete and brick, and will be used for storing fuel and other purposes.

The first story will be some twelve or fifteen feet in height and will contain the rooms for the county officers, and one room for city purposes. It will also have four fire-proof vaults. The external will be built of stone, cut in rustic, like the Bank front.

The second story will be about twenty-two feet high and will contain the Court-Room, Judge's and Attorney's Rooms, Grand Jury Room, and several Petit-Jury Rooms. The Court-Room will be forty-five feet by fifty-four feet, and will open into a large corridor. The ventilating arrangements are ample and perfect. The outside face of this story will be of dressed stone.

The stone out of which the entire building is to be made is a magnesian limestone and is taken from quarries within or just without the corporate limits. Our State Geologist calls this stone "gray massive limestone."

The arms of the Cross not used by the Court-Room, are to be divided by a floor, giving in three of the arms a third story. Two of these will be left unfinished ; in the other will be the jail, which is a room about twenty-three by forty-six feet. It will be entirely lined—floor, sides, ceiling—with border-plate iron. Inside this room there are to be eight iron cells, with all modern improvements. This makes our jail above the reach of outsiders and entirely safe, giving at the same time good ventilation and avoiding dampness.

The whole is to be surmounted with a grand dome, made of wood but covered with metal. In the dome is to be placed by the contractor a fifteen hundred pound bell and a large clock with four faces. From the center of the clock to the ground will be just ninety-nine feet. The spire will reach about one hundred and fifty feet from the ground.

The dome is to be octagon, and on four sides will be open blinds and on the other four sides glass doors. A flight of good wide stairs leads to this part of the dome which will be floored and given a room over thirty feet in diameter.

When completed, with wide blinds to all windows and in all respects ready for use, it will cost about seventy-five thousand dollars.

CITY OF WINTERSET DIRECTORY.

Mayor—Eli Wilkin.
Treasurer—J. S. White.
Marshal—T. M. Hyskel.
Recorder—J. McLeod, Jr.
Aldermen—J. M. Andrews, D. D. Davisson, C. P. Lee, J. B. Sturman, W. C. Newlon, Wm. R. Shriver.

CHURCHES.

Baptist—Rev. O. T. Conger, Pastor.
Methodist—Rev. H. H. O'neal, Pastor.
First Presbyterian—Rev. Samuel Dickinson, Pastor.
United Presbyterian—Rev. C. T. McCaughan, Pastor.
Christian—Rev. Paul W. Jellison, Pastor.
Disciples—Rev. J. P. Roach, Pastor.

LODGES.

Lebanon Chapter, No. 11, R. A. M.; meets Tuesday on or before full moon.

Evening Star Lodge No. 43. F. & A. M., meets Friday on or before full moon.

Madison Lodge, No. 136, I. O. O. F.; meets every Tuesday evening.

BUSINESS FIRMS.

Agricultural Implements.—Gould & Howell; D. P. Kenyon, Stone & Sturman; A. J. Kendig, and J. D. Holbrook.

Attorneys.—M. L. McPherson, John Leonard, V. Wainwright, B. F. Murray, H. J. B. Cummings, S. B. Gilpin, T. C. Gilpin, S. G. Ruby, J. S. McCaughan, Eli Wilkin, John Burke, V. G. Holliday, W. H. Lewis, Joseph W. Bartlett.

Bank—National Bank of Winterset.

Book Store—W. P. Cassidy & Son.

Barber—Miller & Co.

Boots and Shoes—McCalman & Co., J. S. White, N. Williams & Co.

Blacksmiths—Gould & Howell, James Monahan, Anderson & Brewer, Jacob Bartholomew, Bisher & Reese.

Butchers—Pursell & Bartlett.

Carpenters—J. Q. White, J. J. Shackelford, D. P. Barker, Thos. M. Wilkinson, J. M. Andrews, Hardesty Snyder, J. W. Jacobs, A. Vanfleet, J. P. Clark.

Dentist—J. C. Coleman.

Drug Stores.—Stout & Sawyer, I. L. Tidrick, D. H. Philbrick, W. W. Yeates.

Dry Goods—J. A. Pitzer & Sons, Sprague & Brown, W. H. H. Dunkle, A. B. Smith, E. W. Jones, W. F. Dillon & Co., T. B. Way.

Groceries.—S. B. Wheelock, M. R. Tidrick, Henry & Leach, Samuel Snyder, James King, Charles T. Jones, Wm. H. Kiser, H. L. Hatch, Shannon & Burnett, A. Crawford, Jonathan Myers, Thomas Mullinix.

Hardware—D. P. Kenyon, Stone & Sturman, Hollingsworth & Co.

Hotels—St. Nicholas, Cavenor & Barnes, proprietors; Madison House, H. L. Hatch, proprietor.

Insurance Agents—H. J. B. Cummings, N. W. Garretson, J. S. Goshorn, James Hanna, A. J. Kendig, J. T. White, Jerome Bartlett.

Furniture—P. J. Stiffler & Co., Hugh Cassidy.

Land Agents—Hutchings & Bevington, W. C. Newlon.

Livery—Glazebrook & Tryon.

Mantua Makers—Mrs. M. Hawley, Mrs. H. Rummel, Mrs. Southan & Jacobs.

Photographers—Ed. Hyder, J. W. Young.

Physicians—David Hutchinson, L. M. Tidrick, D. D. Davisson, E. L. Hillis, J. B. Duff, A. C. Baldock, A. J. Russell, A. J. Morris, S. B. Cherry, G. M. Rutledge.

Restaurant and Bakery—Shannon & Burnett, Salisbury & Thornburgh.

Surveyors—J. W. Brownell, A. W. Wilkinson.

Harness Makers—E. G. Laidley, R. D. Stewart.

Wagon Makers—Wm. R. Shriver, Wm. Eberly, John Shrackengast, A. Hornback, Samuel Betts.

Chair Makers—McIntyre & Stone.

Saloons—George Miller, W. E. Matthews, John Hohn.

Beer Brewery—Morris Schrader.

Provision Store—J. D. Holbrook.

Jewelers—J. H. Barker, M. Bailey.

Printing Offices—Madisonian Office, Sun Office.

Queensware—David Shull.

Billiard Saloon—J. H. Porter.

Stone Masons—David Harris, John McLeod, Jr., Henry Smith, Caleb Clark, Thos. Hardy, L. Barrett, D. Dombrin, Robert Hughes.

Tailors—A. D. Taylor, G. W. Coon.

Plasterers—T. L. Fraley, D. S. Boughton, C. H. Short, Jesse Truitt, N. A. Harlan.

Gunsmith—Wm. Shannon.

Painters and Glaziers—R. Bain, H. C. Farnsworth, J. F. Bropst.

Veterinary Surgeon—W. D. Baily, John Dill.

Brickmakers—A. DeCou, S. Noel.

ATTORNEYS OF WINTERSET.

The following individuals compose the "Bar" of Winterset, to-wit:

Hon. M. L. McPherson, Hon. John Leonard, Hon. B. F. Murray, Major T. C. Gilpin, S. G. Ruby, Col. H. J. B. Cummings, V. Wainwright, Samuel B. Gilpin, J. S. McCaughan, Eli Wilkin, John Burke, V. G. Holliday and W. H. Lewis. For ability and a thorough knowledge of their profession, the Bar of Madison county is unsurpassed by that of any county in the State.

Hon. M. L. McPherson.

M. L. McPherson, one of the oldest settlers in Madison county and at the present time one of the most successful lawyers of Western Iowa, is of Quaker origin, and was born in the State of North Carolina. While quite young, his father migrated to the State of Indiana, in which State he grew to manhood. He received his education at Green Castle, Indiana. After leaving school he turned his attention to the study of law. In 1847 he migrated to the State of Arkansas, with a view of practicing his profession, but the unhealthy climate of that State and his natural aversion to slavery, caused him to soon seek a location where he could breathe God's pure air uncontaminated with the miasmatic influences of human bondage. He returned for a short time to the State of Indiana; and in 1850 he started to seek a home in the new State of Iowa. His arrival at Winterset is described by an early settler somewhat as follows: At the first settling of the county the streams were often impassable in the spring, and the wayfaring man had to trust himself to the mercy of the waves or remain until the floods were assuaged. This was the case in the spring of 1850. Few persons were seen in the small village of Winterset. But one bright day, when the roads were hardly navigable, and the streams in good swimming order, the monotany of the town was disturbed by the entrance of a stranger. He was barefoot, had his pants rolled up and his coat off; but he was a perfect pattern of manhood and health, and he signified his intention of making the village his home. Soon the inquiry went abroad, what will he follow for a living? This was answered by the stranger—M. L. McPherson—who soon convinced the people of the county that he was a worthy follower of Blackstone, and that he was ready to practice law, teach school, or do most any other respectable business for a livelihood.

As the law business was limited, he taught school for a short time after his arrival. He has been very successful as a lawyer and has a very large practice, extending throughout most of the counties of south-

western Iowa. He is ever zealous in the cause of his client, and exerts
a great influence over a jury. He is a man of fine personal character,
and a firm believer in practical Christianity. He is generous and
patriotic, and always evinces a lively interest in all matters of a public
character. He represented this portion of the State two terms in the
State Senate, and was regarded as one of the leading members of that
body. During the war he was a Captain in the Commissary Department, and at its close came home with the rank of Brevet-Colonel.
He was one of the "original Abolitionists," and by his labors on the
stump did much to advance the principles of Freedom; and he has
always been identified with the best interests of Madison county. His
success is another evidence of what energy and unfaltering application
to business and devotion to principle will do when nature has provided
a good head and generous heart.

John Leonard

Is one of the oldest residents of the county. He came to Winterset,
we believe in 1852, and has been identified with the best interests of
the county ever since. He was born in Knox county, Ohio, and was
educated at the Dennison University, at Granville, Licking county,
Ohio. After leaving College he located in Morrow county, Ohio, and
was elected county surveyor. The duties of that office not occupying
the whole of his time, as a recreation he took up the study of law. He
made such rapid progress in his reading that after a time, owing to
physical inability, he was better prepared with the knowledge he had
gained, to make a living in the practice of law than in any other manner; and he put out his "shingle" in Mt. Gilead, the county seat of
Morrow county, Ohio. But after a couple of years practice, he started
for the West, and located at Winterset. He has now, perhaps, the
largest practice of any lawyer in south-western Iowa. He is a man of
great perseverance and tenacity of purpose, and attends strictly to his
business. He impresses those around him with the idea, that every
one, like himself, should attend strictly to their own affairs; that
"favors" in law are only granted on "terms," and that those at the
head of affairs of a public nature, should control them to the best interests of the people, without suggestions or aid from the people. He has
been a close student, is logical in his conclusions, and is more successful
in the management of a case, and in arguing points of law before the
Court than as an advocate before a Judge. If once fully enlisted in a
cause, he bears down with such vehemence that a mighty weight is
required to balance the scale. As an attorney he is the most successful
in the West. He is a man of temperate habits, and a devout member

of the Baptist Church. He, together with his son-in-law, Fred'k Mott,
now Circuit Judge, with the aid of a few others, built the large Baptist
church edifice which now ornaments and graces the city of Winterset.
Of them it might be said that they "carried the Church along on their
shoulders."

V. Wainwright

Is a lawyer of great natural and acquired abilities, a fluent speaker and
a good debater. He is well read, and is very thoroughly conversant
with all that pertains to the law profession. He has only been a resident of the county some five or six years, but during that time he has
built up for himself a large and rapidly increasing practice. In politics
he is democratic, and he is the only democratic lawyer in the county.
He is able and thorough in all that pertains to his profession; and he is
in all respects, a gentleman and a Christian.

Frederick Mott.

Frederick Mott, who is at the present time our Circuit Judge—2d
Circuit, 5th District—came to Winterset about fourteen years ago. He
is a graduate of an Eastern College, and for a number of years he was
the Principal of a flourishing Academy of learning in Vermont; and
also of a College at Upper Sandusky, Ohio. He is a lawyer of large
legal attainments, an accomplished scholar, and a man of great natural
and acquired abilities. He has always been identified with the best
interests of the county, and he has always taken an active and leading
part in all matters of a general or public welfare. He is one of the
live and stirring members of the Baptist Church; and his labors in the
church and Sabbath school have been awarded with great success. As
Judge, he is giving universal satisfaction. We predict for him an
enviable reputation and the highest judicial honors of the State.

B. F. Murray

Studied law in 1857 and 1858 with Messrs. Leonard & Mott, and was
admitted to the practice of law in 1859. In 1867 he was elected to rep-
resent Madison county in the State Legislature. He filled that office
with credit to himself and with honor to his constituents. He is a
fluent speaker and a young man of great natural ability, and has
earned and acquired for himself a good reputation and practice.
Should his health permit, we anticipate a useful and brilliant future in
store for him.

S. G. Ruby

Is at the present time one of the prominent lawyers of Madison county.

He emigrated to the county with his father, in an early day, at which time he was a small boy. Before he was of age he studied law with G. N. Elliott—once an eminent lawyer of this county. After he had sufficiently prepared himself he was admitted to the practice of law in the District and U. S. Courts of Iowa. He is at the present time the able Prosecuting Attorney of the county. He been very successful in whatever he has undertaken. He is a young man of great energy and ability, and he is eminently deserving of the exellent reputation which he has already acquired.

Col. H. J. B. Cummings

Has been a resident of Winterset since the year 1855, and he has always borne a conspicuous part in all that pertains to the best interests and welfare of Madison county. He is a lawyer of note, and has the reputation of having no superior in that part of his profession which requires the "getting up of legal papers or documents." He is at the present time the able editor of the Winterset *Madisonian*.

J. S. McCaughan

Studied law with Messrs. Leonard & Mott, and was admitted to the practice of law in 1868. He is a thorough scholar and a close student. He is a smooth, graceful and fluent speaker. Assiduous in his business and affable to all, he is bound to win his way up to affluence and honor.

Eli Wilkin and John Burke

Are young attorneys who have resided in the county but a short time; but they are already working into a good practice, and are earning a flattering reputation for themselves. They are young men of exceeding good ability, good students, and are of unreproachable habits. They are made of the right material and are bound to succeed.

Gilpin & Gilpin,

Lawyers, and brothers; both well read and thoroughly posted in the law profession. They were both soldiers and served with great distinction through the late war. T. C. Gilpin enlisted as a private and was mustered out a Brevet-Major. He was elected County Judge in 1857, and he is at the present time County Auditor. He is a kind-hearted, straight-forward, Christian gentleman, and is one of the "shining lights" of the Presbyterian Church, and has been Superintendent of its Sabbath School for a number of years past. Samuel B. Gilpin was admitted to the practice of the law at the March (1868) term of Court. He is a young man of great natural power and genius. He is a fine orator and speaker, and he has all the ability to make an eminent lawyer. We predict for him a brilliant success.

W. W. McKnight,

One of the successful and prominent business men of Madison county, came to Winterset as early as '53 or '54. For many years he was a leading and popular merchant of Winterset. He had but a very small capital to commence with, but by a strict attention to business, urbane deportment, and being a good financier, he won the confidence and esteem of the public, and has retired from the mercantile business with a handsome competence. He is now one of the principal proprietors of the National Bank of Winterset; and to him belongs the honor of originating and putting into successful operation that flourishing institution. As a financier he has no superior in the county.

C. D. Bevington,

Another successful business man of Madison county, came to the county at an early day, with very limited means; but by untiring industry and good financiering, he has become one of the wealthiest men in the county. He has been a very extensive dealer in live stock; but of late years has been a dealer almost exclusively in lands and real estate. He is at the present time President of the National Bank of Winterset. He is another illustration of what untiring industry and indomitable perseverance will accomplish.

Thomas Garlinger

Came to Madison county in 1855, and settled in Crawford township, on what is now a part of Aaron Howell's farm. At the time he came into the county all his worldly goods consisted of an old wagon, two horses, two cows, and sixty-two dollars and a half in money. But he had what is often better than a large fortune—an iron constitution, an indomitable will and untiring industry. The first Fall after he came here, a prominent merchant, doing business in Winterset at that time, refused to trust him a few weeks for half the price of a cooking-stove, regarding him as a man of too limited circumstances to trust. To-day, Tom Garlinger is worth over a hundred thousand dollars, and is the richest man in Madison county; and is, to all appearance, as strong, industrious and energetic as ever. He has made his money in buying and selling live stock. As a stock dealer, his operations during the last five years, amount to hundreds of thousands of dollars. Within the three months ending May 1st, 1869, he paid out for cattle and hogs alone, over thirty-three thousand dollars. He has now in Madison county nearly seventeen hundred acres of land under cultivation, and nearly seventeen hundred acres of unimproved land. He is liberal and generous to benevolent and charitable purposes,—unusually so for a wealthy man; and is a useful man for the county in which he lives.

Dr. David Hutchinson,

A prominent physician of Madison county, has been resident of Winterset during the last seven or eight years. As a scientific physician and surgeon, he is, perhaps, unsurpassed by any physician in the West. He commenced his medical career at an early period of his life. Having resolved at the age of twelve years to devote himself to the medical profession, he began to prepare himself; obtained a classical education, and entered the medical profession while quite young. He has been an active practitioner of medical surgery for the last thirty-three years, and during the whole of that time an active and industrious student; as he possesses a vigorous constitution, it has permitted him to pursue his studies unremittingly, so that he has not only accumulated a vast fund of general and medical knowledge, but likewise a very large and extensive library of very valuable works on the different branches of medical science. His library comprises about a thousand volumes of medical books, embracing not only the most recent standard authorities, but also some very rare works on Microscopic Anatomy, and Histology. His library is especially rich in works of Pathology, embracing perhaps a greater variety in that department than is to be found in private libraries. His collection of medical journals is also very extensive, embracing the Dunglison Medical Library and Intelligencer; also forty volumes of the London Lancet, forty volumes of the American Journal of the Medical Sciences, the Lancet and Observer from 1842, the Chicago Journal from 1846, Braithwaite's Retrospect, Ranking's Abstract, and several other journals, both American and foreign. The Dr. is himself an author on medicine. The Rhode Island State Medical Society awarded him the prize on an essay, in 1847, the competition for which was held out to all the states of America, and also to Europe. He is also the author of an essay on the Physiology and Pathology of the spleen, which attracted considerable attention at the time of its publication, not only in this country, but in Europe. He has also many volumes on Horticulture in his library.

THE OLD LOG COURT-HOUSE.

Before any church or school-buildings were erected in the county, meetings were held in the residence of Mr. Blair and other private dwellings. Soon after the sale of lots in Winterset the county built what is known as the "Old Log Court-House," a large, double log-cabin, which stood on the lot now known as Monumental Square, and was torn down but a few years ago. This building was used for a court-house, school-house, meeting-house, and for County Clerk's, County Judges's and County Recorder's offices. And the house was also a temporary resting place for weary travelers, and its doors were open to all who wished to enter, at all hours, summer and winter. California emigrants would often remain in this hospitable building for days and weeks at a time. Among the early ministers who preached in it, we might mention the names of Reverends John Hooten, John Guiberson, Syrus Spurlock, J. T. Cason, and Jones of Greenbush. Behind those old bass-wood logs, and beneath the old clap-board roof, many an erring wanderer has had pointed out to him the way that leads to truth and righteousness, and who can tell the benefit the world may have derived from the words of truth and wisdom given with soul-inspiring eloquence within the walls of that old Log Court-House!

Here large congregations would gather, of ladies clothed in calico and sun-bonnets, and of men in their "home-spun," to listen to the preaching of the blessed Gospel; and yet a more devout and attentive audience never assembled in the fine and aristocratic churches of the East. And the command "Love thy neighbor as thyself," was common to them all, and when they parted the hand of friendship was clasped with wishes for the health, happiness and prosperity of each other. Here a "saint and sinner class" would often meet, and the class-leader would often find the room filled with members, travelers and outsiders, and he would invariably call upon all in the house, one by one, to tell the state of their minds, and many a heart has thus been opened to religious thoughts which never had a place there before. A little episode occurring at one of these class meetings furnished us by an early settler, would not be inappropriate here: John Spurlock, an eminent class-leader, to whose piety the early settlers were wont to look up to as without a rival, arrived late at the meeting appointed at the "Old Log" one sabbath morning. The audience, however, were excusing him in their own minds, as a very heavy rain had fallen on the night before. He finally came in, however, quite flushed, and deeming an apology necessary for his tardiness, he remarked that he had to remain longer because he "had to let out that *damned water*." There was great surprise, and every one looked at each other in amazement. They wondered whether their good old class-leader had fallen from grace or gone mad! But he was not long in noticing the astonishment his words had produced, and began to call back his language, and he then explained what he meant. He had been letting out the water that had covered his corn in the furrows of his entire field. That was all.

The first Sabbath School of the county was held in the Old Log Court-House in '53 and '54. Members of all denominations interested themselves in its welfare. E. R. Guiberson and Wm. B. Ruby were the first superintendents, and William Pitzer, and Martin B. Ruby were the active *working* members of the school, and they were the means of accomplishing great good in the Sunday School cause.

THE OLD LOG JAIL.

During the year 1851, the county authorities found it necessary to deal out justice to a few horse thieves and other violators of the law, who would once in a while make their troublesome appearance in the county. Accordingly it was deemed best to build a jail where all offenders would be incarcerated and given time to repent of their misdeeds. And a two-story bass-wood log jail was soon erected on the lot where Glazebrook and Tyron's hay scales now stand. The jail did not answer very well the purpose for which it was built, and many an erring criminal broke from its unhospitable quarters, and in the language of an early official, " escaped, and is escaped ever since."

We remember one individual who had taken board and lodging at the county expense believed it to be to his best interests to try and seek his way to a more congenial climate, and he sought to obtain his freedom by burning a hole through the log floor. It was not long, however, before he found he had merely "jumped from the frying pan into the fire." The smoke began to smother him and he was in great danger of burning to death, frightened half out of his wits he hallooed lustily for help; luckily help came just in time to save him and the jail.

The jail long since condemned, was torn down about three years ago. The same logs are now used in the stable of the Rev. C. T. McCaughan.

THE SOLDIERS' MONUMENT.

To honor and perpetuate the memory of the many brave soldiers who went forth from Madison county to battle in defence of their country, and who sacrificed their lives on the altar of patriotism, the citizens of the county have erected a marble monument. The people of the county have every reason to be proud of this tribute to the noble dead. The brave boys are gone, but chiseled deep in many a loving heart, their memory is as lasting as the marble shaft that has thus been erected to their memory. Coming generations, will, when those who are living now are gone, point to this column and recount the exploits of the dead, and thank God that they who survived the brave dead, had the public spirit to erect a monument to Virtue and Valor and Patriotism. While America thus honors those who fell for liberty, Liberty is safe in the hands of her sons.

The subject of building a Soldiers' Monument in Madison county, was first suggested by some correspondent through the Madisonian, and he further suggested that the Madison county Agricultural Society should first move in the matter. Accordingly, at a meeting of the officers and members of the Agricultural Society, held in October, 1865, a Soldiers' "Monument Committee" was organized consisting of the following members: H. J. B. Cummings, President; Flora Winkly, Secretary; J. J. Davies, Treasurer; and Mr. E. W. Fuller, Mrs. Mary A. Hutchings, and Miss Emma McCaughan, Executive Committee. Sub-Committees were appointed in each township in the county, whose duty it was to solicit contributions for the Monument. A number of festivals, lectures, and exhibitions were given in Winterset during the winters of '65 and '66, for the benefit of the Monument, and school exhibitions were often given in the country, and various other plans were resorted to to assist in the building of the monument. For the success of the enterprise, much praise is due to the untiring efforts of the President of the Committee. For persevering, executive ability, he is, perhaps, unsurpassed by any man in Madison county. The ladies, too, worked with heart and soul for the success of the enterprise, and are deserving of the greatest praise.

The County Board of Supervisors donated for the use of the Monument, the lot on which the "Old Court-House" stood, also the "Old Jail" lot. The Society afterwards sold the jail lot and bought another lot adjoining the Old Court-House lot, and thus obtained a very beautiful piece of ground, one hundred and sixty-six feet square. The Monument was dedicated and erected on this lot. It was dedicated on the 7th of October, 1867, with appropriate ceremonies. Dr. Wm. L. Leonard and Hon. M. L. McPherson made the dedicating orations. In December following, the marble column was erected, and the Monument completed.

The base of the Monument is composed of native stone, standing six-and-a-half feet above the level of the park, and upon this rises fourteen feet of beautiful American marble, making the Monument twenty feet high.

The park—now designated as Monumental square—is located in a very desirable portion of town. And it is fenced with a neat pine fence. The grounds are now placed in the charge of the City Council, who will see that the grounds are ornamented and kept in good repair.

MADISON COUNTY WAR RECORD.

During the late war, Madison county responded nobly to the call for volunteers. According to the Adjutant-General's Report, Madison county was represented in eighteen different regimental organizations, and furnished seven hundred and ten men; which was largely in excess of the quota required of her. This number does not include men who enlisted more than once, nor officers who held different commissions, but counts only the highest commissions. The number of commissioned officers was forty-two, as follows : One Colonel, three Majors, one Brevet Lieutenant-Colonel, fourteen Captains, fourteen First Lieutenants, and two Second Lieutenants.

H. J. B. Cummings, Colonel, 39th Iowa Infantry.

George N. Elliott, Lieutenant-Colonel, 39th Iowa Infantry.

Dr. Wm. L. Leonard, Sergeant, 39th Iowa Infantry.

Frederick Mott, Quartermaster, 39th Iowa Infantry.

S. G. Guiberson, Captain, Co. A., 39th Iowa Infantry.

Oliver C. Ayer, First Lieutenant, Company A., 39th Iowa Infantry.

Charles S. Armstrong, First Lieutenant, Company A., 39th Iowa Infantry.

J. B. Rawls, Second Lieutenant, Company A., 39th Iowa Infantry.

John P. Jones, Second Lieutenant, Company A., 39th Iowa Infantry.

J. M. Browne, Captain, Company F, 39th Iowa Infantry.

Thos. W. Stills, Captain, Company F, 39th Iowa Infantry.

Adolphus Bradfield, Captain, Company F, 39th Iowa Infantry.

William Anderson, First Lieutenant, Company F, 39th Iowa Infantry.

Dr. S. B. Cherry, Surgeon, 47th Iowa Infantry.

J. S. Goshorn, Captain, Company E, 47th Iowa Infantry.

J. D. Jenks, Brevet Lieutenant-Colonel, 1st Iowa Cavalry.

Dr. D. B. Allen, Surgeon, 30th Iowa Infantry.

Wm. R. Shriver, First Lieutenant, 1st Iowa Cavalry.

William Pursell, Captain, Company I, 4th Iowa Cavalry.

J. R. Lambert, First Lieutenant, Company I, 4th Iowa cavalry.

William Hastings, First Lieutenant, Company I, 4th Iowa cavalry.

William Early, First Lieutenant, Company I, 4th Iowa Cavalry.

E. W. Raymond, Quartermaster-Sergeant, Company I, 4th Iowa Cavalry.

Wm. W. Buchanan, Second Lieutenant, Company E, 5th Iowa Cavalry.

M. R. Tidrick, First Lieutenant, Company G, 3d Iowa Infantry.

R. A. Stitt, Adjutant, 4th Iowa Infantry.

D. E. Cooper, Captain, Company F, 4th Iowa Infantry.

A. J. Tisdale, Captain, Company F, 4th Iowa Infantry.

Leander Pitzer, First Lieutenant, Company F, 4th Iowa Infantry.

John A. Kelly, First Lieutenant, Company F, 4th Iowa Infantry

John M. Cooper, Second Lieutenant, Company F, 4th Iowa Cavalry.

David S. Smith, First Lieutenant, Company K, 11th Iowa Infantry.

George Gregory, Second Lieutenant, Company K, 11th Iowa.

J. W. Stiffler, Second Lieutenant, Company K, 10th Iowa Infantry.

J. H. Goolman, Captain, Company H, 23d Iowa Infantry.

S. G. Beckwith, First Lieutenant, Company A, 23d Iowa Infantry.

J. L. Shipley, First Lieutenant, Company H, 23d Iowa Infantry.

J. D. Ewing, First Lieutenant, Company H, 23d Iowa Infantry.

John E. Ford, Captain, Company F, 30th Iowa Infantry.

Robert E. Martin, First Lieutenant, Company C, 33d Iowa Infantry.

Of the above named officers, J. D. Ewing, Leander Pitzer, O. C. Ayer and J. P. Jones, were killed in battle, or died of wounds received while in battle. They were all brave and noble men ; and their names are honored and revered by all who knew them.

In giving a brief notice of the war record of Madison county, the following strange narrative, which we clip from the *Cincinnati Commercial*, should very appropriately occupy a prominent place in the history of Madison county, for the hero is none other than Wm. C. Newlon, a Madison county Soldier :

The War Spirit of an Iowa Soldier.

[From the Cincinnati Commercial.]

It was immediately after the battle of the Hatchie. The dead of that terrible conflict had been laid beneath the mould while the wounded had been brought to the church building, or placed in the spacious apartments of the wealthy disloyalists of Bolivar. Among the number of unfortunates was William C. Newlon, a Sergeant in Company G, 3d Iowa Infantry. His leg had been so badly shattered and torn by a musket shot as to render an amputation unavoidable. He was informed of such a necessity, but not a murmur or word of complaint escaped his lips. Nor did the intelligence seem to cast over his face the least perceptible shade of seriousness. The table was prepared; the instruments were placed conveniently, and everything put in readiness for the operation. He was brought out on the verandah and placed upon the table; his poor shattered, torn and half fleshless leg dangling around as if only an extraneous and senseless appendage. There was no sighing, no flinching no drawing-back or holding-in. There was not a simple feeling of dumb resignation, nor yet of brute indifference; but a soldierly submission—a heroic submission—without a question or a sigh. He indulged freely in conversation respecting the operation, until the chloroform was applied. From the wakeful and rational state he glided into the anæsthetic without the convulsive

motion of a single muscle, and without the utterance of a single inco-
herent sentence; but glided into it as the innocent and weary child
glides into the sweet embrace of a healthful and restoring sleep.

The operation was performed. The arteries all ligated; the stump
cleansed, and the last suture just in that instant applied. During the
entire operation he had scarcely moved a muscle. Just at this time
the large body of prisoners taken in the engagement were marched up
the street, and were nearing the house where the maimed and bleeding
soldier lay. The streets were all thronged by soldiery, and hundreds
of them rushed to get a near sight of the vanquished (prisoners) while
they rent the heavens with their loud huzzas. A full regiment pre-
ceded the column of prisoners; and when just opposite, the band struck
up, in full force, the inspiring air of "Hail Columbia." In a moment
—upon the very instant—the color mounted to his face! He opened
his eyes half wonderingly, and raised his head from the pillow with
the steadiness and dignity of a God. The scene of the conflict came
back to him, and he thought his noble regiment was again breasting
toward the enemy, through a shower of shot and shells. His brave
comrades he deemed, were falling one by one around him, just as they
had done in that dreadful hour of fratricide and carnage. The spirit
of the battle came over him, and his features assumed an air of bold,
fierce and fiery and unyielding determination. He broke forth into
exclamations the most terrible and appealing I had ever listened to in
all my life.

"Louder with the music! Louder! Louder! Louder! Burst the heavens with your strains! Sweeter! Softer! Sweeter! Charm the blessed
angels from the very Courts of Heaven! Victory! Victory! Onward!
Onward! No flagging! No flinching! No faltering! Fill up the vacan-
ies! Close up! Fill up! Fill up! Step forward! Press forward! Your
comrades' graves! The fresh graves of your slain! Remember the
graves of your comrades: Blue Mills! Blue Mills! Shelbina! Shelbina! Hager Wood! Shiloh! Shiloh! Shiloh! For God's sake
onward! Onward, in Heaven's name onward! Onward! Onward!
See! the devils waver!—See them run! See! See! See them fly!
FLY!! FLY!!!"

During the outbursts of passion his countenance kindled and grew
purple, till his look seemed that of diabolism! Such a fury marked
his lineaments that I instinctively drew back. But there was "method
in his madness." He only erred in mistaking time, and in misplacing
himself and his position, which the martial music and the "pomp and
circumstance of war" in the public streets would have a natural tendency toward producing. In the very middle of his fury, he seemed

suddenly to comprehend his mistake. He ceased abruptly, his whole frame in a tremor of emotion. He looked around on the faces present, and without a word laid down his head. He grew meditative as he seemed to realize a full sense of his unhappy situation. At length his eyes gradually filled with tears and his lips grew slightly tremulous. He quietly remarked—"Well boys, good bye, good bye; I should do but sorry fighting on a wooden leg." He again relapsed into silence, and was shortly afterwards carried away to his room.

W. M. B. 78*th* *Ohio.*

NEWSPAPERS OF MADISON COUNTY.

In 1856, Mr. James Ilor bought a second-hand press, type and material of the Sandusky (Ohio) *Register* office, loaded them on his wagon and hauled them to Winterset. The press was a venerable one, for it had been used in publishing the Sandusky *Register*, and other papers in the Western Reserve, of Ohio, for more than forty years. This press is now used in the *Gazette* office, at Adel, Iowa. With this material James Ilor commenced the publication of the *Iowa Pilot*, at Winterset, in the summer of 1856. Mr. Ilor published a very neat six column paper for a few months, but he then let it run down to a very small size, publishing occasionally a paper about as large as a sheet of foolscap. About this time, the Republican party, just fairly organized in the county, were making every effort to increase their strength. Accordingly, a few of the leading members of that party, seeing the great advantage that a good newspaper would be to their party, formed a joint-stock company and purchased of Mr. Ilor his press and printing material. The following persons composed the company : B. F. Roberts, M. L. McPherson, J. A. Pitzer, John Leonard, William Pursell, and others. Mr. Albert West and H. J. B. Cummings were the chief editors of the paper while it was in the hands of the company. Under their control the paper was enlarged and the name changed to the *Madisonian*, and it was otherwise very materially improved. As might be expected, the paper proved very expensive to the company, and they were soon glad to get rid of it.

In the fall of 1857, J. J. Davies bought the office, and he published the *Madisonian* until the fall of 1862. During one year of this time, he was assisted by Mr. E. H. Talbott, Esq.

In 1862, Mr. Oliver H. Ayers bought the office, and he published the *Madisonian* about one year, when he enlisted in the army and sold the office to J. M. Holliday. Mr. Holliday also published the paper for about one year, when he sold out to Mr. C. S. Wilson. Mr. Wilson, after publishing the paper about one year, sold it to Mr. H. M. Ewing.

Mr. Ewing also published the paper about one year and then sold out to Mr. E. W. Fuller. Mr. Fuller published the paper two years, when he sold out to Davies & Ewing. Davies and Ewing published the paper a little more than one year, when they sold out to H. J. B. Cummings, the present efficient editor and proprietor.

The *Madisonian* has always been a Republican newspaper and has done much for the advancement and best interests of the county, and bears the reputation of being one of the best country newspapers in the State of Iowa. Terms, two dollars per annum.

The Winterset *Palladium* was started in 1859 by I. C. Browne. It was Democratic in politics and was a good looking six column sheet. After publishing the paper nine months, Mr. Browne moved the office to Lewis, Cass County, Iowa, and started the Cass County *Messenger*.

The Winterset *Sun* is a lively semi-weekly paper. It was commenced in September, 1868, by C. S. Wilson & J M. Holliday. It is a lively and well edited paper and has a very large circulation in the city of Winterset. It is Republican in politics. A. J. Housington has lately purchased Mr. Holliday's interest in the *Sun*. Its proprietors design soon to enlarge its size. Terms, two dollars per annum.

A. F. & A. MASONS.

Evening Star Lodge No. 43, of A. F. & A. Masons, Winterset, Iowa, was organized August 13th, 1853, with the following charter members:

D. C. McNeil, W. M.
G. A. Beerbower, S. W.
Geo. Bennett, J. W.
J. A. Pitzer, Treasurer.
Addison Knight, Sec'ry.
J. G. Scott, S. D.
R. P. Bruce, J. D.
S. L. Burlingame, Tyler.

Since the organization of the Lodge, the various Worshipful Masters have been as follows:

D. C. McNeil,...............	1853.	D. B. Allen, ...	1861.
J. G. Scott, ...	1854.	Fred'k Mott, ...	1862.
W. W. McKnight, ...	1855.	A. J. Kendig, ...	1863.
W. W. McKnight, ...	1856.	M. R. Tidrick, ...	1864.
J. G. Scott, ...	1857.	V. Wainwright, ...	1865.
John Leonard, ...	1858.	V. Wainwright, ...	1866.
W. W. McKnight, ...	1859.	M. R. Tidrick, ...	1867.
William Pursell, ...	1860.	V. Wainwright.	1868.

The present officers of the Lodge are as follows:

V. Wainwright, W. M.
T. C. Gilpin, S. W.
H. J. B. Cummings, J. W.
Wm. Pursell, S. D.
Peter F. Lynch, J. D.
A. B. Smith, Treasurer.
O. A. Moser, Secretary.
T. H. Pendleton, Tyler.

The Lodge has a room well furnished, in the third story of Judge Pitzer's store building, and it now numbers about seventy members in good and regular standing. Regular meetings on Tuesday evenings, before the full moon in each month.

INDEPENDENT ORDER OF ODD FELLOWS.

Madison Lodge No. 143, I. O. O. F. was organized at Winterset, April 25th, 1865, with the following charter members:

J. H. Barker, N. G.
Dr. S. B. Cherry, V. G.
W. G. Walker, Sec'ry.
J. O. Kirkwood, Treasurer.
Wm. Compton, Conductor.
A. J. Adkinson, Warden.
E. O. Burt, I. G.

The present officers of the Lodge are as follows:

P. J. Stiffler, N. G.
A. J. Adkinson, V. G.
J. Bartholomew, Sec'ry.
C. P. Lee, P. S.
R. Bain, Treasurer.
J. H. Barker, Warden.
D. Burnett, I. G.

The Lodge has a very nice room, beautifully furnished, in the second story of Sprague & Brown's store building; and it numbers over forty members in good and regular standing. Its regular meetings are held on every Tuesday evening.

MADISON COUNTY AGRICULTURAL SOCIETY.

The Madison County Agricultural Society was organized in 1856. It has held its Fairs annually, ever since its organization. The first Fair was held on Cedar Creek, just north of P. M. Boyle's residence. The people of the whole county turned out *en masse* to attend the Fair, and it is said to have been more interesting than any of the succeeding Fairs. But all fairs must necessarily be interesting and attractive when the people generally interest themselves in its success. The Society now owns magnificent grounds one-half mile west of Winterset. The grounds comprise about eighteen acres, and are enclosed with a good substantial fence. It contains a good, smooth half mile track, and wells sufficient to answer all purposes. The Society is now entirely out of debt, and contemplates the erection, during the present season, of good substantial buildings and sheds on the grounds, for the use of the Society. It is now in a flourishing condition, and gives every prospect of accomplishing a vast amount of good. The officers of the Society from its organization have been as follows:

1856—Elias Stafford, Pres.	1863—A. J. Adkinson, Pres.
1856—W. W. McKnight, Sec.	1863—C. S. Wilson, Sec.
1857—Wm. Jones, Pres.	1864—A. J. Adkinson, Pres.
1857—Elias Stafford, Sec.	1864—C. S. Wilson, Sec.
1858—A. J. Adkinson, Pres.	1865—A. J. Adkinson, Pres.
1858—Elias Stafford, Sec.	1865—J. J. Davies, Sec.
1859—David Stanton, Pres.	1866—A. J. Adkinson, Pres.
1859—J. I. Denman, Sec.	1866—M. Houston, Sec.
1860—W. J. Patterson, Pres.	1867—A. J. Adkinson, Pres.
1860—J. J. Davies, Sec.	1867—M. Houston Sec.
1861—P. M. Boyles, Pres.	1868—C. B. Lothrop, Pres.
1861—J. J. Davies, Sec.	1868—D. E. Cooper, Sec.
1862—P. M. Boyles, Pres.	1869—M. Glazebrook, Pres.
1862—J. J. Davies, Sec.	1869—E. G. Perkins, Sec.

POST-MASTERS OF WINTERSET.

Enos Berger was the first Post-Master of Winterset. John A. Pitzer was the next Post-Master, and served the county several years in that capacity. Thomas Bird and Wm. M. Knowlton, were the next to receive the postal honors. Mastin Glazebrook received the appointment in 1864, and he served with great satisfaction, until the change of administration in 1860, when J. J. Davies received the appointment as Post-master, in which capacity he served until the summer of 1867. Francis Marion Cassidy then received the appointment, and he is at the present time our very faithful and accommodating Post-master.

POST OFFICES OF MADISON COUNTY.

Winterset—Francis Marion Cassidy, Postmaster.

Clanton—in Monroe Township—Wesley Wilson, Postmaster.

Ellsworth—in Crawford Township—O. Crawford, Postmaster.

Kasson—in Monroe Township—Benjamin Blythe, Postmaster.

Middle River—in Webster Township—Otho Davis, Postmaster.

North—in Madison Township—George Clemons, Postmaster.

Earlham—in Madison Township—Martin Cook, Postmaster.

Ohio—in Ohio Township—Samuel Walker, Postmaster.

Peru—in Walnut Township—H. C. Wright, Postmaster.

St. Charles—in South Township—L. P. Thompson, Postmaster.

Venus—in Grand River Township—Martin Jessup, Postmaster.

Debord's Point—in South Township—Marius Debord, Postmaster.

FIRST COURT HELD IN MADISON COUNTY.

The first court held in Madison county, met May 31st, 1849, in a store and saloon, which was given up for the use of the court, for the time being. William McKay, of Des Moines, was the Judge. He took his seat back of the counter, and the attorneys and clients in front.

The following persons composed the first Grand Jury:

Hampton Jones, David Cheneworth, Lewis Baum, Irwin Baum, M. C. Debord, E. J. Hinkle, Noah Bishop, David Foil, Andrew Evans, William Hinshaw, J. C. Casebier, and Lewis Brinson.

VANMETER

Is a nice little town situated on Coon River, in Dallas county, fourteen miles north-east of Winterset, and nearly three miles north of the Madison county line, on the Chicago, Rock Island & Pacific Railroad. It is on the south bank of the river, one-half mile below the confluence of North and South Coon Rivers. Naturally, it belongs to Madison county, because rivers are natural boundaries, and a principal part of its trade comes from Madison county. Its location is good, for nature has done much for it. It is a good wood station for the railroad, for there is plenty of timber accessible. And there is also a good prospect that plenty of coal will be found convenient to the town. Water can be conveniently procured by digging from twelve to thirty feet, which is of a good quality. There is abundance of good stone within half a mile of the town. The town was first named Tracy, but has been changed because the railroad company refused to recognize that name. Its present name is in honor of Mr. Jacob R. Vanmeter, who has for years been one of the live men of Dallas county. The town was laid out by Wm. F. D. Wilson, in April,

1868. The first business building was built by William Whitmore, and used as a grocery. Dr. D. A. Bunce came to the place soon after and hung out his sign. The McCoy House, the best building in the place, was erected in May, 1868. The town has improved rapidly, though not in favor by the railroad company, and now contains sixty-five houses, and a population of about two hundred and twenty-five souls. The public school of the place is attended by sixty pupils, and is now under the supervision of J. M. Mosena, a teacher of experience and ability. The first sermon ever preached in the town limits, was delivered in the bar-room of the McCoy House, by Rev. T. D. Adams, a Methodist preacher. The town is represented by the following business men : Clayton Brothers have a good stock of dry goods and groceries and they are reliable business men. J. D. Ellis keeps a general store and is doing a good business. Those who deal in groceries exclusively are, Maticks & McKey, J. J. Moore, and G. H. Wood. They are all liberally patronized. The two drug stores in the place are owned by Dr. C. M. Dodge and Dr. E. L. Russell. They are also practicing physicians. A. Tindle keeps a neat house and grocery. The boot and shoemakers of the place are Christoff & Doty. Logan Doty is the only harness maker in the place. J. C. Taylor owns and runs a steam saw-mill. Getchel & Tichenor have an extensive lumber yard here kept by Stephen Adams and are doing a good business. The two hotels are the McCoy House and the Graham House. Peter White has a large stock of hardware and is rapidly building up a trade. The four physicians of the place are Doctors D. M. Bunce, E. L. Russell, C. M. Dodge and H. C. H. Fitzgerald. Dr. Fitzgerald is a graduate of the medical college at Keokuk. W. B. H. Wilson, one of the oldest residents of the county, is Postmaster. The large flouring mill of Vanmeter & Ellis, the most extensive mill in the county, and one of the best in the State, is located here. The cost of this mill was about forty thousand dollars. The railroad company have now determined to erect a depot at this point, which will give new life to the town. The Methodists, the only organized religious denomination of the place, are building a very neat church edifice. The morals of the place are good, and it is a very desirable location for business men of all classes.

DE SOTO.

Although this thriving town is not situated in Madison county, yet it is located so close to its line and receives so large a portion of its trade that it is eminently deserving of a place in the history of the county. The town is located on the Chicago, Rock Island & Pacific Railroad, in Dallas county, on a beautiful eminence or hill, fourteen miles north of

Winterset. It was laid out early in the spring of 1868. The original town plat, embracing one hundred acres, was owned by G. J. & H. G Vanmeter and Thomas Hemphill, who donated the land as a free gift to the Railroad Company; they being possessed by nature with broad and generous views, had sufficient foresight to see the necessity of the gift. The Railroad Company afterwards bought one hundred and sixty acres adjoining the town and have laid it out in three and five acre tracts, which will afford valuable sites for residences. The town now contains about one hundred houses and about five hundred inhabitants. The inhabitants are a live, energetic, go-a-head, whole-souled people, all proud of their town and thankful that they live in so good a location. Some fine houses are now in process of building, and the town gives every indication of a rapid growth.

Scarcely was the survey completed by Capt. A. J. Lyon, then County Surveyor, when the site was named. It was christened De Soto, and its god-father was a railroad man. Why that name was suggested history does not tell us. Certainly not in honor of the great explorer, for men are so wise now-a-days that even names must be practical as well as pretty.

De Soto himself was not a success, although he had more than ordinary enthusiasm and courage, but though he failed to find the "Fountain of Youth" he discovered the Mississippi river, which, if the term may be allowed, is his monument, as it holds his remains, so if he failed in one thing he grandly succeeded in another. De Soto was probably chosen because it was pretty and easily spoken. Conductors who have to "call off" the stations twice a day do not like hard names. De Soto slips off the tongue as easy as "St. Patrick's Day" from a hand organ. At all events De Soto, the town, is a success, and has all the enthusiasm of its namesake with none of his vagaries.

The survey was completed March 27th, 1868. Upwards of three hundred lots were embraced in the original survey, of which two hundred and fifty have been sold, bringing from twenty-five dollars to five hundred dollars each.

The situation of De Soto is favorable. It is within a mile of the south fork of the Coon river, which affords excellent water privileges. Bulger Creek runs through the one hundred and forty acres adjoining the town on the south, which is valuable for stock purposes. It is bounded by heavy bluffs, which probably contain rich deposits of coal, that will ere long be developed. The land is elevated and rolling, which lends a charm to the scenery and affords choice building sites, and protects the place from much of the mud and filth found in many Western towns. Half a mile to the east is the stone quarry belonging to Julius Vanmeter, which yields an excellent variety and almost inexhaustible supply of sandstone, durable and easily dressed.

Another advantage, which has been considerably improved, is the clay deposit near the place, which makes excellent brick.

There is no timber immediately adjoining the town, but it is but a short distance to the river on the north where there is an abundance. Bulger is also lined with excellent timber near by.

An important advantage in De Soto's favor is the railroad interest centered there. Several officers of the road hold town property, and it is natural to suppose that they will use their influence to promote the growth of the place. The company have already built a fine depot, commodious enough for a city of 10,000 people—a large water tank, that is supplied from a spring sixty rods distant, the water being conducted through cast-iron pipes. There is also a turn-table here, the only one between Des Moines and Casey, in Adair county. It is expected that during the year the Company will build a round-house with a capacity for several engines, at this place. If this is done, De Soto will be a division station for freight. The division next east is at Brooklyn, ninety-two miles distant, and the one to be next west, will be at Atlantic, in Cass County, sixty miles distant. It may be noticed that De Soto is not the central point between the two stations, but as the Company is interested in the town and not interested to a great extent in the other stations toward Des Moines, the expectations of the De Soto people may be realized.

The farming country around De Soto is good. It is considerably settled up, but there is still large room for more good farmers.

The first house, or shanty, was built by Wash Smith, who, by the way, was one of the early settlers of Madison county. About the next house finished was by Henry Merryman. Lyon & Hemphill next put up a real estate office.

The business firms of De Soto, at the time of the writing of this book, April 1869, was about as follows :

Real Estate.—Lyon & Hemphill were the first to open a real estate office. It may be said of them that "they have sold De Soto." Until recently they were the only real estate agents in the place. They have a large interest in De Soto. Several buildings have been built by them —the most noticeable one is the two-story brick not yet completed, which measures 44 x 65 feet, with stone basement. It will be finished off in the most approved style. Lyon & Hemphill have their hands full of business and are likely to have for a long time.

Hall & Wyman have recently gone into the real estate business. Mr. Wyman came to De Soto in October and engaged in the hardware business. About the first of December, 1868, he sold his stock to Hards & Smith. Mr. Wyman then took in Mr. Hall as a partner, and engaged in the land business. They bought forty acres adjoining the town plat north on the Adel road. They have also bought twenty-eight town lots. They have lately built a handsome new office. There is no doubt about their success. They are business men and gentlemen to deal with.

Dry Goods.—A. Collins was the second who offered dry goods and groceries for sale in the town. He built a fine two-story frame building, using the lower story as a store-room. He has a large stock of dry goods, groceries, &c., and an extensive trade. He is permanently located, and believes in De Soto. He is also Postmaster, and, being a Radical, will probably enjoy the office the next four years.

J. B. O'Neal & Co., are enterprising young merchants. The "Co." are brothers. They also have a store at Newton. Their store always looks attractive, and they sell a large quantity of goods. They tell us that most of their trade comes from Madison county. They commenced business in August. Having a good deal of the fight-it-out-on-that-line spirit, they will succeed.

E. D. Smith & Co., keep a general assortment of dry goods and groceries. They commenced business in August in the building now occupied by R. Hellyer. Having sold that they built another where they are having a satisfactory trade.

Hardware—W. E. Parmelee was the first man who brought on a stock of hardware. He sold out his stock to W. C. Newman. He will continue in the store as an agent for Mr. Newman.

Hard & Smith, manufacturers and dealers in hardware, stoves and tin ware, bought out Mr. Wyman in November. They design keeping a general assortment of agricultural implements. They are young men, also, and are bound to succeed.

Furniture.—Robert Hellyer was among the very first to commence business in De Soto. He first engaged in the grocery trade. He and Mr. Owen built the fine two-story brick store, which they sold to J. D. Cavenor. Mr. Hellyer then bought Smith's building and commenced to sell and manufacture furniture. He employs two hands. His stock is large and so are his sales.

Bakers—W. H. Brown & Bro., first engaged in the grocery business, but soon sold out their stock to J. D. Cavenor. They are nearly ready to start a bakery. They are in the fine two-story building built by J. W. Eldridge. They propose to run a cart to Adel and Winterset.

Drugs.—Dr. S. B. Campbell & Co., opened a fine drug store. Dr. Campbell, besides having had a large experience as a practical

apothecary, took a course of study at the Chemical Labratory at Ann
Arbor, Michgan. Associated with him is Dr. A. P. McCullough, who
hung out his shingle in the new railroad town. The Doctor
is a graduate of Rush Medical College of Chicago; is a gentle-
man of culture and is meeting with the success that he deserves. Dr.
F. C. Stewart is another highly educated and successful physician.
Dr. Thos. M. Cummock, a popular physician, is also a resident of
De Soto.

Groceries.

The merchants all keep groceries, but N. Murray is the only one who
keeps groceries and nothing else. He bought the fine brick store formerly owned by J. D. Cavenor, and has it well stocked with all kinds
of groceries.

Restaurants.

D. M. Farrar keeps a restaurant and oyster saloon. He has $900 in
store building and residence.

A. M. Kibby keeps an oyster saloon and restaurant. He keeps a
good house. He will build a new residence in the spring.

M. M. Harrah, restaurant keeper, opened the last of May, was the
first man who brought any goods to the place. C. & M. M. Harrah
keep a livery stable. They also own the stage line running to Adel.

The Revere House, a large three-story frame, was built by the Railroad Company. It is now owned by Capt. A. J. Lyon, and its present
popular lessee and landlord is L. H. Doty, a man of small stature but
big heart.

Miscellaneous.

The Depot is kept by A. Smart, a public spirited citizen never behind
in any good enterprise. Mr. Lewis is the telegraph operator, a good
looking unmarried young gentleman.

Chase & Brothers, carpenters and contractors, came to De Soto in
May. They have built a dozen houses and are ready for more jobs.

J. W. Eldridge brought on a stock of lumber early in July. He
keeps a complete stock, also coal and lime.

Sargeant & Stevens, harness makers, commenced business August
1868. They have a good trade and do good work.

J. A. Spaulding opened a shoe shop in September, 1868. He has all
the boots and shoes to make that he wants.

H. I. Jones keeps an eating-house and takes boarders. His house,
one and a half story high, costing $1,000, is always kept in good order.

Mr. Hellyer, brother of R. Hellyer, keeps a meat market in the basement of Cavenor's building.

There are two blacksmith shops in De Soto. They are kept by B. F. Way, Wm. Cole & Son, and Frank Gilman.

H. G. Van Meter's Flouring Mill is but a mile and a half distant. An addition was built to this mill last summer at a cost of $5,500. This is one of the best mills in the county.

Julius Van Meter sold his interest in the mill last year. His farm of 1080 acres joins De Soto on the north.

The citizens of De Soto have shown their liberality by building a school-house and church by stock subscription. The building is 21x48 feet, and cost $900. It is occupied alternate Sundays by the Presbyterian and Methodists. Rev. John E. Darby, formerly an old resident of Madison county, is the Methodist pastor; and Rev. E. Bayles is the Presbyterian minister.

Messrs. Wm. Kerrick & Co., carpenters and joiners, and A. Kerrick, sign and house painter, who were old settlers in Madison county, are also residents of De Soto, and are doing a thriving business.

Looking back to this time last year when there was not a solitary house where there is now a thriving town of 500 inhabitants, we are reminded of the age of progress we live in, and what railroads will do. We cannot have too many.

DEXTER.

Dexter is a new town on the C., R. I. &. P. R. R., thirty-five miles west of Des Moines, and twenty miles north-west of Winterset. It was laid out about June 30th, 1868. At that time there was only one building, and that was occupied by Mabe Marshal, who was the owner of the land which now forms the town site. It is located on the north half of the north-east quarter of section 31, township 78, range 29 west, lying just one half mile east, and three-fourths of a mile north of the south-west corner of Dallas county. It is surrounded by a magnificent country, being the best parts of Dallas, Madison, Adair and Guthrie counties.

The following are among the leading business firms of Dexter at the present time:

Agricultural Implements and Seeds.—E. O. Burt & Co.

Dry Goods and Groceries.—A. E. Dutton; Wilshire & Myers; C. W. Roland; J. D. Osborn, and —— Cheesman.

Hardware and Agricultural Implements.—Carruthers & Bro.; Rogers Helm & Co.

Lumber Dealers.—Vanorman & Bro.; Chas. O. Bass, agent for Getchell & Tichenor.

Livery Stable.—O. F. McVey.

Boots and Shoes.—James Kirkland.

Real Estate Exchange and Bank.—L. J. Barton, & Co.
Real Estate Agent and Notary Public.—H. Freeman,
Druggists.—Hunter & Bros., and J. G. Stanley.
Grain Dealers.—J. Allen, and E. Jackson.
Blacksmiths.—Fisher & ——
Hotel.—Dexter House, J. J. Young, Landlord.
Saddlery and Harness.—Frank Battee.

Dexter now contains over one hundred houses and over four hundred inhabitants; and new houses are springing up as if by magic. Property owners are ornamenting their homes with shade trees, and shrubbery and are setting out all varieties of large and small fruits. There is no school-house or church building as yet, but arrangements are making to build one during the present season. Religious services, sabbath schools and prayer meetings are held regularly at the present time in the depot building, and all are well attended.

The Western Stage Co., run a coach daily, (carrying the U. S. mail) from Dexter to Panora, via Redfield. This, in connection with the constant arrival and departure of trains with freight for Dale City Morrisburgh, Redfield and Panora, and the constant influx of strangers hunting land, teams loading with lumber, the sound of hammer saw and plane, the stone masons trowel and the shrieks of the locomotives of the five or six daily trains, makes a scene of busy life not surpassed by many towns of far greater age and pretentions.

The town contains at the present time, eleven dry goods stores, two hardware, two drug stores, one agricultural implement store, two lumber yards, two groceries, one boot and shoe shop, two grain buyers, one livery stable, two meat markets, one saddle and harness shop, one hotel, two milliners, two blacksmith shops, one wagon and carriage shop, one cabinet shop, two real estate agents, one exchange office, one barber shop, three physicians, three notaries—but no lawyer—three boarding-houses and two restaurants.

There is a vein of excellent coal two and one-half miles north-west of the town that is sufficiently large to furnish the town and surrounding country with an inexhaustible supply of fuel. Stone of excellent quality, is also found in abundance within two miles of town, which is very valuable for building and lime purposes. Good brick clay is also found convenient to town. With these advantages, and an enterprising class of citizens, Dexter cannot fail to be a place of some importance.

The citizens of Dexter are moral, intelligent and refined. They are fully aware of the advantages of their town and the demands of the times, and invite those seeking homes in a healthy, growing place, to visit Dexter and compare its advantages with other places, feeling that it

has nothing to lose thereby.   There is plenty of room for moral, energetic men to build up a good trade, and get a good home cheap, what
more can be wanted?

STUART.

Stuart is the name of a new town on the C., R. I. & P. R. R., on the
n. w. qr. of sec. 4, T. 77, R. 30. It is located in Lincoln township, Adair
county, Iowa. It was laid out in the spring of '69, by Charles Stuart,
who owned the land on which it is situated. It is the first station
west of Dexter, and is 42 miles west of Des Moines. It now contains
about a dozen houses and a railroad depot; and it has every prospect
of becoming soon a good-sized, flourishing railroad town. It is located
on a high, beautiful prairie, and the country around it comprises the
best portion of Adair county, and is a continuation of what is known
as the "Quaker Divide." Abundance of coal has been found within
two and a half miles of the station. Its situation in the midst of so
beautiful a farming country, its future prospects can not be otherwise
than bright. The prices of dwelling and business lots are low, in comparison with those of other railroad towns. The inhabitants of this
new railroad town offer liberal inducements for good moral and industrious mechanics and business men of all kinds to come and settle in
their midst, where they can obtain for themselves and their families
comfortable homes, in a good country.

GUTHRIE STATION.

This flourishing railroad town was laid out about the 20th of December, 1868, by the railroad company. It is situated on the Chicago,
Rock Island & Pacific Railroad, fifty-five miles west of Des Moines, in
Guthrie county, one and one-half miles north of the Guthrie county
line, and near the centre east and west, and but a short distance from
the head of North River. The town now (June 1869) contains thirty-
two houses and a population of two hundred souls. New houses are
being rapidly built, and new-comers are coming in thick and fast, and
the town has flattering prospects of future growth and prosperity.

Guthrie Station is the principal station for Dale City, Panora, Guthrie
Center and Morrisburg on the north, and for Fontanelle, Greenfield,
and Holliday on the south. All of the above points have good, heavy
settlements surrounding them. The surrounding country is of surpassing beauty and fertility, and comprises the west-end of the famous
"Quaker Divide." There is plenty of coal, stone and timber convenient. A large and flourishing grist-mill is located on Coon River,
just four miles north of Guthrie Station, owned by John Preston; and
John Linsdale has a large woolen factory, located at Dale City, which
is also about five miles north of Guthrie Center.

Among the large farmers in the immediate vicinity of Guthrie Center, we will mention the names of the following: G. B. McPherson, John Hitchcock, and William Davis. There are two organized societies of Christians in the town, viz: the Methodists, under the administration of Rev. Mr. Sweeney, and the Presbyterian, with Rev. H. H. Kellogg for Pastor. Arrangements are already being made by the Presbyterian society to build a church during the present summer. A good school already exists and is well supported.

The "raw prairie" may yet be purchased within reasonable distance for from ten to twenty dollars per acre. Improved farms command from twenty to forty dollars per acre. The town lots range in price from fifty to two hundred and fifty dollars each. There is one hotel in the town, kept by N. Gregory, and it is an excellent point for another hotel. A harness shop and a livery stable are much needed in the town.

Business Notices.—George B. McPherson keeps constantly on hand a large assortment of building material.

Gregg & Wear, dry goods and general merchants. This old and reliable house study the wants of the public, and are worthy of confidence.

H. N. & J. M. Ross, hardware, stoves, and farming implements. Have the agency for all the best reapers and harvesters.

C. S. Henderson & Co., general merchants.

Samuel Stultz is the Postmaster.

Any one wishing further information in regard to Guthrie Station can correspond with G. B. McPherson, or with Hill & Swisher, real estate agents.

COUNTY OFFICERS.

In the early days of the county there were no political divisions among the people. The county was almost entirely democratic in politics. The first officers of the county were as follows:

Commissioners—David Bishop, Wm. Combs and Wm. Gentry.
Clerk—G. W. McClellan.
Recorder—P. M. Boyles.
Treasurer—Joseph K. Evans.
Prosecuting Attorney—Alfred D. Jones.
Surveyor—Alfred D. Jones.

The first political contest was in August, 1851, between the Democrats and Whigs. Both of the political parties were in the field, with forces drilled and well officered, but the Democracy triumphed. The whole number of votes cast was 224. It was as follows:

For County Judge—John A. Pitzer..........................154
For County Judge—*John Spurlock* 70
For Sheriff—Silas Barnes 129
For Sheriff—*Otho Davis* 87
For Recorder—I. D. Guiberson 118
For Recorder—*Enos Berger* 102
Whigs in italics.

The next election, August, 1852, was closely contested; every man at his post. The contest was for Clerk of the District Court. The candidates, I. G. Houk and Alfred D. Jones, each had 131 votes—a tie. This, according to law, had to be decided by casting lots. Houk came out first best, and made as good and efficient an officer as the county ever had.

The election of 1853 was one of note. The Whigs, or as they termed themselves, the "People's Party," went to battle with a vigor and with a determination to conquer, while the Democratic party were divided, and consequently defeated. Enos Berger, Whig, was elected Recorder and Treasurer, over L. McCarty; and L. S. Garrett was elected Sheriff, over P. M. Boyles.

In April, 1855, there was a different contest at the ballot-box. It was for or against a "Prohibitory Liquor Law." The contest was quite warm; all the available forces on each side were out, and the vote showed, for Prohibitory Law, 168, against the law, 343.

The first organization of the Republican party was during the year 1855. H. J. B. Cummings had the honor, we believe, to draft the first resolutions, organizing the party. The contest was on the County Judge. The candidates were John A. Pitzer, Republican, and E. R. Guiberson, Democrat. At this contest all the appliances were used, from the "stump" to "bushwhacking" and "button-holeing." Pitzer was elected Judge. At this election Dr. L. M. Tidrick, Democrat, was elected Treasurer and Recorder, Wm. Combs, Democrat, was elected Sheriff; William Davis, Democrat, was elected Surveyor; and Dr. J. G. Scott, Republican, was elected Coronor.

In 1856, the election was for Senator and Representative. M. L. McPherson, Republican, was elected Senator, over John Hilton, the Democratic candidate. B. F. Roberts, Republican, was elected Representative over David McCarty, Democrat. The Senatorial District was then composed of Warren, Madison, Adair and Cass counties. The Representative District was composed of Madison, Adair and Cass counties. At this election, C. D. Bevington, Democrat, was elected County Clerk over L. R. Boxly, Republican.

In 1857, John A. Pitzer, familiarly known as the "old war-horse," again entered the field as a candidate for County Judge. He had a noble competitor for his opponent, I. G. Houk; but he distanced him in the race, and was again elected County Judge. At this election J. K. Evans, Democrat, was elected Sheriff over Wm. Compton, Republican. David Bishop, Republican, was elected Treasurer and Recorder, over Otho Davis, Democrat. To illustrate what a change has taken place in the public sentiment within the past ten years, we will add that the vote for striking out the word " white, " in the article regulating suffrage in the State Constitution in this county, stood as follows: "For striking out the word white," 47 votes; "Against striking out the word white," 1144 votes! A great contrast to the vote ten years afterwards, on this same question, when it was carried by a handsome majority.

In 1858 the contest was confined to the office of County Clerk. The candidates were William Pursell, (Republican), and C. D. Bevington, (Democrat). The contest was the warmest political fight ever made in this county, unless we except that on the office of County Treasury in 1868. The Democrats won the victory, and C. D. Bevington was elected Clerk.

In 1859, Mr. M. L. McPherson was again elected to the office of State Senator, from this District. D. S. Tannehill was his competitor. T. D. Jones, (Democrat), was elected Representative over David Bishop, (Republican). E. R. Guiberson, (Democrat), was elected County Judge, over A. Ballentine, (Republican). I. G. Houk, (Democrat), was elected Treasurer and Recorder, over James Shepherd, (Republican). Samuel Hamilton, (Democrat), was elected Sheriff, over Wm. Jones, (Republican). Lewis Mayo, (Democrat), was elected County Superintendent; James Shepherd, (Republican), was his competitor. Dr. D. B. Allen was elected Coroner. Total number of votes cast, thirteen hundred and sixty-four.

In 1860, the fight was on the office of County Clerk; E. A. Huber, (Democrat), was elected Clerk; Lytle Faurote, (Republican), was his competitor.

The vote for county officers, in 1861, was as follows:

> For *Representative—A. Hood*......................................688
> For *Representative*—C. D. Bevington......................653
> For **Treasurer and Recorder**—I. G. Houk................700
> For *Treasurer and Recorder—J. Carmean*..............689
> For *Sheriff*—Samuel Hamilton...............................685
> For *Sheriff—Lewis Garrett*.....................................671
> For *County Judge*—Lewis Mayo.............................779
> For *County Judge—T. D. Jones* 668

Republicans in Italics.

In 1862, John Leonard, (Republican) was elected District Attorney, over W. H. McHenry, his competitor. M. R. Tidrick, (Republican), was elected County Clerk, over E. A. Huber, his Democratic competitor.

The vote for county officers in 1863, was as follows:

For Representative—John E. Darby...........................999
For Representative—Joseph W. Lane....................618
For Sheriff—H. C. Carter......................................781
For Sheriff—S. H. Guye.......................................608
For Treasurer and Recorder—R. A. Stitt...............784
For Treasurer and Recorder—A. W. Ford..............612
For County Superintendent—H. W. Hardy..............995
For County Superintendent—O. H. Perry................618

NOTE.—At this election N. W. Garretson was elected County Judge, and E. S. McCarty, County Surveyor, but we could not learn who their competitors were.

In 1864, M. R. Tidrick was again elected County Clerk; O. H. Perry was his competitor this time. O. A. Moser, (Republican) was elected County Recorder, over Lewis Mayo, (Democrat). The total number of votes cast at this election was 1,395.

In 1865, the vote on county officers was as follows:

For Representative—J. M. Browne...........................984
For Representative—V. Wainwright.......................566
For County Judge—N. W. Garretson 993
For County Judge—Lewis Mayo.............................562
For County Treasurer—R. A. Stitt........................989
For County Treasurer—Ed. McLaughlin.................556
For Sheriff—J. F. Brock.......................................988
For Sheriff—S. S. Guiberson................................570
For County Surveyor—O. A. Moser......................1000
For County Surveyor—Simeon Rutty......................564
For County Superintendent—J. S. Goshorn..............987
For County Superintendent—J. T. Seevers................566

In 1866, the officers elected and the vote cast, was as follows:

For County Clerk—M. R. Tidrick............................1191
For County Clerk—O. F. McLaughlin.....................630
For Recorder—O. A. Moser..................................1180
For Recorder—N. E. Wilder.................................641
For County Surveyor—W. H. Lewis...(no opp.)......1181

Republicans in Italics.

The election of County Officers in 1867 was as follows;

For Representative—B. F. Murry..........................1072
For Representative—George W. Seevers.................. 766
For County Judge—T. C. Gilpin...........................1172
For County Judge—Willis H. Compton................. 738
For County Treasurer—Wm. H. Leonard.............. 994
For County Treasurer—E. G. Perkins.................... 902
For Sheriff—J. F. Brock.............................1178
For Sheriff—Wm. H. Clampitt........................... 721
For County Surveyor—P. G. Andrews..................1168
For County Supervisor—J. L. Andrews................. 52
For County Superintendent—W. H. Hardy.............1154
For County Superintendent—Geo. W. Schnellbacher 745

The contest for the year 1867, was for the office of County Treasurer. It was, perhaps, the warmest strife for office ever made in the county. The fight first took place in the Republican Nominating Convention. The friends of both Leonard and Perkins made desperate efforts to control the Convention. Bitter feeling and considerable confusion arose in the Convention. Doctor Leonard was made the choice of the Convention. And the Perkins faction went home very much dissatisfied with the proceedings, and they soon induced Perkins to run as an independent candidate. Both factions marshalled their hosts, and made strenuous and unremitting efforts to elect their candidate. The Democrats made no nomination for that office. There was much acrimony and bitterness of feeling at that time, but we believe all parties are now on sociable and agreeable terms.

OFFICERS OF MADISON COUNTY FOR 1869.

Clerk of The District Court—Daniel E. Cooper.
County Auditor—Thos. C. Gilpin.
County Treasurer—Wm. L. Leonard.
County Recorder—Osiah A. Moser.
County Sheriff—Jonas F. Brock.
Superintendent of Common Schools—Henry W. Hardy.

OFFICERS OF THE CITY OF WINTERSET FOR 1869.

Mayor—Eli Wilkin.
Recorder—J. Mc Leod, Jr.
Treasurer—J. S. White.
Marshal—T. M. Hyskel.
Aldermen First Ward—John M. Andrews.
                      John Sturman.
                      Wm. R. Shrivier.

Aldermen Second Ward—D. D. Davisson.

Wm. C. Newlon.

C. P. Lee.

BOARD OF SUPERVISORS.

In the year 1861, the system of County Board of Supervisors were organized in the various counties of the State, by act of the Legislature; the following persons composed the

FIRST BOARD OF SUPERVISORS IN MADISON COUNTY.

Josiah Arnold, of Center Township.
William McDonald, of Jefferson Township.
Otho Davis, of Webster Township.
Henry A. Myers, of Jackson Township.
Milton Thompson, of South Township.
J. C. Scott, of Grand River Township.
Lewis Crawford, of Madison Township.
Oliver Crawford, of Crawford Township.
Ira S. Smith, of Lee Township.
Ashford Lake, of Walnut Township.
J. D. Hartman, of Ohio Township.
Harbert Harris, of Monroe Township.
David Stanton, of Penn Township.

THE BOARD OF SUPERVISORS IN 1863.

David McCarty, Chairman,	A. Bonham,
J. W. Lane,	S. Ross,
O. Crawford,	H. Hann,
S. Ralston,	A. Bennett,
E. H. Venard,	G. A. Beerbower,
Wm. H. McDonald,	H. Harris,
S. Harter,	W. J. Davis.
L. N. Clark,	

THE BOARD OF SUPERVISORS OF 1865.

William H. McDonald, Chairman,	M. M. McGee,
George W. Roberts,	Thos. H. Pendleton,
O. Crawford,	Simeon Hamblin,
J. M. Browne,	Abihu Wilson,
E. H. Venard,	W. J. Davis,
P. M. Boyles,	H. C. Smith,
S. A. Ross,	J. C. Scott,
B. F. Brown,	A. Hood.
James Allen,	

BOARD OF SUPERVISORS OF 1869.

William Anderson, Chairman, Ohio Township.
John McLeod, Sr., Center Township.
J. D. Whitenack, Madison Township.
D. F. Turney, Lee Township.
Daniel Francis, Penn Township.
James Goare, Douglas Township.
Van B. Wiggin, Union Township.
George B. Breeding, Scott Township.
I. N. Hogle, Lincoln Township.
C. Hughart, Crawford Township.
Thos. W. Stiles, South Township.
William Smith, Walnut Township.
Harbert Harris, Monroe Township.
O. B. Bissell, Jackson Township.
A. M. Hart, Webster Township.
J. J. Greer, Grand River Township.

SIMPSON CENTENARY COLLEGE.

The excellence of Iowa's schools and colleges has become proverbial, and ranking among the best and most flourishing is found Simpson Centenary College, located at Indianola, in our neighboring county of Warren. We see no need of our Madison county citizens sending their sons and daughters to colleges in Eastern States, when an institution, offering all the advantages of a university and scientific course, is to be found close to our own doors. We believe in Iowa men patronizing Iowa institutions, and that our Iowa boys and girls can be educated as thoroughly at home as they can in foreign parts. We commend this college to all who have sons or daughters whom they propose to educate, as an institution in every way worthy of their support. Indianola can boast of having no beer, billiard or saloon of any kind within its limits, or within five miles of the city, hence no temptations to indulge in that which destroys both body and soul are presented.

PENN TOWNSHIP.

Penn township is bounded on the north by Dallas county, on the south by Jackson township, on the east by Madison township, and on the west by Adair county, and it is the north-west corner township of the county. This township embraces the most beautiful portion of the "Quaker Divide" and it is said to be one of the most charming townships of land to be found anywhere in the State of Iowa. The soil is a dark loam, entirely free from stone, and exceedingly fertile; ready

and admirably formed by nature for the use of the plow and the husbandman. The township is almost entirely destitute of timber, and
there is scarcely an acre of rough or waste land in the whole township.
The prairies are high, and have a gently waving or undulating surface,
and its general appearance is as grand as any garden spot. Upon be-
holding this lovely country, the heart very naturally borrows from
Bryant the following rhapsody:

> —— "My heart swells while the dilated sight
> Takes in the encircling vastness. Lo! they stretch
> In airy undulations far away,
> As if the ocean in its gentlest swell,
> Stood still, with all his rounded billows fixed
> And motionless forever.
>
> Man hath no part in this glorious work ;
> The hand that built the firmament hath heaved
> And smoothed these verdant swells, and sown their slopes
> With herbage, planted them with island groves,
> And hedged them round with forests. Fitting floor
> For his magnificent temple of the sky—
> With flowers whose glory and whose multitude,
> Rival the constellations."

This township has been improved within the past two years, faster
than any other portion of the county. In 1867 it contained only a population of 225, it now contains a population of 454.

C. P. Wright and James Jeffries were the first settlers in the township; they came in '56, David Stanton, Thomas Wilson, and J. E.
Darby settled in the township in '57.

Among the large and extensive farmers in the township at the present time, are the following individuals, viz: Wheeler and Conger,
(they have one section of land under cultivation), Rankin and Bell,
David Stanton, Daniel Francis, Thomas Wilson, Christopher Wilson,
D. C. Holmes, A. H. Armstrong, Abihu Wilson, and others.

Wheeler and Conger deal very extensively in live stock. Stanton
and Francis deal quite extensively in lands and real estate.

Allen Barnett has lately commenced a very fine nursery in this township. He designs to make it a permanent and reliable nursery.

Messrs. Wheeler, Conger, Ford, Rankin, and one or two others have
one *little* field enclosed with one fence, which contains over five thousand acres of land.

The inhabitants of this township are mostly Friends or Quakers.
They are industrious, honest and frugal; generous, kind-hearted and

religious; intelligent and temperate; and, as a class, are amongst the best people in the world to live with.

The township has six good school-houses, all in a flourishing condition.

There is some good stone in the township, out of which some fine stone houses have been built. North Branch and the south fork of North Branch pass through the township.

Pilot Grove is a beautiful body of natural forest trees, of about six or seven acres in extent, and it is the only timber in the township worthy of mention. It is said to have derived its name from the fact that it is situated on high ground, and can be seen for miles around; and the California and other emigrants passing through the county at an early day, and the early settlers of the surrounding country would "pilot" their course by it. It is on the farm of David Stanton, who has built his residence in the midst of the grove.

The man who has a farm in Penn township is cheerfully and independently fixed for life.

MADISON.

Is bounded on the north by Dallas county, on the south by Douglas, on the east by Jefferson, and on the west by Penn. North Branch passes through the south part of the township, along which stream there is a large growth of heavy timber. The north-half is a high and gently rolling prairie, as beautiful and pleasing to the eye as any garden spot. It is on the divide between North Branch and Coon River, and is widely known as "Quaker Divide," taking this name from the fact that most of the people residing on the divide are Quakers or Friends.

Derrick Bennett, now a citizen of Winterset, made the first permanent improvement north of North Branch. In 1852 he settled on and improved the farm now owned by William Barnett; and to him (Bennett) belongs the honor of making the first "breaking" on that divide. Soon afterward William Fee came and settled on the farm on which he now resides. In 1853 and 1854 John Brown, J. W. Burnett (now of Winterset) White Burnett, John Wilson, together with his sons Abihu, Christopher, and Henry, all settled on the same divide. In 1854, Benjamin Powell and his sons, William Coe, and Michael and Jacob Gabbert, settled in the eastern part, north of North Branch.

James Brewer settled on the south side of North Branch, as early as 1849, and he was, perhaps, the first settler in Madison township. In 1852, Henry Groseclose, Henry Rice and a man named

Hannahs, took claims along North Branch, on the south side. In 1852 John Todd came and improved a farm at a place now known as Worthington. Mr. Todd remained at this place nine years and improved a large farm, and he done much toward improving and settling up that part of the township. In 1853 he set out a large orchard, which were the first fruit trees ever planted north of North River, in Madison county. Following soon after Mr. Todd, George T. Nichols, Leroy Anderson, and others, settled in the same neighborhood.

Jacob Bennett settled where he now resides, in 1851 and 1852, and bought out the claims of James Brewer, Absolom Bedell, and all the claim-holders on the south side of North Branch, and he has been for many years one of the largest farmers in the township.

The first school taught was in a building built especially for that purpose in 1853, by Jacob Bennett; and it was taught by Samuel Kirkland. The township now has five schools, all in good flourishing condition. The Friends have also a very neat and substantial meeting-house.

The lively little railroad town of Earlham is also located in this township, of which we speak more fully elsewhere.

The farmers located here, especially the Friends on "Quaker Divide," have paid much attention to the raising of fine stock.

Among the more substantial farmers, we would mention the names of Conger & Wheeler, George T. Nichols, Wm. Fee, Wm. Barnett, Martin Compton, David Mills, Seth and Milton Wilson, and others.

Considering the natural advantages of Madison township, her abundant supply of timber, water, stone, coal and the magnificent prairies, and the excellent class of people who reside there, she will rank as one of the best townships in the county.

EARLHAM.

Earlham is a village recently located on the C., R. I. & P. R. R., and is the only railroad town in Madison county at the present time. It is situated on the s. hf. of the s. w. qr. of sec. 6—77—28. Its distance from Winterset is about 13 miles. The land on which it is laid out was originally entered by Seth Wilson, Sr., and conveyed by him afterward to Mr. David Hocket. Last Autumn, B. F. Allen, Esq., of Des Moines, purchased the land of David Hocket, for $20 per acre. When Mr. Allen bought the land, it was understood that he intended to make a town of it, and several parties immediately began to arrange for building. Before the town was surveyed two or three houses occupied the site of the future village. Martin Cook, who had built a store-house a half mile west of the place, removed it to Earlham at once; and Dr. M. R. Lyons commenced building a dwelling and a drug store. When the town came to be laid out, Martin's store was found to occupy a part of two lots and a street; and Dr. L.'s building stood squarely in the centre of a street 100 feet wide. Of course these gentlemen had some moving to do. As soon as the survey was completed by the railroad engineer, lots were offered for sale at prices ranging from $25 to $125. Martin Cook bought the first lot in the new town, and many others followed in rapid succession. Before the village had existed 15 days one half at least of the lots were owned by men who intended to improve them as soon as the weather and other circumstances would permit. A side railroad track had been put down late in the fall, and a section house and water tank erected by the Railroad Company.

Sometime during the winter, Messrs. Getchel & Tichenor of Des Moines, established a lumber yard at Earlham; and later Messrs. Thompson & Maddern, of Davenport, opened a competing yard. These establishments furnished material for building, and, notwithstanding the season and weather were the worst possible for such operations, business houses and dwellings began to go up with at rapidity and steadiness, that demonstrated at once the determination of the new settlers to build up the town. The result is that scarcely five months since the first stake was planted in the frozen earth, Earlham contains at least thirty-five buildings, many of which are first class for a country village.

The name for the town was chosen by Mr. Milton Wilson, and was taken from the Earlham of Indiana, noted for its Quaker College. It was this circumstance, we suppose, that suggested to the minds of the first settlers the idea of making it a college town. However suggested, it was their first idea, and was immediately acted on. A stock company was organized for the purpose about two months ago, and the plan is steadily and surely maturing. Something like $5000 worth of the stock has been taken, and since the best men in the county are interested in the enterprise, there is no doubt of its ultimate success. It has been resolved that at least $10,000 worth of stock shall be taken before any step toward building shall be taken. This amount will be subscribed for by July 1st, 1869. The citizens have also subscribed about $1200 for the purpose of erecting a Union Chapel for Divine service.

Any one at all familiar with the surroundings of Earlham can have no doubt of its future prosperity. Railroads, churches, schools, &c., are great developers of towns; but their ultimate success and prosperity depend almost solely on the country surrounding them. All towns look to the farming community, more or less, for support. In this respect Earlham is peculiarly fortunate in its location. For productive powers, variety of soil, ease of cultivation; amount of land in proportion to the whole susceptible of cultivation; for the purity of the water and healthfulness of the air; for its beauty and for its every natural advantage, the country around Earlham can well bear comparison with any other section of Iowa, or with any country in the world. A large proportion of the land within six or eight miles of town is under cultivation. The assessed value of the township, as per assessment just completed for 1869, is, exclusive of the village, within a fraction of $300,000.

One mile south of town is a quarry of peculiar stone, which is now being opened by its recent purchaser, Mr. J. E. Parkins, formerly of Winterset. He bought it of Milton Wilson, two months since, for $2000. Competent judges in Chicago and New York have pronounced this stone inferior to none known in the West, for building purposes. When first taken from its bed it is extremely soft, and almost as easily worked as chalk. Exposure to the air, however, renders it as hard as granite. Mr. P. has a force of twenty-five or thirty men quarrying the rock and dressing it on the ground, ready for shipment. We understand that he has secured the contract for building the Railroad depot at Earlham of this stone. He has erected a patent lime kiln near the quarry, and will be able to turn off a car load of lime daily, when he gets the thing in running order.

Mr. Seth Wilson, from Madison county, has a fine large hotel, nearly ready for the reception of guests. In so good a house, and under the care of such a gentlemanly landlord, a traveler can spend a day or two very agreeably in Earlham.

The Railroad Company have appointed Martin Cook, Esq., their agent at this place, and the selection is certainly a happy one, for "Mart" is a good and capable fellow.

Dr. M. R. Lyon has a drug store in operation here, and is at present the only practicing physician in Earlham.

Joseph Cook has erected an agricultural warehouse, and does a commission business generally.

Messrs. Cammack & Hill are about to erect a large building for the same business. They are competent and experienced gentlemen, and are favored with the full confidence of business men and the community generally.

Barnett & Hawkins are already occupying their large store-room, (60 feet deep,) and have filled it with a splendid assortment of general merchandise

A. & T. E. Barnett have a number one grocery establishment. They are live, energetic young men, and they are doing a good business.

But we cannot specify even a tenth of the different firms and enterprises in this flourishing young city. The depot will be commenced immediately and rapidly pushed to a completion. According to the most reliable authority, Earlham is to be the *permanent division station* of the railroad, an honor that De Soto now enjoys temporarily. There is good reason also to believe that the B. W. & D. M. R. R. will intersect the C., R. I. &. P. R. R. at this point.

The high road to prosperity is broadly open to this infant town, and without doubt Earlham is destined to be one of the best towns between Des Moines and Council Bluffs. It certainly possesses sufficient advantages to raise it to that distinction; and we have no doubt that its enterprising inhabitants will use them well to that end.

JEFFERSON.

Is bounded on the north by Dallas county, on the south by Union, on the east by Lee, and on the west by Madison. North Branch passes through this township from west to east. There is abundance of good timber along this stream. Badger Creek also passes through the north part, but there is no timber on its banks. There are large quarries of good lime-stone on North Branch; and good coal is also found in considerable quantities along its banks. The surface of the country along the streams is quite broken and rough; but in other portions the prairies are high, grand and rolling, and there are dotted over them here and there many beautiful farms. The north part comprises a portion of that beautiful prairie lying between North Branch and Coon River, known as "Quaker Divide."

William Payton, St. Baur, and J. M. Brown were the first settlers. They came in 1853. D. H. Rose, George Gotshall, and Thos. Nicholson, settled here in 1854; and S. W. Nicholson, Wm. Schoen, and George Fisher came the season following.

The following residents own large and extensive farms: Adam and Simon Shambaugh, Jackson Smith, Wm. McDonald, Daniel Hazen, M. A. Knight, J. H. Hartenbower, Jacob Peyton, Anthony Myers, William and C. H. McClery, Robert Shields, Emerson Hazen, William H. Brewster, A. M. Peters and others.

Mr. Payton has a fine mansion, a good orchard, and other valuable improvements on his farm. John M. Mitchell and St. Baur have also excellent orchards on their farms; and most of the farmers have young and thrifty orchards planted out.

Adam and Simon Shambaugh are extensive wool growers, and they have at the present time over five thousand head of sheep.

A good saw mill is located on North Branch, owned by John Wiggins, which is doing a good business.

Religious worship and Sabbath Schools are held in the various school-houses of the township.

LEE

Is the northeast township of the county. It is bounded on the north by Dallas county, on the south by Crawford township, on the east by Warren county, and on the west by Jefferson township. There is but little timber, but it is a magnificent township of high rolling prairie. A large portion of this prairie is as beautiful as any that " ever laid out of doors." Badger Creek passes from west to east nearly through the center, and is its principal stream.

A man named Heaton, who resides in Pennsylvania, owns a section of land near the center of the township. The whole section lays high and dry, but gently rolling, in almost every direction, making it as grand as a garden spot. In 1858, Mr. Heaton laid off and staked this land into lots, with the intention of making a town there. It was his intention to build a large seminary there, to cost not less than $100,000. Many of the lots were contracted for at prices ranging from fifty to three hundred dollars each, and great expectations for a thriving town were raised. In the Summer of '58, Mr. Heaton, and quite a large number of citizens met on the ground, and speeches were made by B. F. Roberts and others, setting forth the great importance of a Seminary of learning at this point, etc. By the terms of sale, two-fifths of all money received for sale of lots was to be given towards the building of the seminary, and the remaining three-fifths was to draw six per cent interest, which was also applied for the benefit of the institution. Heaton, before leaving, executed a bond, in the sum of $50,000, which is registered in the Madison county records, for the faithful application of all moneys accruing according to the terms of the contract. From some cause, which we are unable to give, the praiseworthy enterprise was abandoned, and there is nothing at this day to show for the town of Heaton, but the stakes that were driven in the ground to mark out the lots.

The township of Lee is well adapted to agriculture and stock raising, the soil being inexhaustibly fertile, and well watered with small streams and springs. Its contiguousness to the Capital of the State, will warrant it an enviable place for homes.

In 1858 Lee was divided, and the west half is what now comprises Jefferson township. The township took its name from Harvey Lee, an early settler in the sounty. Mr. James Rothill settled on section thirty-one in 1852 and was its first settler. Soon after, James Lane, an Irishman, settled on section one, who soon afterwards sold his claim to Allen Majors. In '53 Andrew Hubbardand Esquire Flinn settled on sections four and eight. In '54, Geo W. Roberts and James Malone settled in the township. Soon after, Malone sold out to Thos. Cavenor, and Mr. Cavenor sold in '64 to N. W. Johnson. Mr. Johnson is an old Connecticut sea captain, and is the most extensive farmer here. His farm consists of a section and a half of land, and he is a very extensive dealer in live stock ; he generally buys all the surplus corn that his neighbors have to sell. And he is said to bear a good name, which " is better than rubies or precious stones."

Andrew Hubbard set out the first orchard in 1859. His trees yielded him eighty bushels of apples last Summer. L. N. Smith, George W. Roberts and Thomas England, also have very nice orchards, all bearing fruit. To illustrate the rapid growth of trees, in this soil, we will mention that L. N. Smith set out a cottonwood tree in '59, which was only three inches in circumference near the ground, but the same tree will now girt four feet and ten inches.

The most extensive farmers in the township are Captain Johnson, Geo. W. Roberts and Emerson Hazen.

It contains three schools, all in good flourishing condition.

JACKSON.

Is bounded on the north by Penn, on the south by Webster, on the east by Douglas, and on the west by Adair county. North River passes through it from west to east. There is on this stream an abundance of good timber and stone ; it also has timber sufficient for its own use, and also Penn, which depends mainly upon Jackson for its timber. The general surface of the country is somewhat rolling, just enough so to make a delightful farming country. With plenty of tim- ber and stone convenient, with the richest soil, with grand, rolling prairies, with abundance of good pure water for man and beast, with a good moral and energetic class of inhabitants, the citizens of this township very justly take a great pride in their homes, and feel that they have as good a country as the heart could desire to live in.

There are many large farms here, among them are those owned by William Early, O. B. Bissell, Noah Sulgrove, the Ralston Brothers, Joseph Davis, J. A. Davis, A. J. Speers, Thomas Early, Hindman Brothers, Dr. D. Hutchinson, John and Thomas Graham, the Rose Brothers and Samuel Bunn. Some of these large farms contain a section or very near a section of land each. The Ralston Brothers, William Early and the Graham Brothers have planted out five hundred acres of corn, each, this present season, (1869.)

Alfred Rice and a man named Phelon, were the first settlers in the Township. They came as early as 1850. Willis Rose, Samuel Bunn and O. B. Bissell settled here soon after. Rose and Bunn bought out the claims of Rice and Phelon.

William Early and Noah Sulgrove deal very extensively in live stock.

O. B. Bissell has a large orchard, of over three hundred trees, in good bearing condition. John Early has also a good orchard.

Rev. John E. Darby lived here many years and taught the first school. There are now five excellent school-houses, and religious worship and sabbath schools are held regularly in the several school-houses.

DOUGLAS,

Is bounded on the north by Madison, on the south by Lincoln, on the east by Union, and on the west by Jackson. Douglas like Union, is divided up into very desirable proportions of prairie and timber. North River and Cedar Creek pass through it, flowing from west to east. Numerous springs and streams also exist in various portions of it. Nature seems to have lavished her choicest favors on this part of the county. It contains, almost all over its entire surface, beautiful and desirable locations for farms. Many of the first settlers in the county chose their claims here, and it is to-day the most thoroughly settled township in the county; but few quarter sections but what are more or less improved. It contains at this time a population of 919.

Irvin Baum, its first settler, settled on the place where he now resides, May 14th, 1846. William and Jacob Combs came the same year. Clayton Pitzer settled on the farm where Matthew McGee now resides in '47; Robert Evans, George Fry, Jacob Fry and Jackson Howard settled in the township in '47. R. P. Bruce and Jonathan Myers settled on the farm where they now reside, as early as '49. Eli Sulgrove, Noah Sulgrove, Emanuel Sulgrove and Sherwood Howerton also settled here at an early day.

Among the large farmers are the following persons, viz:

Thomas McDonald, James Black, R. P. Bruce, James Foshier, M. M. McGee, I. S. Ford, Jonathan Myers, J. C. Wilson, Robt. Evans, Eb. Hays, Andrew Bennett, John, Norris, John Cooper, I. W. Moody, Joshua Bennett, Robert Duff, Jacob Reichart, and others. James Foshier has six hundred acres fenced in for his farm.

Albert Getchel has a magnificent and thrifty orchard of over six hundred large bearing trees. This orchard is the best in the county, and is worth a fortune to any man. George Sceevers, Jonathan Myers, Jacob Sickles, William Baird and M. M. McGee have also nice orchards.

A good steam saw-mill was erected in 1855 by Jonathan Myers and Martin Ruby. The mill is now owned by Samuel Kirkland, and is doing a thriving business. There are various church organizations and religious services and Sabbath Schools are held in the various school-houses.

Early Reminiscences.

Irvin Baum had the misfortune to lose his house by fire in a few days after it had been finished. It was a log-house, 18 x 20 and it was the largest house in the county at that time. In a few days afterwards, his neighbors, without giving him any notice, came and put him up another good substantial house.

In '47 William Combs had his fence destroyed by fire, while he was absent in Missouri on business. His neighbors gathered together on Sunday, and put up a new fence for him, and thus saved his crop from being destroyed by stock. Many instances might be given of the kind-heartedness and whole-souled feeling existing among the early settlers.

The early settlers made regular appointments to meet as often as once a week for social times, and they would roast a deer or two when they came together, and they would have a feast and good time generally.

During the severe winter of '55, the deep snow had so frozen and crusted on the top that it became impracticable for horses to travel on it ; and the severe weather had continued so long, that some of the settlers were becoming short of food ; under these circumstances Jacob Combs, William Combs, Irvin Baum and Lewis Baum, determined on going to the mill to procure meal, and to do this they were obliged to beat the snow with wooden mauls, all the way to Compton's mill on Middle River ; and in this way their horses were enabled to travel and they to obtain their meal. This is only one of the many hardships which the early settlers had to undergo.

UNION

Is bounded on the East by Crawford, and on the West by Douglas; on the North by Jefferson, and on the South by Scott.

Nature has lavished on it her richest favors. For equitable and proportionable distribution of nice rolling prairies, pleasant groves, heavy timber, rich soil, and stone and water privileges, perhaps it cannot be surpassed by any Congressional township in the State. Many of the first settlers of Madison County picked out their claims here as their choice for their homes. They availed themselves of the magnificent sites for homesteads along the beautiful groves, skirting the several streams. And many of the first settlers of the county are still living, evidently well contented that their lot had been cast in so favorable a location.

It is now well settled, with a moral, thriving and energetic class of people, and it contains at the present time about seven hundred and twenty souls. Among the first settlers of Union township are, the Guye colony, P. M. Boyles, John Beedle, Amos Cass, John Evans, a Mr. Wilhite, and a Mr. Wallace; all of whom came as early as 1846. All of the above settlers, with the exception of the two latter, are still living where they first staked their claims. In 1847, Leonard Bowman, David Cracraft, Alfred Q. Rice, and Henry Rice settled in the township. And Bassil Pursell, James Brown, George Magnus, John B. Sturman, and Charles Farris, made homes for themselves and families here as early as 1847. After this, settlers came in so thick and fast, that we cannot keep track of them.

There are many large and extensive farmers in this neighborhood. Thomas Garlinger, the most extensive farmer in the county, has in this township twelve hundred acres of land, a large portion of which is under improvement.

In 1854, John Cracraft put up a large steam grist mill on the place now owned by Thomas Garlinger. His mill obtained a good reputation, and he done a very extensive business; but by bad management, he broke up in the course of a few years, and his machinery was sold to satisfy the claims of his creditors. The engine and boiler of this mill, are now used to run the Madison Woolen Factory. There are six good substantial school-houses, and Religious meetings and Sabbath Schools are held in all of them. Eli Cox resides here, in a large brick residence, the largest dwelling house in the county.

Considering its natural and acquired advantages together with the good class of inhabitants that reside here, it is a most desirable place to live in.

CRAWFORD

Is bounded on the north by Lee, on the south by South, on the east by Warren county, and on the west by Union.

North River, Cedar Creek and Midde River all flow directly through it from west to east. On all of these streams there are large growths of timber. There is an abundance of lime-stone and some coal is also found. And it is the best watered in the county; numerous springs and small streams providing the very best of stock water for every locality. The surface of the country is very rough and rolling; much more so than any other township in the county. Yet there is not any great quantity of land but what is susceptible of cultivation; and there are many choice locations here and there, for fine farms. A large portion of the township is but little settled.

Hiram Hurst, the first white settler in Madison county, settled here in 1846, on Middle River, and on what is now known as the old Cason farm. In 1849 Thomas Cason and J. J. Cason settled here. J. B. McGinnis, William Weekly, Thomas Stewart, Jacob Kinkannan, Jackson Nelson and George Salisbury all settled here as early as 1850 and 1851. In 1852, widow Shreves, and her sons, John, Jonah and Jonathan Shreves, settled here.

The following individuals are among the large and substantial farmers of the township: Aaron Howell, Oliver Crawford, Joseph McGinnis, John Holton, George Blosser, John Potter, Ephraim Potter, Elvis Stout and Jonah Shreves.

Aaron Howell has a farm of over nine hundred acres under cultivation. He is a living example of the rich reward that Iowa soil repays the faithful husbandman. He came there fourteen years ago, with but a few hundred dollars in his pocket, but by economy, perseverance and diligence, he "dug gold out of the ground with his plowshare," until he has now become one of the richest farmers in Madison county. He has a magnificent bearing apple orchard of about one thousand trees, and he is one of the extensive stock dealers of Crawford township.

J. M. Huglin is the proprietor of an excellent grist mill and saw mill on Middle River; and he is doing a very popular and extensive milling business. There is also another good saw mill, (steam) which is owned by Messrs. Carson & McDowell.

There are several religious organizations and religious services and Sabbath schools are held in the various school-houses.

ANECDOTE.—There is a large black walnut tree in Middle River Valley, on the farm of John Holton, which is worthy of note. It is about six feet in diameter, and it looms up gracefully and beautifully about one hundred feet high. Its lower branches are about nine feet from the ground, and spread out about forty feet in every direction, the ends touching, or very nearly touching the ground. At an early day, camp meetings were held under its ample folds, and other public meetings and gatherings have often been held there. A little incident once occurred here, which is too good to be lost, and we therefore publish it. In 1858, B. F. Roberts and H. J. B. Cummings, were two prominent speakers in the Republican ranks of Madison county, and they had gathered together the people of the surrounding neighborhood under the pleasant shade of this black walnut, for the purpose of addressing them upon the great political issues of the day. Among the audience were three or four ladies. Cummings was proceeding with his speech, and all went smoothly on for awhile, until some wag in the crowd climbed up into the tree, above the speakers head, and he beckoned to the others to follow. They did so, one at a time, slowly and quietly, until *every man present was hidden in the foliage of the tree above the speaker's head!* and in this plight he was left to finish his political harangue to the ladies, who were the only *fellow citizens* he could observe. The Colonel was afterwards heard to remark that "the hardest thing he ever did in his life was to *finish that speech!*"

WEBSTER

Is bounded on the West by Adair county, on the East by Lincoln township; on the North by Jefferson, and on the South by Grand River. Middle River enters near the north-west corner, and passes almost diagonally across it. The surface of the country is somewhat rough and broken, especially south of the river; and, comparatively speaking, the land does not lay so well as in other townships of the county. There is an abundant growth of timber, and an inexhaustible supply of stone on Middle River. It is admirably adapted to the growth of stock. There are many points and projections of prairie which would make beautiful forty and eighty acre farms. A good German settlement would make a very paradise out of it.

The earliest settler, is John H. Baugh. He came here as early as 1850. Theodore Wight, L. D. Skidmore, Dexter Howard, James Harman, Patrick Large and John Vancil, also settled here in 1852, soon afterwards, came Otho Davis, J. R. Drake, and A. M. Hart. Most of the above named early settlers are still residents of the township, and argue well for the permanent character of the inhabitants.

Among the large substantial farmers of Webster, are the following persons: Theodore Wight, Otho Davis, John H. Baugh, John Ettien, John Schnellbacher, John W. Hunter, H. C. Smith, I. Harris, and others.

The town is located in the north-west corner. It contains a large saw mill, owned by Otho Davis, and a good country store is carried on by Davis & Zearing. Abel Graham is the resident physician.

Besides the saw mill above mentioned, there is another saw mill in the township, owned by a German firm, named Schaeffland & Co. Both mills are doing a good business.

Among the good orchards in the township we will mention the one owned by Otho Davis. His orchard, sometimes, produces as much as three hundred bushels of apples in one season.

Religious worship and Sabbath Schools are held in all the schoolhouses.

Good water and stone abound; and there are some fine stone farm houses in the township.

LINCOLN

Is bounded on the north by Douglas, on the south by Monroe, on the east by Scott, and on the west by Webster. Middle River courses through the township from west to east, a little north of the center. There are large bodies of heavy timber and inexhaustible supplies of limestone. Coal is also found cropping out of the bluffs along the banks of Middle River. The surface of the country, in the central portion in the vicinity of Middle River is quite broken and rough; but in the southern and northern portions, the prairies are beautiful and just rolling enough to make the most desirable farms. There are numerous small streams and springs providing abundance of live fresh stock water for every section of land. The greater portion of the township is now occupied and under improvement; though there are occasionally fine locations scattered here and there which are not yet occupied that would make elegant farms. The north portion is all fenced in with beautiful and valuable farms.

Daniel Vancil, C. D. Wright and Absalom Thornburgh, were the first settlers, they came as early as 1847, and took "claims" in the timber, along Middle River. Elijah Perkins and James Bertholf also settled here as early as 1849. (Elijah Perkins traveled all the way from the hills of New Hampshire, with an ox team, when railroads were in their infancy, and before the "iron horse" had turned its course to the Westward.) Alexander Bertholf and his sons, Alexander, Zachariah, George and James, Joshua Gentry and Rev. John Heaton came here as early as 1850. Wm. Harman, Mr. Skidmore and John Macumber also settled here soon after.

In 1852, James Bertholf and a Mr. Hogg, each, erected saw mills on Middle River, which were amongst the earliest mills in the county. They would also grind corn at these mills, and they were designated as "corn crackers."

There are many large and substantial farmers among whom are the following: John Macumber, Alexander Bertholf Josiah McKibben,

Elijah Perkins, Benjamin Hartsock, Alexander Lorimore, B. F. Lori-
more, Jacob Linard, William Cameron, Dr. William L. Leonard,
John Hooton, Nathan Newlon, Jacob Linard, Geo. A. Beerbower, D.
G. Martin, Samuel Gordon, Samuel Duncan, Isaac Hogle, Isaac Ruby,
Rev. John Reed, John Huffman, James W. Evans, and others.

John Macumber and Wm. Hartsock deal quite extensively in stock.
A. W. and B. F. Lorimore are very extensive wool growers. They have
now over 5,000 head of sheep.

C. Fink, Elijah Perkins, Rev. John Hooten, Wm. Cameron, Isaac
Ruby, D. G. Martin, Harrison Evans, Rev. John Reed, John Brown,
Alex. Lorimore, have good bearing apple orchards on their farms.

There are many fine residences here; among which we will
mention those of Jacob Linard, John Macumber, and White & Co.,
and the Factory Farm; the three latter of which are built of stone.
The one on the Factory Farm was built by Hon. B. F. Roberts, and
is three stories in height. Many other substantial improvements
might be spoken of had we the space to spare.

The Methodists have a church organization, and religious worship
and Sabbath Schools are held in the various school houses.

The famous Woolen Factory of Messrs. J. T. White & Co., is located
here, a description of which we herewith furnish:

Madison Woolen Mills.

The " Madison Woolen Mills " were built in 1865 by J. T. White and
N. W. Munger. They are situated one and a half miles west of Winterset, on the Council Bluffs road.

The buildings are of stone, 40 x 50 feet, three stories high, with a wing
20 x 55, containing engine, boiler and dye-room. In addition to this
there is a three-story stone dwelling, a two-story ware-room, 20 x 40 and
some half a dozen dwellings for operatives, all together making quite
a little village.

The machinery for this establishment was manufactured expressly
for Messrs. White & Munger at Lawrence and Worcester, Mass., and
Staffordville, Conn., and comprises two pickers, one duster, two setts
40-inch manufacturing cards, two double acting roll cards, two 240 spindle jacks, one fifty spindle twister, one three yard wide fancy Crompton loom, one yard wide fancy Crompton, two yard wide Stafford, three
two and a half yard wide Day & Lovejoy.

The finishing machinery consists of upright fulling mill, scourer,
teazling-gig, shearing-machine, press, cloth winder, dye works, etc.

This machinery combines all the latest improvements, and is of the
same style of that used in the best New England factories. The rooms
are heated by steam pipes connecting with the boiler.

This establishment furnishes employment to twenty-five operatives, and turns out about 30,000 yards of goods annually, which, together with yarn and rolls consumes some 60,000 pounds of wool.

These goods were awarded the "first premium" at the District Fair at Des Moines last fall, and are deservedly popular wherever they are known and worn. For durability, warmth, and beauty of finish, they are unsurpassed in the State.

Messrs. White & Munger have recently sold a half interest in this establishment, to Robert Herron of Vermont, and William Sutton of Pennsylvania, both life long manufacturers, who will bring to the management of the establishment a large and varied experience, and untiring energy. The interests of wool growers, and of all who wear woolen goods are certainly safe in the hands of these gentlemen.

There is a great natural curiosity in Lincoln, of which we give the following description :

"Devil's Back Bone."

About five miles west of Winterset on Middle River, is a peculiar formation of nature bearing the euphoneous title of "Devil's Back Bone" or "Hogback." This back bone of his Satanic Majesty bears quite a local notoriety. If the ridge were surrounded by a large body of water it would simply be termed a promontory. As it is, it is merely a high, rough, rocky ridge, so narrow that at the top there is only room for a wagon road. Middle river, running from east to west, strikes this high ridge, which is over two hundred feet above the water level, and then bears in a circuitous route away, and some two or three miles further down its course bends around until it passes on the other side of the same steep, high ridge. From water to water, directly through the ridge, is less than one hundred feet. An early settler in that neighborhood, named John Harman, together with his sons, tunnelled the ridge through solid rock occupying three years time to do the work. They thus obtained a water fall of twenty feet, making it the most desirable site for a mill in the western country. A large room has been made in the rock around the mill end of the race, making as delightful a bathing place as can be found anywhere. A large grist mill and saw mill has lately been erected at this point by Messrs Wilkin & Co. This back bone is quite a curiosity and worth going a long distance to see.

SCOTT

Is bounded on the North by Union, on the south by Walnut, on the east by South, and on the West by Lincoln, Middle River and Jones' creek are principal streams. Middle River passes through the north part of the township, from west to east, and Jones' creek flows through the southern part. The divide, lying between Middle River and Clinton, is widely known as "Hoosier Prairie," and it derived its new name from the fact that many of its early settlers came from the "hoosier" State. A greater portion of it is what is termed a *flat* or *level* prairie; and it is said to be the most level or least rolling prairie in the county; in the breaks, near the streams, however, the surface of the county is very rough and broken. There are many beautiful farms on "Hoosier Prairie" and in other portions of Scott township. A greater portion is "taken up," or in process of cultivation; and the entire township has more of the appearance of an old settled county, than any other township in the county. Inexhaustible quarries, of the very best lime stone, are found all along the bluffs of Middle River; and coal is also found in various places; many springs and small streams exist here and there throughout the township, making it a very desirable locality for the raising of stock. A large spring comes out of the bluff from beneath the residence of John Dryden, which furnishes water power sufficient to run a saw mill; and on the farm of the widow Wilkinson, there are no less than seven springs.

David Bishop, Henry McKinsie, Wm. Alcock, and John Wilkinson were its first settlers. They took "claims" in the township as early as 1847. Henry McKinsie settled on the farm now owned by W. W. McKnight. John Wilkinson's widow still resides on the claim which he had first chosen. Ephraim Bilderback put upon his farm a blacksmith shop, which was the first blacksmith shop in the county. Wm. Alcock still resides on the farm which he had first chosen.

John Rogers, Marious C. Debord, John Landers, Whitley Allen, John Hinkel, Joel Graves, Wm. Hogg, Josiah Struthers, Josiah Smith, Isaac Debusk; all came into the township as early as 1849 and '50.— John Hinkle, John S. Holmes and Wm. Bowlsby settled here soon after.

The following persons are among its large and substantial farmers: W. W. McKnight, John Rogers, John Hinkle, Marius C. Debord, Geo. Close, Mitchel Robinson, J. S. Holmes, Geo. Hamner, J. R. Silliman, John Jones, John Landers, A. J. Campbell, Benj. F. Reed, Ed. Herrald, A. J. Adkinson, James Harris, B. Lake, John Dryden, Porter Ralston, B. F. Carter, Geo. A. Breeding, and others.

J. R. Silliman, John Rogers, Wm. Hogg, and A. J. Campbell are heavy dealers in stock, B. F. Bowlsby also deals to some extent in stock.

Wm. Alcock, James Short, John Rogers, Noah King, John Hinkle, and John Landers have good bearing apple orchards on their farms.

There are several church organizations in the township. The Methodists have three organizations, holding their meetings, one at the Lincoln school-house, and one at Elm Grove, the other at the Harbert or Hinkle school-house. The Evangelical Christians have an organization, and they hold their meetings at the Lincoln and the Stevens school-houses. Religious services and Sabbath Schools are held in all of the school-houses.

;SOUTH.

South township is bounded on the east by Warren county, on the west by Scott township, on the north by Crawford, and on the south by Ohio. For stock-raising and agricultural purposes this township is blessed with superior advantages. Clanton creek runs through it, near the centre, from the south west to the north east. Along this stream there is a fine large growth of oak and other valuable forest trees. The heaviest growth of timber in the county, and scarcely surpassed in the State, is found along the banks of this stream. There are also numerous smaller streams, furnishing good stock water for almost every section of land. Stone abounds on Clanton creek, and good veins of coal are found on Brush creek.

The township is very well settled, and there is not very much unimproved land remaining. Unimproved prairie ranges from five to ten dollars per acre; and improved farms from ten to thirty dollars per acre.

The first settlers here were the Clanton colony, of which we have made mention elsewhere. George Hartman, Jesse Young, N. S. Alcock, David Smith, the Casons, the Casebiers, and others came as early as 1851.

Among the extensive farmers are J. M. Johnston, Jeff. Rhyno, James Phipps, N. S. Alcock, J. M. Browne, Joel Clanton, Hogan Queen, and others.

There are a number of fine bearing orchards; among them we might mention those on the farms of J. M. Johnston, N. S. Alcock and Joel Clanton.

Hogan Queen has a beautiful farm-house, which would do honor to the nabobs of older and more pretentious localities. It is a large two story and a half stone mansion, located by the side of a very beautiful grove. He has also a very large and extensive barn close by. J. M. Browne and James Phipps have also large and magnificent residences.

In South township is located the village of St. Charles, of which we give a description below:

ST. CHARLES.

St. Charles is a small village situated on the Winterset and Indianola road, about twelve miles south east of Winterset. It is located on a high prairie, near the timber of Clanton creek. It contains about seventy houses, and about three hundred inhabitants. The town was laid out as early as 1851, by George Hartman and Jesse Young, who at that time owned the land on which the town site is located. In a short time after the village was laid out it grew into a flourishing place But during the war no improvements of importance were made. (For the little village of St. Charles was largely represented in the war, Capt. J. M. Browne having raised a full company in that village and vicinity.) During the last two years it has taken another start, and it is now growing quite rapidly. The village is surrounded by one of the best farming countries in the world. The soil, stone, timber and water privileges surrounding it, will compare favorably with the most favored localities in the state. And its central location between Winterset and Indianola, in the midst of a well settled farming community, make it a good point for business.

The village contains at the present time two hotels—one kept by William Barton, and the other by M. E. Clanton; two dry goods firms —Smith & McClure, and Browne & Thompson; three resident physicians—Drs. A. B. Smith, L. J. Forney, and Wm. M. Anderson; and also one grocery story; all of which are doing a good business. It has also one saddle and harness shop, one blacksmith shop, two cabinet shops, one wagon shop and one boot and shoe shop.

It has three church buildings and one school-house, which speaks well for the village. The religious denominations are the Methodists, United Presbyterians and Disciples.

It has also a large three-story flouring mill, known as the "Madison Mills." This mill is owned by Messrs. McClure, Ergenbright & Co., and it is doing a very extensive and constantly increasing business.

GRAND RIVER

Is the south-west township of the county. It is bounded on the west by Adair county, on the south by Union county, on the east by Walnut township, and on the north by Webster township. The surface of the country is mostly rolling and rough, but there is a great deal of choice prairie land in this section of country. There is a large body of heavy timber on Grand River, which is the principal stream. The timber grows principally along the valleys of the streams, which are narrow and deep, and can hardly be seen from the high prairies. Persons traveling along the divides, would very naturally conclude that there was but very little timber.

James Nelson was the first white man who settled here. He came in 1852, and took a claim on what is now known as the John Bray place. Ransom Moon was the next settler. He came in February, 1852, and took a claim in the timber, on "Moon Branch," where he built him a pole cabin, 12 by 14 feet square. In the spring he moved to his "prairie home," near the center of the township, where he now resides, surrounded by all the comforts of a good farm home, with groves, orchards, &c. Alvin Greer came in March following, and took a claim on a beautiful point of land between Grand River and Barker Branch; but failing to get money in time to enter it, some heartless wretch entered it and drove him off. He afterwards settled in the edge of Adair county, but during the war he went in defence of his country, and was killed. In May, 1853, Samuel Barker, and his sons, O. W. Barker, J. C. Barker and Elihue Barker, and his brother, J. C. Barker, together with A. J. Hasty, settled in what is now known as the Barker settlement. Samuel Barker was a Baptist minister, and a man of some means and of great energy of character. He entered 2,000 acres of land in that township, and done more, perhaps, toward settling the township than any other man in it. He has been deceased a number of years, but his aged and respected widow still resides on the old homestead. Elihue Barker served with great distinction as a soldier, during the war. He is now a resident of Arkansas, and is, at the present time a State Senator, representing the fifth senatorial district of that State. O. W. Barker still resides on the claim which he entered. His farm, which is one of the largest and best in the township, has several miles of good Osage Orange Hedge fencing on it, and he is surrounded with all the comforts common to a substantial Iowa farmer.— A. J. Hasty and J. C. Barker still live on their "claims," which they have greatly improved. Mr. Hasty is one of the substantial men of the township. He, together with O. W. Barker, are the principal stock dealers of this neighborhood; and they are said to be the owners of some of the best blooded cattle in western Iowa. John H. Bray, James Pierson and Hiram Pierce settled in the township as early as 1853, Phillip Osburn, J. J. Greer, E. Pindle, Wm. Kivitt, Mr. Doty, John Granfield, and others also settled here within a year or two afterwards.

It now contains about six hundred souls; and its inhabitants are, as a class, moral and religious. The Methodists, Missionary Baptists, and Christian denominations have each live and flourishing organizations here. Meetings are held in each of the five school-houses. An unusual interest is taken in the Sabbath School cause, and Sabbath Schools are held in all the school-houses, under the charge of industrious and efficient superintendants and officers. They are evidently proud of their school facilities, and are doing all they can to " train up their children in the way they should go, that when they are old they will not depart from it."

It has most excellent water facilities and it is admirably adapted for the raising of stock.

The prairie land is held from two to twelve dollars per acre; the timber from five to forty dollars; and improved farms range from ten to forty dollars per acre. There are two saw mills; one owned by A. J. Hasty, and the other by Daniel Shepherd, and both are doing a good business.

There is an abundance of wild fruits, such as crab apples, plums, berries, &c., and there are several large bearing apple orchards. In an early day the settlers found plenty of wild game in the timber, such as deer, elk, turkeys, and smaller game. It is also related that they used to find wild hogs in the timber. The hogs were long legged, and wild and fleet as deer. They had been left by a colony of Mormons, who had wintered at Mt. Piscah, in Union county, in 1847 or '48.

It contains excellent water facilities, and it would at the present time be a grand location for a grist mill.

Other matters of interest might be spoken of concerning this township, but it is, to a great extent, the same as the general history of the county, which we speak of more fully elsewhere in the book; suffice it to say, that it is in all respects, a very desirable township for those seeking new homes.

MONROE

Is bounded on the north by Lincoln township, on the south by Union county, on the east by Walnut township and on the west by Grand River. Clanton Creek passes through near the center, from west to east; and there is a large body of heavy timber on this stream, especially at Big Grove. There are on Clanton, large quarries of good limestone. The surface of the country is quite rolling and it is in many places quite rough; it is more so than any other township in the county, and there is considerable of what is termed waste land in the township; yet there are many elegant locations for fine farms, as beautiful as any heart could wish for. There are many small rivulets and valuable springs in the township, and abundance of good range for stock; which makes it very desirable for those engaged in stock raising. And the farmers are paying a great deal of attention to the raising of fine stock; and we are pleased to state that business proves very renumerative to their pockets. There have been considerable emigration here of late, and it is at the present time improving very rapidly.

An Irishman named Malone, and James Britton and Isaac Nichol, are among its earliest settlers. They settled here as early as 1852. William Boling, John Bancroft, Lewis and George Linton, Phillip and John Moore, William Claim, William Berry and John Berry settled in the township in 1853, and 1854. Frank Bosworth, Samuel Hamilton, N. Clark, and H. Harris settled here soon afterwards.

The Methodist and Missionary Baptists have church organizations here and meetings are held regularly.

WALNUT

Is bounded on the north by Scott township, on the south by Clark county, on the east by Ohio township, and on the west by Monroe. The north branch of Clanton enters it in section 7, and passes from west to east, through sections 17, 16, and to the centre of 15, where it forms a junction with South Branch, which enters the township in section 19. After the two branches come together, they pass on down through sections 10, 11 and 1. This stream furnishes sufficient water for milling purposes during the greater portion of the year.

Plenty of timber and inexhaustible supplies of limestone exist along the bluffs of the streams. A good saw mill was erected on this stream 1853, by Aaron Hiatt and B. F. Browne. It is now owned by Benjamin Reed. The surface of the country is generally quite rolling, and in some places quite rough, with fine first and second bottoms along Clanton creek. The soil is a rich dark loam, yielding luxuriantly every kind of grain and vegetable common to the latitude. Wheat, corn and oats are the main productions. There are some fine springs, and good wells are found by digging from fifteen to twenty-five feet. Thus with springs, wells and streams, it is abundantly supplied with water.

Its first settlers were Samuel Peters, A. J. Stark and Geo. W. Teague, who came in 1849. John Marshall, James A. Emerson, Abijah Marsh, A. L. Bryant and Wm. J. Guthrie settled here as early as 1850. Samuel Peters, John Marshall, James A. Emerson and William J. Guthrie still reside in the township. Abijah Marsh moved to Des Moines some years ago, and was elected City Marshal; and while serving in that capacity, in a fit of passion, he killed a man named King, fled to Texas, and was arrested in that state by a Polk county sheriff; but while the officer was on the way with him to Des Moines, he jumped off the boat and was drowned in the Mississippi river.

There are no very extensive farmers in this township. From 100 to 140 acres being about the extent of the farms owned by any one man. A great deal of attention has been given to the raising of tame fruit.

Hardy varieties of the apple, cherry and plum flourish exceedingly well. The gooseberry, strawberry and grape are becoming very plentiful. Aaron Hiatt is the most extensive fruit raiser in the township. He has exhibited at our county fairs for a number of years past the most choice and luscious varieties of fruit. Others have good apple orchards, among them are Jacob Brown, John Marichel, J. A. Emerson, B. F. Browne, David Hollowell, Isaac Rager, Daniel Baker, N. Foster, A. Simmons and the Painters.

There are six sub-districts and one independent school district. Seven schools were in flourishing operation during the past winter, at an average cost of nearly forty dollars per month. There are two church buildings; one Methodist, known as the Ebenezer church; and the other the Christian church at Peru. Both buildings are good, substantial frame edifices. The Methodists have also church organizations at Pleasant Grove and at Harmony school-house. Sabbath schools are held in the churches and in several of the school-houses.

There are two post offices, one called Ohio, of which Samuel Walker is post master; the other is at Peru, H. C. Wright, post master. B. F. Browne had been the post master of Peru for twelve years.

Hog's Back.—There is situated on Clanton creek, about a mile and a half east of Peru, a peculiar shaped hill or high piece of ground, which is known as Hog's Back, and is quite a curiosity; in shape and form not widely different from "Devil's Back Bone," spoken of elsewhere in this book. It is a steep bluff, about one hundred and twenty-five feet high, and about three quarters of a mile in length. On the top of the ridge, for a distance of about half a mile, there is barely room sufficient for a wagon track. Clanton creek courses along on one side of the ridge, and a small stream on the other, forming a junction near the end of the ridge. This high ridge is composed mostly of limestone rock, and a peculiar greasy, reddish clay. The clay is supposed to be what is known in many places as "paint clay," but no experiment has ever been made with it. It exists in great quantities, and may prove to be of great utility and value.

Peru.—This is the name of a small village situated in Walnut township, in section three. The town was laid out in '53, by Aaron Hiatt, who was proprietor of the land on which it was located. The town now contains one store, one blacksmith shop, one cabinet and wagon shop, one shingle manufactory, one steam saw mill, one church, fifteen or twenty private residences, and about seventy inhabitants. A large stone school-house is in process of erection at the present time in the village.

OHIO

Is bounded on the east by Warren county, on the west by Walnut township, on the south by Clark county, and on the north by South township. The prairies are high, beautiful and rolling, and the soil is of great fertility, producing in great abundance all kinds of grain. South River, quite a large stream, flows through the southern portion of it and there are heavy growths of good timber along this stream. A good article of stone coal has been found in several places. There are numerous small streams and quite a number of excellent springs exist on the prairies in different localities. These springs are never, dry, and they never freeze up in the winter time. It is, therefore, peculiarly adapted to stock raising.

Andrew Hart and M. S. Douglas were its first settlers. They came in 1854. They were both rebels, and when the war broke out they sold out and moved south. Noah Bishop, and John Cregor, Henry Cregor, Solomon Delong, A. G. Martin, William Farson, and J. D. Hartman also settled here at an early day.

The most extensive farmers are, J. D. Hartman, Noah Bishop, William Anderson, and David Bradshaw.

Meetings and sabbath schools are held in the various school-houses.

There are some good bearing orchards; among them is one planted out in 1860, by A. G. Martin, which is now in good bearing condition.

For quiet rural home places, it offers very superior attractions.

Written expressly for Davies' History and Directory.]

GOD BE PRAISED!

BY JAMES ELLIS.

A few short years, what change has come
O'er thee, thou glorious Madison!
Thy sons have toiled, and fought, and won
A victory on these wilds alone :
Yet not alone! His mighty hand
Led on this brave and struggling band ;
He gave them nerve, and strength, and heart ;
And nobly have they done their part.
With thankful hearts, our voice is raised
In one loud anthem—God be praised !

Our Pioneers! As they advance
Sweet Nature wakes from out her trance ;
And Plenty, with an open hand,
Scatters abundance through the land.
The primeval soil its richness yields ;
And corn in blossom decks the fields ;
Fruits, ripe and luscious, meet the eye,
Foretelling riches by-and-bye.
For all these gifts our voice is raised
In one loud anthem—God be praised !

And when the sun-burnt Autumn nears,
Tanning with brown the wheaten ears,
Each thankful heart bows low its head,
To Him above for mercies shed ;
The farmer smiles with honest pride,
Clasping his darling by his side ;
While children, ruddy, round them play ;
And Nature beams on all, that day.
For all His love, our voice is raised
In one loud anthem—God be praised !

Then, come—poor wanderers from afar—
And join Progression's onward car:
We proffer thee a home and wealth,
With Nature's gifts—full, robust health.
Thy fading cheek shall sink no more—
Here joys in plenty are in store;
Here worth is honored and esteemed—
The rich, the poor are equal deemed.
For this true right, our voice is raised
In one loud anthem—GOD be praised!

Here Freedom reigns: in whose glad face
A thousand promises we trace,
Of worldly blessings—Freedom's Gifts—
When from the earth, the Slave-King lifts
His tyrant hand, and bids appear
The GOD with visage mild and clear—
Whose birth, these prairies wild will tell,
To Indians rude in mead and dell.
For thee, sweet Liberty! our voice is raised
In one loud anthem—GOD be praised!

Sweet Madison! we view with pride
Thy many virtues spreading wide.
Long may thy Star of Progress shine,
And blessings wait on thee and thine;
May every breeze that floats around,
Come laden with some joyous sound;
That Heaven with choicest gifts may bless,
And grant thee health and happiness.
For all thy sons, our voice is raised
In one loud anthem—GOD be praised!

CENSUS RETURNS OF MADISON COUNTY,

From its First Settlement to the Present Time.

Population in 1849................... 701
Population in 1850................1174
Population in 1851................1492
Population in 1852................1832
Population in 1854................3122
Population in 1856................5508

Population in 1857................7071
Population in 1860................7337
Population in 1853................7934
Population in 1865................8214
Population in 1867................9764
Population in 1869...............11817

COUNTY STATISTICS, 1869.

No. of dwelling-houses........ 2,117
Families............................. 2,158
White males................ .... 6.148
White females................... 5,666
Total white population........11,814
No. of colored males........... 2
Colored females.................. 1
Total population.................11,817
Entitled to vote.................. 2,587
Foreigners not naturalized.. 17
Militia........................ 2,055
Blind 5
Deaf and dumb.................. 2
Insane............................ 2
Acres enclosed....................89,939
Acres in cultivation............69,419
Acres in spring wheat........15,223
Acres in winter wheat......... 14
Acres in corn.............. 33,573
Acres in oats...................... 5,927
Acres in buckwheat............ 66
Acres in barley................... 3
Acres in rye...................... 99
Acers in Potatoes............... 649
Acres in onions................. 5
Acres in tame grass............ 2,595

Acres in flax..................... 1
Acres in sorghum.............. 520
Acres of trees planted for
    timber.......................... 134
Acres of hops.................... 11
Rods of hedging................56,039
No. fruit trees bearing........14,757
No. not bearing.................46,293
No. grapes bearing.............11,785
No. not bearing.................20,796
Horses............................. 6,194
Cattle............................. 12,453
Hogs.............................19,987
Sheep............................30,171
Mules and asses.................. 548
Milch cows........................ 3,816
Work oxen........................ 270
Dogs.............................. 1,891
Hives of bees..................... 1,242
Bushels of spring wheat...133,434
Bushels of winter wheat... 101
Bushels of corn..............1,018,369
Bushels of oats............... 101,887
Bushels of buckwheat........ 326
Bushels of barley............. 217
Bushels of rye.................. 897

Bushels of potatoes.............76,918
Bushels of clover seed......... 2
Bushels of onions.............. 367
Bushels of grass seed.......... 57
Bushels of apples.............. 6,267
Pounds of grapes...... ....19.352
Pounds of honey...............11,940
Pounds of Butter.............242,879
Pounds of cheese................ 5,252
Pounds of wool in 1868......110,224
Pounds of hops................. 26

Gallons of sorghum............45,498
Tons of tame hay.............. 2871
Tons of wild hay.............13,397
Value farm produce, 1868....613,260
Value of stock sold...........329,225
Value of agricultural im-
    plements,...... 143,714
Value of Manufactures...... 58,996
Bushels of coal.................. 85
Value of other minerals...... 679

CENSUS RETURNS BY TOWNSHIPS.

CENTER.

No. of dwelling-houses........ 288
No. of families.................... 326
No. white males.................. 807
No. white females.............. 751
No. colored males.............. 1
No. colored females............ 1
Total population................. 1,560
No. entitled to vote............ 400
No. of Militia.................... 330
No. of fruit trees in bearing 1,842
No. fruit trees not in bearing 2,956
No. of grape vines bearing.. 4,575

No. grapes vines not bearing 2379
No. of horses of all ages..... 268
No. of cattle of all ages...... 222
No. hogs of all ages............ 690
No. of milch cows............. 155
No. of dogs...................... 67
No. of bee hives............... 26
No. bushels of apples......... 16
No. pounds of grapes 365
No. pounds of honey........... 200
No. of pounds butter made.. 500

PENN.

No. of dwelling-houses...... 89
No. of families.................. 92
No. white males................ 239
No. white females. 215
Total population 454
No. entitled to vote............ 110
No. militia........................ 112
No. acres of land enclosed.. 4326
No. acres of land under cul-
    tivation................... 4,239
No. acres of spring wheat... 8229
No. acres of corn.............. 1,185

No. acres of oats................. 296
No. acres of potatoes........... 28
No. acres of sorghum......... 18
No. acres planted for timber 57
No. rods of hedging planted 3,812
No. fruit trees in bearing... 222
No. of fruit trees not in
    bearing................. 1,070
No. grape vines in bearing 150
No. of grape vines not in
    bearing...................... 797
No. of horses of all ages..... 314

No. of cattle of all ages...... 334
No. of hogs of all ages......... 540
No. of sheep of all ages........ 657
No. of mules and asses....... 37
No. milch cows.................. 134
No. of work oxen.............. 16
No. of dogs........................ 74
No. hives of bees.............. 13
No. bushels of spring wheat 8,048
No. bushels of corn............41,860
No. bushels of oats............ 7,488
No. bushels of buckwheat... 4
No. bushels of Irish potatoes 4,180
No bushels of onions........... 12
No. bushels of apples......... 75
No. pounds of grapes......... 1,112

No. gallons of syrup from
    sorghum.................... 2,427
No. pounds of honey.......... 143
No. pounds of butter........... 8,760
No. pounds of wool shorn in
    1868............................. 3,122
No. tons hay from tame grass 18
No. tons of hay from wild
    grass.......................... 800
Value of farm produce dur-
    ing 1868........................49,815
Value of stock sold during
    1868............................ 9,942
Value of implements and
    machinery.................... 8,560

MADISON.

No. of dwelling-houses...... 134
No. of families.................. 143
No. of white males............ 405
No. of white females.......... 383
Total population................. 788
No. entitled to vote........... 170
No. of foreigners not natu-
    ralized 8
No. of militia................. ... 125
No. of acres of land enclosed 7,549
No. of acres of land in culti-
    vation.......................... 5,569
No. of acres of wheat......... 1,600
No. acres of corn 2,907
No. of acres of oats............ 507
No. of acres of rye............. 12
No. of acres of potatoes....... 45
No. of acres of tame grasses. 216
No. of acres of sorghum...... 32
No. of acres planted for tim-
    ber............................. 37
No. of rods of hedging plant-
    ed................................. 5,930
No. of fruit trees in bearing. 540

No. fruit trees not in bearing 3,363
No. of grape vines in bear- 196
    ing.............................
No. of Grape vines not in
    bearing......................... 841
No. of horses of all kinds...... 444
No. of cattle of all kinds...... 601
No. of hogs of all kinds...... 2,684
No. of sheep of all kinds...... 2,017
No. of mules and asses...... 72
No. of milch cows.............. 255
No. of dogs........................ 132
No. hives of bees.............. 59
No. bushels of spring wheat 9,818
No. bushels of corn............96,310
No. bushels of oats............. 9,059
No. bushels of buckwheat... 2
No. bushels of rye.............. 329
No. bushels of potatoes........ 6,132
No. bushels of onions.......... 22
No. bushels of apples........... 72
No. lbs. of grapes.............. 1,605
No. of gallons of sirup from
    sorghum..................... 2,397

No. lbs. of honey.............. 887
No. lbs. of butter made.......16,602
No. lbs. of cheese made....... 100
No. lbs. wool shorn in 1868. 5,872
No. tons of hay from tame
   grass........................... 33
No. of tons from wild grass. 604

Value of farm produce du-
   ring 1868....................50,242
Value of stock sold during
   1868......................30,215
Value of agricultural implements and machinery.. 9,892
Value of manufactures in
   1868.......... 827

JEFFERSON.

No. of dwelling-houses...... 109
No. of families................... 113
No. of white males 313
No. of white females........... 285
Total white population........ 578
No. entitled to vote........... 114
No. of militia..................... 128
No. acres of land enclosed... 6,578
No. acres land not enclosed.. 4,832
No. acres of spring wheat... 1,456
No. of acres of corn 2,373
No. of acres of oats............. 299
No. of acres of buckwheat.. 16
No. of acres of potatoes...... 42
No. of acres of tame grass... 101
No. of acres of sorghum..... 29
No. acres planted for timber 12
No. of fruit trees in bearing 456

No. rods of hedging............5,750
No. fruit trees not in bearing 3,906
No. grape vines in bearing.. 138
No. of grape vines not in
   bearing 792
No. of horses of all ages..... 402
No. of cattle of all ages...... 756
No. of hogs.................. 1,119
No. of sheep....................... 2,717
No. of mules and asses........ 26
No. of milch cows.............. 265
No. of work oxen.............. 9
No. of dogs 102
No. of hives of bees 55
No. of bushels spring wheat.10,528
No. of bushels of corn.........86,480
No. of bushels of oats......... 4,283
No. of bushels of buckwheat 42

LEE.

No. of dwelling-houses...... 54
No. of families................... 55
No of white males............. 179
No white females............... 139
Total population................. 318
No entitled to vote.............. 62
No. of militia..................... 44
No. of acres of land enclosed 2,660
No. of acres of land in culti-
   vation 2,143
No. of acres of spring wheat 570
No. acres of corn.............. 1,310
No. of acres of oats............ 102

No. of acres of potatoes...... 39
No. of acres tame grass....... 30
No. of acres of sorghum...... 14
No. of rods hedging planted 225
No. of fruit trees in bearing 180
No. of fruit trees not in bear-
   ing.................. 601
No. of grape vines in bearing 33
No. of grape vines not in
   bearing..................... 317
No. of horses of all kinds.... 213
No. of cattle of all kinds..... 555
No. of hogs of all kinds..... 584

No. of sheep of all kinds..... 1,570

No. of mules and asses........ 27

No. of milch cows.............. 186

No. of work oxen.............. 12

No. of dogs....................... 77

No. of bushels spring wheat 5,340

No. of bushels of corn........40,730

No. bushels of oats.............. 1,883

No. of bushels of Irish potatoes.............................. 5,031

No. of bushels of onions...... 18

No. bushels of apples......... 105

No. of pounds of grapes...... 173

No. of gallons of syrup
from sorghum.............. 909

No. of pounds of honey...... 175

No. of pounds butter made 8,650

No. of pounds of wool shorn
in 1868............................ 5,121

No. of tons of hay from wild
grass............................ 1,216

Value of farm produce for
the year 1868.................37,285

Value of stock sold in 1868..15,301

Value of agricultural implements and machinery.. 2,988

Value manufactures for 1868   340

JACKSON.

No. of dwelling-houses...... 87

No. of families.................. 87

No. of white males.............. 263

No. of white females......... 239

Total population................ 502

No. entitled to vote........... 115

No. of militia..................... 99

No. of acres of land enclosed 5,728

No. of acres not enclosed..... 3,815

No. of acres spring wheat... 1,160

No. of acres of corn.............. 1,785

No. of acres of oats.............. 247

No. of bushels of buckwheat   6

No. of bushels of potatoes...   33

No. of acres tame grass........   46

No. of acres of sorghum......   25

No. acres of hedging planted 2,491

No. of fruit trees in bearing   163

No. of fruit trees not in bearing.............................. 2,020

No. of grape vines in bearing   123

No. of grape vines not in
bearing......................... 458

No. of horses of all kinds...   331

No. of cattle of all ages........   725

No. of hogs of all ages.........   651

No. of sheep of all ages........ 1,344

No. of mules and asses........   26

No. of milch cows..............   169

No. of work oxen..............   25

No. of dogs.......................   108

No. of hives of bees............   39

No. bushels of spring wheat 6,773

No. bushels of corn.............60,430

No. bushels of oats.............. 6,530

No. bushels of Irish potatoes 4,104

No. bushels of onions.........   25

No. bushels of apples..........   155

No. lbs of grapes................   395

No. of gallons of syrup from
sorghum 2,813

No. of lbs. of honey...........   416

No. of lbs. of butter...........11,730

No. of lbs. of cheese...........   358

No of lbs. of wool shorn in
1868.............................. 4,324

No. of tons of hay from tame
grass...........................   46

No. of tons of hay from wild
grass............................ 1,188

Value of farm produce........36,611

Value of stock sold during
the year 1868.................11,775

Value of agricultural implements............................10,426
Value manufactures for 1868 9,509

Value of other minerals than
coal 150

DOUGLAS.

No. of dwelling-houses......	149	No. of work oxen...............	22
No. of families...................	150	No. of dogs.........................	223
No. of white males............	484	No. of hives of bees............	124
No. of white females.........	435	No. bushels spring wheat...12,911	
Total white population......	919	No. bushels spring corn...115,388	
No. entitled to vote...........	209	No. bushels of oats............10,038	
No. of militia.....................	162	No. of bushels of rye.........	87
No. acres of land enclosed..	9,719	No. bushels Irish potatoes	7,190
No. acres land not enclosed.	7,562	No. bushels of onions........	29
No. of acres of spring wheat	1,758	No. bushels of apples.........	416
No. of acres of corn...........	3,354	No. bushels of grapes.........	3,152
No. of acres of oats............	683	No. gallons of syrup...........	4,055
No. of acres of buckwheat.	7	No. lbs of honey...............	835
No. of acres of rye..	10	No. lbs. of butter made......20,126	
No. of acres of potatoes......	71	No. lbs. of cheese made......	200
No. of acres of tame grass...	373	No. lbs. wool shorn in 1868..12,608	
No. of acres of sorghum.....	54	No. tons of hay from tame	
No. acres planted for timber	9	grasses.......................	344
No. rods of hedging planted	8,856	No. tons of hay from wild	
No. fruit trees in bearing....	1,936	grasses.......................	1,035
No. grape vines in bearing	1,238	Value of farm produce du-	
do not in bearing	5,826	ring the year 1868...........53,283	
No. fruit trees not in bearing	6,038	Value of stock sold during	
No. of horses of all ages.....	605	the year 1868..................50,252	
No. of cattle of all ages.....	1,055	Value of agricultural imple-	
No. of hogs of all ages......	1,944	ments, machinery, and	
No. sheep of all ages..........	2,429	wagons..........................14,099	
No. of mules and asses........	65	Value of manufactures for	
No. of milch cows..............	245	1868..............................15,854	

UNION.

No. of dwelling-houses......	118	No. of acres of land enclosed	7,352
No. of families...................	118	No. of acres under cultiva-	
No. of white males............	368	tion..................................	5,873
No. of white females...........	353	No. of acres of spring wheat	1,105
Total population.................	719	No. of acres of corn............	2,211
No. entitled to vote...........	141	No. of acres of oats............	401
No. of militia......	107	No. of acres of rye.............	45

No. of acres of potatoes...... 47
No. of acres of tame grasses 348
No. of acres of sorghum..... 35
No. of rods of hedging
   planted 3,380
No. of fruit trees in bearing 1,816
No. of fruit trees not in bear-
   ing.................................. 5,210
No. of grape vines in bear-
   ing.................................. 1,343
No. of grape vines not in
   bearing............................. 2,127
No. of horses of all ages..... 357
No. of cattle of all ages...... 893
No. of hogs of all ages........ 1,152
No. of sheep of all ages...... 3,312
No. of mules and asses........ 48
No. of milch cows.............. 296
No. of work oxen............... 12
No. of dogs....................... 121
No. of hives of bees........... 197
No. of bushels of spring
   wheat 12,312
No. of bushels of corn........115,511
No. of bushels of oats......... 4,964

No. of bushels of buckwheat   20
No. of bushels of barley..... 118
No. of bushels of rye.......... 2
No. of bushels of potatoes... 5,323
No. of bushels of onions...... 21
No. of bushels of apples...... 1,480
No. of lbs of grapes............ 164
No. of gallons of sirup from
   sorghum 3,178
No. of lbs of honey............ 1,291
No. of lbs of butter made...16,363
No. of lbs of wool shorn in
   1868 7,098
No. of tons of hay from tame
   grass............................. 421
No. of tons of hay from
   wild grass 524
Value of farm produce in
   1868 47,150
Value of stock sold during
   1868.........................39,111
Value of implements and
   machinery 6,851
Value of manufactories in
   1868 3,607

CRAWFORD.

No. of dwelling-houses...... 116
No. of families.................. 115
No. of white males............ 337
No. of white females......... 316
Total population............... 653
No. entitled to vote........... 130
No. of foreigners not natu-
   ralized............................. 2
No. of militia.................... 86
No. acres of land enclosed... 6,418
No. acres of land in cultiva-
   tion 5.142
No. acres of spring wheat... 1,003
No. of acres of corn............ 2,478
No. of acres of oats............ 407

No. acres of buckwheat...... 9
No. acres of potatoes......... 83
No. acres of tame grass...... 139
No. acres of sorghum......... 38
No. rods of hedging planted20,508
No. fruit trees in bearing 1,743
No. fruit trees not in bear-
   ing.................................. 1,870
No. grape vines in bearing 818
No. of grape vines not in
   bearing........................... 432
No. of horses of all ages...... 432
No. of cattle of all ages...... 1,220
No. of hogs of all ages...... 1,662
No. of sheep of all ages...... 1,875

No. of mules and asses...... 27
No. of milch cows............. 324
No. of work oxen............. 47
No. of dogs...................... 140
No. bushels spring wheat.. 8,344
No. bushels of corn.......... 29,939
No. bushels of oats........... 6,203
No. bushels Irish potatoes 9,073
No. bushels of onions........ 34
No. bushels of apples........ 826
No. lbs of grapes............. 650
No. of gallons sirup made
  from sorghum............... 3,891
No. lbs of honey............... 657
No. lbs butter made.......... 25,162

No. lbs cheese made........... 50
No. lbs wool shorn in 1858 4,105
No. of tons hay from tame
  grasses...................... 193
No tons of hay from wild
  grasses......... 563
Value of farm produce
  during the year 1868...... 34,706
Value of stock sold during
  the year 1868............. 22,581
Value of agricultural im-
  plements, machinery,
  and wagons................. 9,460
Value of manufactures for
  1868................... 3,788

WEBSTER.

No of dwelling-houses........ 72
  do families,.................... 73
  do white males.............. 194
  do white females........... 183
Total population.................. 377
No entitled to vote............. 79
  do of militia...... 69
  do acres of land enclosed 2,735
  do acres in cultivation... 1,571
  do acres of spring wheat 358
  do acres of corn............. 788
  do acres of oats............. 184
  do acres of potatoes........ 27
  do acres of tame grasses.. 29
  do acres of sorghum........ 17
  do rods of hedging plant-
    ed............................. 864
No. of fruit trees in bearing 382
  do not in bearing........... 1,140
  do grape vines in bearing 135
  do not in bearing........... 326
No of horses of all ages......... 281
  do cattle of all ages......... 415
  do hogs of all ages......... 614
  do sheep of all ages........ 1,068
  do mules and asses......... 20

No. of Milch cows.............. 148
  do work oxen................. 52
  do dogs 81
  do hives of bees.............. 47
  do bushels spring wheat..5,390
  do bushels of corn.........30,990
  do bushels of oats..........4,772
  do bushels of rye............ 19
  do bushels of Irish pota-
    toes..........................2,830
  do bushels of onions...... 21
  do bushels of apples........ 174
  do lbs of grapes............. 480
  do gallons of sirup from
    sorghum..................1,710
  do lbs of honey.............. 280
  do lbs of butter made.....10,058
  do lbs of cheese.............. 100
  do lbs of wool shorn in
    1868.........................3,843
  do tons of hay from tame
    grasses...................... 46
  do tons of hay from wild
    grasses....................1,108
Value of farm produce in
  1868.........................32,342

Value of stock sold in 1868...15,477   Value of manufactures in
Value of agricultural imple-   1868.......................... 700
   ments and machinery 7,841

LINCOLN.

No. of dwelling-houses......	152
do families.....................	157
do white males..............	446
do white females...........	412
Total population.................	858
No. entitled to vote.........	182
do militia	113
do acres of land enclosed	7,231
do acres of land not en-	
closed....................	5,259
do acres of spring wheat	1,143
do acres of corn.............	2,365
do acres of oats..............	414
do acres of potatoes........	42
do acres of tame grass...	358
do acres of sorghum......	29
do rods hedging planted	7,042
do fruit trees in bearing	848
do fruit trees not bearing	3,269
do grape vines bearing...	653
do grape vines not bear-	
ing	1,418
do horses of all ages......	453
do cattle of all ages.......	893
do hogs of all ages.........	929
do sheep of all ages........	3,379
do mules and asses.........	36
do milch cows..............	307
do work oxen..............	10
do dogs......................	143

No. of hives of bees............	85
do bushels spring wheat	9,129
do bushels of corn.........84,110	
do bushels of oats...........	6,054
do bushels of buckwheat	40
do bushels of barley......	99
do bushels Irish potatoes	5,651
do bushels of onions......	24
do bushels of apples......	387
do pounds of grapes......	3,864
do gallons of sirup from	
sorghum.................	2,910
do pounds of honey......	821
do pounds butter made...24,724	
do pounds of cheese.......	160
do pounds of wool shorn	
in 1868...................24,705	
do tons of hay from tame	
grasses....................	394
do tons of hay from wild	
grasses...................	1,647
Value of farm produce for	
1868 70,079	
Value of stock raised during	
the year 1868.................21,165	
Value of agricultural imple-	
ments and machinery...15,427	
Value of manufactories for	
1868.............................	970

SCOTT.

No. of dwelling-houses.....	183
do families....................	183
do white males............	502
do white females.........	488
Total population..............	990

No. entitled to vote........	214
do militia............	183
do acres land enclosed	10,035
do acres in cultivation..	7,461
do acres of spring wheat	1,278

No. acres of corn............ 3,346
do acres of oats............. 731
do acres of rye............ 10
do acres of potatoes...... 59
do acres of sorghum..... 57
do acres of tame grass.. 504
do rods of hedging
planted 3,831
do fruit trees in bearing 1,950
do fruit trees not in
bearing.................. 3,988
do grape vines in bear-
ing...................... 784
do grape vines not in
bearing.................. 1,297
do horses of all ages..... 515
do cattle of all ages...... 1,650
do hogs of all ages........ 2,252
do sheep of all ages...... 3,164
do mules and asses 61
do work oxen............... 19
do milch cows 381
do dogs....................... 132
do hives of bees........... 159
do bushels of spring
wheat.................... 13,055
do bushels of corn........ 116,588
do bushels of oats........ 11,995

No. bushels of rye........ 155
do bushels of Irish po-
tatoes..................... 4,824
do bushels of onions..... 21
do bushels of apples...... 804
do lbs of grapes............ 1,559
do gallons of sirup from
sorghum................. 5,437
do lbs of honey............ 1,505
do lbs of butter............ 26,601
do lbs of cheese made... 550
do lbs of wool shorn in
1868...................... 8,400
do tons of hay from
tame grasses.......... 591
do tons of hay from
wild grasses.......... 495
Value of farm produce
in 1868.................. 40,850
Value of stock sold du-
ring 1868................ 40,851
Value of agricultural im-
plements and machi-
nery.........................10,955
Value of manufactures in
1868..........................13,545
Value of minerals, not
including coal in 1868... 305

SOUTH.

No. of dwelling-houses...... 150
do of families................. 150
do of white males.......... 410
do of white females....... 373
Total population................. 783
do entitled to vote......... 166
do of militia 125
do of acres of land en-
closed..... 5,095
do acres in cultivation... 4,123
do acres of spring wheat 755
do acres of winter wheat 12
do acres of corn............. 2,075

No. acres of oats.............. 440
do acres of potatoes........ 25
do acres of tame grass.... 118
do acres of sorghum...... 38
do rods of hedging......... 1,889
do fruit trees in bearing. 910
do fruit trees not in bearing.................... 2,814
do grape vines in bearing 361
do grape vines not in
bearing 466
do of horses of all ages... 361
do of cattle of all ages... 732

do   of hogs of all ages..... 1,380
do   of sheep of all ages... 1,843
do   mules and asses.......... 13
do   of milch cows............ 146
do   of work oxen............ 24
do   of dogs.................... 112
do   of hives of bees.......... 149
do   of bushels of spring
        wheat.........................10,994
do   of bushels of winter
        wheat..................... 110
do   of bushels of corn.....73,425
do   of bushels of oats...... 8,515
do   of bushels Irish pota-
        toes........................ 2,138
do   of bushels of onions..   6
do   of bushels of apples... 345
do   pounds of grapes...... 215

No.   gallons of sirup from
        sorghum.................. 4,244
do   pounds of honey........ 849
do   pounds of butter made10,285
do   pounds cheese made.. 150
do   pounds of wool shorn
        in 1868...................... 5,391
do   tons of hay from tame
        grass.............. 280
do   tons of hay from wild
        grass........... 325
Value of farm produce du-
        ring 1868....................27,719
Value of stock sold during
        1868.........................13,550
Value of agricultural imple-
        ments and machinery 6,790
Value manufactures during
        1868........................... 1,488

GRAND RIVER.

No of dwelling-houses........   96
do   families   96
do   white males..............   272
do   white females............   260
Total population   532
No entitled to vote............   98
No of militia......................   82
do   acres of land enclosed 2,451
do   acres of land in culti-
        vation 2,158
do   acres of spring wheat   396
do   acres of corn............. 1,130
do   acres of oats..............   220
do   acres of buckwheat...   8
do   acres of rye.............   10
do   acres of potatoes........   27
do   acres of onions..........   4
do   acres of tame grass...   16
do   acres of hops   11
do   rods hedging planted 1,841
do   fruit trees bearing.....   452

No.   fruit trees not bearing 1,448
do   grape vines bearing...   96
do   grape vines not bear-
        ing.......................   690
do   horses of all ages......   283
do   cattle of all ages........   437
do   hogs of all ages.........   511
do   sheep of all ages...... 1,465
do   mules and asses.........   17
do   milch cows..............   158
do   work oxen...............   6
do   dogs.........................   104
do   hives of bees.............   47
do   bushels spring wheat 2,885
do   bushels of corn.........17,125
do   bushels of oats......... 2,430
do   bushels of buckwheat   58
do   bushels Irish potatoes 3,287
do   bushels of onions......   13
do   bushels of apples......   68
do   pounds of grapes......   125

No. gallons of sirup made
    from sorghum........ 1,479
do pounds of honey...... 570
do pounds butter made.. 8,031
do pounds of wool shorn
    in 1868.................... 4,478
do tons of hay from tame
    grasses.................... 17
do tons of hay from wild
    grasses.................... 460

Value farm produce during
    the year 1868................15,302
Value of stock sold during
    the year 1868................12,736
Value of machinery and im-
    plements....................... 7,540
Value of manufactories in
    1868.............................. 1,717

MONROE.

No. of dwelling-houses...... 73
do families 73
do white males............ 217
do white females........... 186
Total population............... 403
No. entitled to vote........ 84
do militia..................... 68
do acres land enclosed.... 2,991
do acres in cultivation.... 2,443
do acres spring wheat... 460
do acres of corn............ 1,554
do acres of oats............ 338
do acres of potatoes...... 23
do acres of tame grass... 47
do acres of sorghum..... 43
do rods of hedging
    planted........ 1,990
do fruit trees in bearing 292
do fruit trees not in
    bearing.................. 1,195
do grape vines not in
    bearing.................. 192
do horses of all ages...... 268
do cattle of all ages....... 602
do hogs of all ages........ 785
do sheep of all ages...... 1,051
do mules and asses....... 16
do milch cows.............. 175
do work oxen.............. 8
do dogs....................... 74

No. hives of bees............ 44
do bushels of spring
    wheat...................... 3,046
do bushels of corn........ 43,350
do bushels of oats......... 4,337
do bushels of potatoes.. 3,043
do bushels of onions....... 20
do bushels of apples.... 88
do lbs of grapes............ 142
do gallons of sirup
    from sorghum......... 1,806
do lbs of honey........... 635
do lbs of butter made.... 11,710
do lbs of cheese............. 3,244
do lbs of wool shorn in
    1868........................... 3,120
do of tons of hay from
    tame grasses............... 48
do tons of hay from wild
    grass........................... 922
Value of farm produce
    during the year 1868.... 19,458
Value of stock sold du-
    ring the year 1868........ 14,718
Value of agricultural im-
    plements and machi-
    nery............................. 4,551
Value of manufactures
    for 1868...................... 734

WALNUT.

No. of dwelling-houses	125	No. milch cows	246
No. of families	125	No. work oxen	4
No. of white males	423	No. of dogs	107
No. of white females	367	No. hives of bees	138
Total population	790	No. bushels of spring wheat	7,317
No. entitled to vote	155	No. bushels of corn	22,564
No. of militia	129	No. bushels of oats	7,351
No. acres of land enclosed	7,352	No. bushels of buckwheat	106
No. acres under cultivation	4,175	No. bushels of rye	300
No. acres spring wheat	735	No. bushels of potatoes	5,669
No. acres of corn	2,588	No. bushels of onions	29
No. acres of oats	330	No. bushels of apples	653
No. acres of buckwheat	10	No. lbs of grapes	4,976
No. acres of barley	10	No. gal. sirup from sorg'm	2,669
No. acres of potatoes	27	No. lbs of honey	1,357
No. acres of tame grass	200	Lo. lbs of butter made	2,907
No. acres of sorghum	34	No. lbs of cheese made	70
No. rods of hedging planted	3,023	No. lbs wool shorn in 1868	1,414
No. fruit trees in bearing	704	No. tons hay from tame	
No. fruit trees not in bearing	2,669	grasses	215
No. grape vines in bearing	576	No. tons of hay from wild	553
No. grape vines not in bear-		Value of farm produce in	
ing	1,675	1868	44,377
No. horses of all ages	418	Value of stock sold during	
No. cattle of all ages	881	1868	18,125
No. hogs of all ages	1,510	Value of agricultural imple-	
No. sheep of all ages	1,449	ments and machinery	9,007
No. mules and asses	19	Value of manufactures in	
		1868	3,025

OHIO.

No. of dwelling-houses	102	No. acres of oats	318
do families	102	do acres of rye	1
do white males	293	do acres of potatoes	29
do white females	281	do acres of tame grasses	74
Total population	574	do acres of sorghum	48
No. entitled to vote	148	do rods hedging planted	2,462
do militia	95	do fruit trees in bearing	321
do acres land enclosed	3,402	do fruit trees not in	
do acres in cultivation	2,962	bearing	2,716
do acres of spring wheat	638	do grape vines in bear-	
do acres of corn	1,429	ing	374

No. grape vines not in bearing.................. 657

do horses of all ages..... 299

do cattle of all ages........ 482

do sheep of all ages...... 1,304

do mules and asses........ 9

do milch cows.............. 198

do work oxen............... 4

do dogs.......................... 92

do hives of bees.............. 46

do bushels spring wheat 8,468

do bushels of corn........ 52,722

do bushels of oats........ 5,925

do bushels of buckwheat 13

do bushels of rye......... 7

do bushels Irish potatoes 2,602

do bushels of onions..... 62

do bushels of apples...... 90

No. lbs of grapes.............. 350

do gallons of sirup from sorghum................ 3,737

do lbs of honey.............. 633

do lbs of butter made... 15,590

do lbs of wool shorn in 1868.... 3,197

do tons of hay from tame grasses............ 117

do tons of hay from wild grasses............ 544

Value of farm produce during 1868................ 29,781

Value of stock sold during 1868...................... 11,400

Value of agricultural implements and machinery......................... 5,558

15

LIST OF VOTERS

OF MADISON COUNTY BY TOWNSHIPS.

CENTER.

Anderson G., farmer
Anderson Nat., blacksmith
Alrich Wm., preacher
Andrews J. M., Carpenter
Achison Wm. M., teamster
Adkinson A. J., farmer
Appleton Able, farmer
Barrett Leonard, stone-mason
Bartlett J. W., lawyer
Bartlett Jerome, insurance agent
Ballard Cal., druggist
Bevington C. D., banker
Baxter D., merchant
Brobst Joseph, painter
Burnett J. W., grocer
Bisher J. H., blacksmith
Baldock A. C., doctor
Blystone F. A., tinner
Bailey W. D., veterinary surgeon
Bailey Moses, silversmith
Brownell I. W., county surveyor
Bardrick George, farmer
Bartlett Wm. W., butcher
Brown Jno. W., laborer
Brown Sylvester, laborer
Brown Ed., merchant
Brown Wm. H., carpenter
Boughton Matthew, plasterer
Boughton D. S., plasterer
Baker Henry, gardener
Bell L. B., billiard saloon
Brewer Jno., blacksmith
Burke Jno., lawyer
Betts Geo. W., barber
Betts Samuel, wagon-maker
Bartholomew J., blacksmith
Barker J. H., jeweler
Barker D., carpenter
Bishop W. H., laborer
Burnett Derrick, farmer

Bardrick C. H., farmer
Bowers J. S., farmer
Bishop J. W., teamster
Burns John, farmer
Clark D. W., farmer
Cassidy W. P., merchant
Cassidy Geo., assistant-postmaster
Cassidy F. M., postmaster
Cassidy Hugh, cabinet maker
Crawford Andrew, grocer
Cherry S. B., doctor
Coon C. H., druggist
Coon G. W., tailor
Cummings H. J. B., editor
Catterline Jno., harness-maker
Coon M., carpenter
Carter R. B., artist
Connoran Ed., farmer
Connoran Ed. F., teamster
Clear Jno., teamster
Curtis Richard, laborer
Cocklin J. W., shoe merchant
Clearwater W., teamster
Coleman J. C., dentist
Conger O. F., preacher
Chamberlin C. C., principal High
  School
Choat C. H., billiard saloon
Cart Jacob, carpenter
Connon Wm., stone-mason
Cowen Arch., shoemaker
Cooper D. E., county clerk
Dunkle W. H. H., merchant
Danforth C., clerk
Danforth W. R., tinner
Darnell Geo. F., teamster
Duer F. A., clerk
Davisson D. D., doctor
Dabney W. H. H., farmer
Dabney Albert, merchant

Dill John, laborer
Dill Peter, farmer
Duff Jno. B., doctor
Davies J. J., " Ye Local "
Dillon W. T., merchant
De Cou Jno., farmer
De Cou Amos, farmer
Dickenson Edward, preacher
Dombran D., stone mason
Donahue Dan., watchman
Eberle Wm., wagon maker
Evans E. W., butcher
Ellis M. D., bookkeeper
Everett R. W., farmer
Ferrall Wm., chair-maker
Farrar W. B., teacher
Frailey T. L., constable
Finalson James, book-keeper
Farnsworth H. C., painter
Ford D. S., stock-dealer
Finney Alonzo, laborer
Garlinger Thomas, stock dealer
Garlinger J. E., stock-dealer
Gordon Jonathan, teacher
Garretson N. W., life ins. agent
Glazebrook Mastin, livery-man
Gray A. J., teamster
Gilpin T. C., county auditor
Gilpin Samuel J., lawyer
Gilpin E. N., teacher
Gould B. W., blacksmith
Gaskill C. A., speculator
Gilleland David, farmer
Goshorn Robert,
Gustine John,
Garrettson G. W., teamster
Goodnow F., laborer
Grow F., stone-mason
Huff C., farmer
Hill A. D., carpenter
Hanners Frank, fiddler
Hoisington A. J., editor
Hollingsworth Jesse, hardware
  merchant
Hollingsworth Elbert, farmer
Howell D., blacksmith
Hart Wm. J., laborer
Hutchinson James,
Hutchinson D., doctor
Hornback Abe, wagon maker
Hornback George, clerk
Homan Conrad, farmer
Hardy W. H., co. superintendent
Hanna James, insurance agent
Holliday V. G., lawyer
Holliday James M., editor
Hatch H. L., landlord
Hohn John, stone-mason

Hestwood John, preacher
Hyskell Jacob, hardware merchant
Hawley E. W., butcher
Hillis E. L., doctor
Houk I. G., capitalist
Howard A., teamster
Hubbard Allen, teamster
Harris David, stone-mason
Hammond L. J., turner
Hill John,
Harrell J. S., farmer
Holmes E. F., farmer
Hughes Robert, stone mason
Hammock J. B.
Harlan N. A., plasterer
Hillman Thomas, trapper
Hawkins V., merchant
Hunt Chester, music teacher
Holbrook J. D. provision dealer
Hutchings J. J., real estate agent
Hyskell T. M., City Marshall
Hood A., farmer
Hood James, farmer
Hyder E. S., artist
Henry W. C., grocer
Jones C. B., printer
Jones C., grocer
James Marion, auctioneer
Jacobs John W., carpenter
James Oliver, farmer
Kenyon D. P., hardware merchant
Kirkwood J. O., farmer
King J. S., grocer
Kendig A. J., express agent
Kelso W. C., teamster
Kelso H. C., teamster
Kelso J. C., preacher
Kizer Wm. H., grocer
Knowlton Wm. M., broker
Kinsman Newall, cabinet-maker
Killam Clinton, teamster
Killam Timothy, farmer
Killam J. M., farmer
Kridler E. H., carpenter
Kirk J. W., laborer
Koon George, laborer
Leonard John, lawyer
Leonard S. R., farmer
Lothrop C. B., stage agent
Lewis W. H., lawyer
Lovelace B., carpenter
Leith James,
Lee C. P., cabinet-maker
Lockhart S. W., teamster
Leach R. L., grocer
Lykens L. E., teamster
Lawrence D. G., laborer
Lawrence James R., laborer

Lawrence C.,'laborer
Leith William, shoemaker
Murray N., landlord
Murray B. F., lawyer
Mullinix L., laborer
Mullinix Thomas, grocer
Mackey Tom, printer
McBride C. H., saddler
McBride W. T., saddler
McBride C. P., saddler
McKnight W. W., banker
McPherson M. L., lawyer
McLeod John Sen., stone-mason
McLeod John Jr., stone-mason
McIntire Alexander, chair-maker
McConnelle Wm., carpenter
McCaughan C. T., preacher
McCaughan John S., lawyer
McComas John, laborer
McBeth Thomas, trapper
McKibbin Gideon, chair-maker
McCalman Robert, shoe merchant
Mott Frederick, circuit judge
Merrill G. J., clerk
McDill Martin,
Munger N. W., wool factor
Myres Samuel, carpenter
Mitchel H. S., saddler
Mackey William, cabinet-maker
Mitchel D. H., lime burner
Mitchel Samuel, wool spinner
McCabe W., stage driver
Mathews W. E., saloon keeper
McDole Conrad, farmer
McDale John W., farmer
Morehead A., brick-mason
Miller George C., saloon keeper
McClure J. A., farmer
Miller Hugh H., blacksmith
Mead Jacob, far mer
Newlon W. C., real estate agent
Newell William, laborer
Null William H., clerk
Noel S., brick maker
O'Neal W. H., preacher
Odell Eli, mechanic
Orswell J., wagon maker
Orswell T. W. D., hedge grower
Pitzer J. A., merchant
Pitzer J. M., merchant
Palmer E., teamster
Palmer Cal, teamster
Philbrick D. H,, druggist
Purcell Bassil, farmer
Purcell William, butcher
Prather S. H.,
Porter J. H., billiard saloon
Porter A., saddler

Porter Henry, farmer
Parker Matthew, laborer
Pyres James, laborer
Pryor M. G., teacher
Ruby William B., farmer
Ruby S. G., lawyer
Root Aaron.
Rattliff George, teamster
Rattliff Thompson.
Rees D. F., blacksmith
Renolds W. G., teamster
Rummel H., merchant
Renfro William, brick-maker
Rutledge G. M. doctor
Reed C. W., plasterer
Russell J. C. clerk
Russell A. J., doctor
Robinson George, stone mason
Rains R., baker
Ratliff Robert, stage driver
Stokes James H., printer
Seevers G. W., nurseryman
Shackleford J. J., carpenter
Stone Mell, hardware merchant
Shull D., crockery merchant
Snyder Samuel, grocer
Snyder H., carpenter
Shriver W. R., wagon maker
Shannon J. R., baker
Shannon William, gunsmith
Smith S. B., teamster
Stitt R. A., ex-county treasurer
Stiffler P. J., cabinet maker
Shadley John A., clerk
Smith A. B., merchant
Sprague P. B., merchant
Sprague Allen.
Stone T., chair-maker
Stiffler G. L., teamster
Stiffler A. J., farmer
Stiffler J. W., sawyer
Sprague Isaac, farmer
Strackinghast J. W. wagon maker
Stout M. C. laborer
Sturgeon Thomas, teamster
Seevers T. J., nurseryman
Spencer C. G., teamster
Shotwell J. W. artist
Shannon E. D.
Storrs N. E., preacher
Storrs E. O., teamster
Short C. H., plasterer
Stingley Jesse, farmer
Stiffler John, Senior
Sturman John B., merchant
Smith W. H. H. carpenter
Shepherd John G.
Snyder Joseph, carpenter,

Smith Henry, stone mason
Stingley Absalom, butcher
Stewart R. D., harness maker
Seevers G. W., farmer
Truitt Jesse, plasterer
Tullis John S., deputy-sheriff
Tidrick M. R., grocer
Tidrick I. L., druggist
Tidrick L. M., doctor
Tryon Calvin livery-man
Thornburgh G. W. laborer
Thompson J. H., farmer
Turner G. H., preacher
Taylor A. D., tailor
Thornburgh Lewis, carpenter
Tedford Thomas J.,
Turbett G. A., carpenter
Thompson Dugald, presiding elder
Turner S. S., insurance agent
Terry Luther, stone mason
Thompson A. B. C., farmer
Turner D., teamster
Vaus Cayock James, basket maker
Vaus Cayock S., laborer
Vaus Cayock O., teamster
Van Vleet A., carpenter
White J. S., shoe merchant

White J. T., proprietor woolen factory
White J. Q., carpenter
White W. N., carpenter
Webster S. R., tinner
Wilson C. S., editor
Wasson J., carpenter
Way J. B., merchant
Wilson David, laborer
Wasson Levi, harness maker
Wilkinson T. M., carpenter
Williams N., shoemaker
Williams J. D., shoemaker
Wainwright V., lawyer
Warmsley B. F., dentist
Wortman D., laborer
Wortman J. M., laborer
Williams H. C., clerk
Wilkin Ell, lawyer
Webster Wm., teamster
Wells D., farmer
Wells V. E., farmer
Witburn Robert, stonemason
Wheelock S. B., grocer
Young J. W., clerk
Young A. E., carpenter
Vilyer Frank, stonemason

PENN.

Alger Samuel, farmer
Armstrong Wm. H., farmer
Armstrong Wm. S., farmer
Boyd John H., farmer
Barnett Eli, farmer
Barnett Wilson, farmer
Boyd Thos. M., farmer
Bellows W. H., farmer
Barnett Albert, farmer
Boyd Wm., farmer
Boyd Henry A., farmer
Barnett Allen, nurseryman
Bond Thos., farmer
Culver Jay, farmer
Culver F. F., farmer
Cook Robert, farmer
Courtwright Wm., farmer
Culver John C., farmer
Carter Eph. H., farmer
Clark D. J., stock dealer
Cook J. C., farmer
Clements G. T., farmer
Compton Benj. farmer
Cook Levi, farmer
Davis John, farmer
Dart Orman, farmer
Eldridge Caleb, farmer

Ford W. T., stock dealer
Francis Daniel, farmer
Francis Washington, farmer
Floyd Michael, farmer
Fleming Wm., farmer
Garrett E. R., farmer
Haugh Wm., farmer
Hubbell M. B., farmer
Holmes D. C., farmer
Humer E. V., farmer
Hathaway D. W., farmer
Hochsetler Jacob M., farmer
Inman Samuel, farmer
Ingle James D., farmer
Jay Thos. E., farmer
Jessup Clarkson, farmer
Johnston Oliver P., farmer
Johnson Joseph M., farmer
Johnson Robert V., farmer
Lee Wesley K., farmer
Lee John, farmer
Lee Ebeneezer, farmer
Lewis Henry, farmer
Martin David L., farmer
Mapes E. S., farmer
Mapes Orrin, farmer
Martin Alfred, farmer

Macy Albert C., farmer
Mendenhall Nathan, farmer
Newlon Joshua, farmer
Neff Isaac C., farmer
Nobles Horace, farmer
Ormsbee E., farmer
Robinson Wm. B., farmer
Rogers Wm., farmer
Ross W. A., farmer
Robinson Geo. B., farmer
Rochler W. L., farmer
Rockafield J. A., farmer
Roark James R., farmer
Rogers Seth, farmer
Scott Josiah, farmer
Smith Jesse P., farmer

Stiff Isaac C., farmer
Schlarb Nicholas, farmer
Stanton David, farmer
Tyler Sr. Wm., farmer
Tyler Jr. Wm., farmer
Wilson Abihu, farmer
Wheeler Adolphus, farmer
Wood E. G., farmer
Wilson John, farmer
Wilson Christopher, farmer
Wilson Charles, farmer
Wilson C. C., farmer
Wilson Jesse, farmer
Young Wm., farmer
Zimmerman Philip, farmer

MADISON.

Allen James, farmer
Allen Hiram, farmer
Anderson Leroy, farmer
Anderson J. W., farmer
Alexander James F., farmer
Anderson J. B., farmer
Abrams Joseph, farmer
Brown John, farmer
Bennett Joshua, farmer
Bennett Jacob, farmer
Bennett Francis, farmer
Beezly Wm., farmer
Beezly David, farmer
Beezly Joseph, farmer
Barnett Asa., grocer
Barnett Wesley, farmer
Barnett Ira, farmer
Barnett Wm., farmer
Barnett David, farmer
Barnett Taylor C., farmer
Barnett Dayton, Merchant
Brown Wm. H., farmer
Bunch Wm., farmer
Bowlsby Wm. H., farmer
Bunch Wm. D., farmer
Brown George, farmer
Bridges Losson, farmer
Barnes J. J., farmer
Bowlsby Levi, farmer
Bell Alexander, farmer
Bridleman Samuel, farmer
Bonine John, farmer
Brown Robert, farmer
Bell Henry, farmer
Clampitt Wm. H., farmer
Coe Wm., farmer
Cox Wesley, farmer
Crawford Lewis, farmer

Clark George, farmer
Croft Thomas, farmer
Crawford Henry, farmer
Carter Joseph, farmer
Crawford Samuel, farmer
Cunningham George W., farmer
Clements A. M., farmer
Clements Stewart, farmer
Compton Martin, farmer
Drinkwater Robert, farmer
Duff Wm., farmer
Dickson James, farmer
Duff Eber, farmer
Duff W. T., farmer
Duff David, farmer
Duff J. A., farmer
Elliott Zimri, farmer
Evans J. A., farmer
Evans John S., farmer
Evans Robert, farmer
Fogleson Jesse, farmer
Fogleson Christopher, farmer
Fogleson Eli, farmer
Fogleson Charles, farmer
Fry Geo. C., farmer
Goodale C. C., farmer
Gough J. B., farmer
Groseclose James, farmer
Gabbart Jacob, farmer
Gabbart Michael, farmer
Graham M. J., farmer
Hockett S. H., farmer
Hubbard Robert F., farmer
Hough Franklin, farmer
Hultch John, farmer
Hockett Joel, farmer
Harlow W. R., farmer
Hawkins John, farmer

Hockett David, farmer
Hellgardner Henry, farmer
Klinginsmith Henry, farmer
Klinginsmith Samuel, farmer
Klinginsmith Daniel, farmer
Kilgore Joseph M., farmer
Klingman John, farmer
Lee Wm., farmer
Litton N. W., farmer
Lemar Geo., farmer
Madden P. W., farmer
Marshall Eli N., farmer
McKibben Wm., farmer
Means James, farmer
McCallan D. C., farmer
Mann Ezra, farmer
Mandorff B. F., farmer
McCabe Wm., farmer
Nickels George, farmer
Nicholson J. B., farmer
Oldham Andrew, farmer
Oldham Jesse, farmer
Oldham John, farmer
Peters Anson M., farmer
Pain Francis M., farmer
Parkinson Joseph L., farmer
Powel Ruel, farmer
Powel Elihu, farmer
Paulin W. H., farmer
Quinett Vanderman,
Rankin James, farmer
Roberts Wm., farmer
Rashford N. D., farmer

Surly Wm., farmer
Shultz Thomas, farmer
Stewart Alexander, farmer
Smith Jonathan, farmer
Stewart John M., farmer
Sandham James, farmer
Stephenson Wm., farmer
Simons Joseph D., farmer
Stewart Francis C., farmer
Smith John, farmer
Stewart Hugh, farmer
Stanley Josiah, farmer
Trester Wm. P., farmer
Thompson M. L., farmer
Trester Martin, farmer
Taylor Henry, farmer
Trester John, farmer
Trester Jacob H., farmer
Taylor John S., farmer
Thompson S. F., farmer
Woody James. farmer
Wilson John, farmer
Woolery Joseph W. farmer
Wilson Milton, farmer
Wilson Seth, farmer
Whaley Z. S., farmer
White R. A., farmer
Wuster Charles, farmer
White W. W., farmer
Woosley B. F., farmer
Whitenac kJ. D., farmer
White W. E., farmer
White J. M., farmer

JEFFERSON.

Allen J. B., farmer
Burger Gotlob B., farmer
Burger A. F., farmer
Brown David, farmer
Brown Lewis, farmer
Britton Pleasant, farmer
Brewster, Wm. F., farmer
Brittain Alfred, farmer
Ballentine Hugh T., farmer
Baurr Stanalus, farmer
Baker Wm., farmer
Brooker John, farmer
Brooker G., farmer
Barnhart Wm. A., farmer
Belliefield Peter J., farmer
Black Wm. M., farmer
Ballentine A., farmer
Cook Eddy, farmer
Cooper C. W., farmer
Cooper Frank, farmer
Cooper Morgan, farmer

Cooper M. W., farmer
Clayton W. T., farmer
Crowl Jesse H., farmer
Cooper A. C., farmer
Cooper S. B., farmer
Cromwell M. W., farmer
Cromwell Henry, farmer
Duff Arthur, farmer
Dumkins Jonathan, farmer
Dehart Thomas, farmer
Doak William, farmer
Dizer John, farmer
Edmundson J. W., farmer
Earkhart G. F., farmer
Forbes William, farmer
Falwell Samuel, farmer
Fitch A. P., farmer
Fisher George Jr., farmer
Fisher George Sr., farmer
Folwell Wm. B., farmer
Fletcher Daniel A., farmer

Forbes Francis H., farmer
Gutchell George, farmer
Gutchell Henry, farmer
Guiselman Adam, farmer
Goodson Wm. N. farmer
Goff, Nathan, farmer
Hazen Daniel, farmer
Hazen Rufus, farmer
Honold T. J. farmer
Hazen Rufus, farmer
Hotchkiss Jarius, farmer
Hutchings John, former
Hartenbower J.H. farmer
Jones Wm. A., farmer
Knight M. A., farmer
Kelly John M., farmer
Kirkpatrick John N., farmer
Kopp Arnest. farmer
Kirkpatrick A. R., farmer
Kennedy Thomas, farmer
McClary G. W., farmer
Means John, farmer
Mohler S. L., farmer
McDonald William, farmer
Matthew Meaker Jr., farmer
McDonald William C., farmer
Miller Israel, farmer
Myers Thomas, farmer
Mark James A., farmer
Myers T. S., farmer
Mitchel John J., farmer
McClery William, farmer
Mitchel Darius, farmer
Myers A. W., farmer
Myers W. A., farmer
Myers Anthony, farmer
McComb A. D., farmer
Isaiah Miller, farmer
Nicholson S. J., farmer
Nicholson Thomas D., farmer
Nicholson Thomas R., farmer
Nicholson John M., farmer
Nicholson E. G., farmer
Payton Jacob, farmer
Payton B. W., farmer

Pierson, R. M., farmer
Payton J. F., farmer
Parker Wm. C., farmer
Poffinbarger, S. W., farmer
Payton Joseph W., farmer
Reigle Daniel, farmer
Rogers Isaac, farmer
Reinhart J. W., farmer
Rogers William E., farmer
Rose L. H., farmer
Reigle Jacob, farmer
Reigle John, farmer
Reigle George, farmer
Rose William M., farmer
Reeder E. W., farmer
Rodrick John W., farmer
Shields Robert, farmer
Smith Jackson, farmer
Spencer Joseph, farmer
Smith Abner, farmer
Smith, Jonathan, farmer
Shambaugh A.. H., farmer
Shambaugh S. B.., farmer
Schoen William, farmer
Sebering William, farmer
Shaw John T., farmer
Stewart J. X., farmer
Thompson Henry, farmer
Thompson Robert L., farmer
Trundle Robert, farmer
Trundle John H., farmer
Trundle Aaron, farmer
Thompson D. F., farmer
Urquhart James, farmer
Welch Jefferson, farmer
Walky H. F., farmer
Welch Edward, farmer
Wiggins John, farmer
Welch Harrison, farmer
White Samuel F., farmer
Wilson J. B., farmer
Walker R. A., farmer
Wilsey Uria, farmer
Young Jacob, farmer

LEE.

Allen Wm., farmer
Brooks Frederick, farmer
Brinson Solomon, farmer
Ballou Lewis, farmer
Ballou Loyal, farmer
Burges Frederick, farmer
Brady Michael, farmer
Burkhead A. J., farmer
Bigelow Hiram S., farmer

Bigelow Paul, farmer
Condon Thomas, farmer
Collins Edward, farmer
Comdon James, farmer
Davy Peter, farmer
Duffey Patrick, farmer
Dooley Patrick, farmer
Dooley Jeremiah, farmer
Duffey Michael, farmer

Evans F. M., farmer
Ellis Byron, farmer
England Jonathan, farmer
England T. J., farmer
Flinn A. J., farmer
Glinn Thomas, farmer
Gilleran D., farmer
Hazen Emerson, farmer
Hamilton L. D., farmer
Hubbard Andrew, farmer
Hubbard Peter, farmer
Harvey Charles, farmer
Imes Otho, farmer
Johnson A. W., farmer
Kelly Matthew, farmer
Lynch James, farmer
Lee James, farmer
Laughlin Michael, farmer
Laughlin Peter, farmer
Littlefield A. F., farmer
McCarty John, farmer
Major Allen, farmer
Muloehill Daniel, farmer
Mahar Patrick, farmer
Major George F., farmer

Mack Martin, farmer
Mack Michael, farmer
Peoples Hanibal, farmer
Pace John V., farmer
Rance George W., farmer
Rixter J. B., farmer
Raymond Julius, farmer
Roberts George R., farmer
Stevenson John, farmer
Smith Elias, farmer
Simpson Samuel, farmer
Smith L. N., farmer
Shabell George, farmer
Spillue John, farmer
Smith Cornelius, farmer
Smith James, farmer
Simmons Peter, farmer
Sandusky John, farmer
Turney Austin, farmer
Turney D. F., farmer
Walker Isaac, farmer
Wooden Henry, farmer
Wright M. E., farmer
Watson J. H., farmer
Wallace John, farmer

JACKSON.

Bruitt Otto, farmer
Barnes Harrison, farmer
Brotherton Miles, farmer
Bard James W., farmer
Bissell O. B., farmer
Bunn Samuel, farmer
Butterfield Nathaniel, farmer
Combs B. E., farmer
Combs J. N., farmer
Colzin Daniel, farmer
Comp Henry, farmer
Cline Fred, farmer
Cranson George, farmer
Conway Charles, farmer
Davis Joseph, farmer
Davis Henry, farmer
Davis W. J., farmer
Daniels Michael, farmer
Dabney Henry, farmer
Dabney J. W., farmer
Darnell George A., farmer
Duff Robert, farmer
Darnell James, farmer
Darnell B. F., farmer
Darnell, William R., farmer
Duff James, farmer
Early John, farmer
Estell R. A., farmer
Early William, stock dealer
16

Edmonds Enos, farmer
Epard W. S., farmer
Epard Anderson, farmer
Epard John W., farmer
Early Thomas, farmer
Ford I. S., farmer
Ford Wm., farmer
Ford, J. M., farmer
Finney Nelson, farmer
Finney Lorenzo, farmer
Gordon Harrison, farmer
Garrett Simon, farmer
Garrett Elias, farmer
Graham John M., farmer
Gordon R. B., farmer
Gordon Robert, farmer
Hart A. M., farmer
Hockenberry M. C., farmer
Hasty Martin, farmer
Henderson Daniel, farmer
Hindman Samuel, farmer
Hindman J. C., farmer
Hindman R. M., farmer
Hamilton Samuel, farmer
Hindman Thomas, farmer
Leizure J. T., farmer
Lyon Benjamin F., farmer
Low Phillip D., farmer
Linn Henry, farmer

Low Samuel, farmer
Mears J. W., farmer
McDaniel, A. H., farmer
Mabbett William, farmer
McKimson William, farmer
McMarshall E. M., farmer
McDill D. H., farmer
Miller J. S., farmer
Means J. W., farmer
Nesselrode John, farmer
Phillips J. S., farmer
Phillips John, farmer
Phillips William, farmer
Prentice N. F., farmer
Perkins, E. G., farmer
Palmer T. W., farmer
Ralston Robert, farmer
Reynold J. A., farmer
Ralston Samuel M., farmer
Ralston James B., farmer
Rose George, farmer
Ralston John, farmer
Reigle Thomas, farmer
Rees John, farmer
Rose John, farmer
Shuck Samuel, farmer
Speer Andrew S., farmer

Sipple Frank, farmer
Stewart Samuel G., farmer
Stewart R. W., farmer
Steel James, farmer
Schoepflin Martin, sawyer
Schoepflin Henry, sawyer
Salisbury Thomas, farmer
Stickler Emanuel, farmer
Stewart Thomas, farmer
Sulgrove Noah, stock dealer
Stewart John M., farmer
Sherman Clark, farmer
Smith George, farmer
Shock E. W., farmer
Titcomb Stephen, farmer
Thrasher Nelson, farmer
Teering Henry, farmer
Tobin H., farmer
Wolverton G. W., farmer
Williams John E., farmer
Wentermantel William, farmer
Welch A. G., farmer
Wilson John, farmer
Wilson John G., farmer
Williams John E., farmer
Zeering Henry, farmer

DOUGLAS.

Abrams James, farmer
Applegate Andrew A., farmer
Anderson Wm., farmer
Acheson Wm., farmer
Acheson John A., farmer
Alexander Wm. H., farmer
Acheson John R., farmer
Abrams Stephen, farmer
Abrams David, farmer
Applegate D. B., farmer
Allgeyer Charles, farmer
Amy John L., farmer
Bennett Edward, farmer
Baxly Francis, farmer
Brinson Zebulon, farmer
Bennett Andrew, farmer
Barrett Joseph, farmer
Bishop James K., farmer
Brown John W., farmer
Bard Wm. K., farmer
Baum Irvin, farmer
Bardrick George, farmer
Brown Bradly B., farmer
Black James, farmer
Brooks Samuel, farmer
Bruce Richard, farmer
Bruce Francis M., farmer

Brooks Wm., farmer
Bruce John A., farmer
Brittain Wm. F., farmer
Brooks Samuel, farmer
Bard John S., farmer
Beck J. G., farmer
Cooper Warren D., farmer
Clark John P., carpenter
Church Seymour, farmer
Chase Augustus, farmer
Chase Seth, farmer
Cooper John M., farmer
Cox Jonathan, farmer
Cooper D. E., Co. clerk
Cardly Armstead, farmer
Cline Sr. David, farmer
Cooper J. W., farmer
Cole Wm., farmer
Chase Wm., farmer
Cole Oliver, farmer
Chase George B., farmer
Clay Henry C., farmer
Cline William R., farmer
Cline Jr. David, farmer
Dewit George C., farmer
Dalson George B., farmer
Dayton Isaac R., farmer

Dabney Isaac W., farmer
Duff Robert, farmer
Duff Samuel W., farmer
Dayton Samuel U., farmer
Evans Jacob, farmer
Evans Alexander, farmer
Evans Wm., farmer
Evans Asa Wesley, farmer
Evans Robert A., farmer
Evans Hugh, farmer
Ellis Shobal, farmer
Eyerly Daniel H., farmer
Flanigan Edward, farmer
Fuller George, farmer
Flinn James, farmer
Fisher James, farmer
Flanigan John, farmer
Ford A. W., farmer
Ford Irvin S., farmer
Garlinger Thomas, farmer
Graves Elihu, farmer
Goare James, farmer
Gustine Lemuel, farmer
Gatchel John, farmer
Gatchel Albert, nurseryman
Gideon Henry, farmer
Goshorn J. S., insurance agent
Gustine Jonathan S., farmer
Gray A. Sultan, farmer
Gatchel David, farmer
Gibson William E., farmer
Henry Martin V., farmer
Harris Henry, farmer
Henry Emanuel, farmer
Hays William S., farmer
Harlan Asa, farmer
Henry Samuel, farmer
Henry William I., farmer
Hobson James M., farmer
Hannah Reuben, farmer
Hamler Cyrus E., farmer
Harford Daniel A., Carpenter
Hollingsworth John, stone mason
Hays Ebeneezer, farmer
James Stephen, farmer
Jack Benj. F., farmer
James Josiah, farmer
Johnson George A., farmer
Leizure William H., farmer
Leach James A., farmer
Lapella John H., farmer
Leech James W., farmer
Lucas Wm. J., farmer
Leach Josiah L., farmer
Leach John, farmer
Kale Thomas J., farmer
Kale Alfred, farmer
Kale Wilson, farmer

Kirkland Samuel, sawyer
Kinsman Herman A. farmer
Kinsman James W., farmer
Kinsman Dennison, farmer
Means Samuel, farmer
Myers Jonathan, farmer
Malone Michael, farmer
Moody Israel W., farmer
McCarty Bradford, farmer
Miller Israel, farmer
McCarty David, farmer
McDonald Joseph F., farmer
Manahan James, farmer
McDonald Robert F., farmer
McDonald Cyrus B., farmer
Mills Albert C., farmer
McDaniel F. M., farmer
Musgrave James, farmer
McGee Matthew, farmer
Norris Alfred, farmer
North John W., farmer
O'Laughlin Michael, farmer
Ogburn Edward, farmer
Oliver Launcelot, farmer
Peed Edward farmer
Powell David C., farmer
Packard Marcus A., farmer
Perkins Wm. K., farmer
Paulin Isaac P., farmer
Pickel Marcus, farmer
Rehard John, farmer
Rinker Wallace E., farmer
Ruth James, farmer
Ruth John, farmer
Roseman Edward M., farmer
Rogan Sr. James, farmer
Rush Joseph, farmer
Rogan Jr. James, farmer
Rutlege Archibald M., farmer
Sanford Philo, farmer
Sutler Austin W., farmer
Sulgrove Eli, farmer
Shafer Andrew, farmer
Sutler Benj. F., farmer
Sutler Henry, farmer
Sutler George, farmer
Salisbury John, farmer
Sutler Samuel G., farmer
Shepherd Jesse P., farmer
Smith Asa B., farmer
Stump Marcellus, farmer
Speers Jesse, farmer
Seevers George W., farmer
Stickler Jacob, farmer
Shepherd Joseph, farmer
Shepherd James R., farmer
Stickler John, farmer
Shepherd H. T., farmer

Sulgrove Emanuel, farmer
Thomas Oliver H., farmer
Terry Elmore G., preacher
Thompson J. W., farmer
Tannehill Wm. C., farmer
Taylor Levi, farmer
Tracy Geo. W., farmer
Terry Wm. C. farmer
Ward Lycander C., carpenter
Wheeler Geo. L., stock-dealer

Woolery Eli, farmer
Warden Malcom W., farmer
Wood Wm. D., preacher
Welch Samuel, farmer
Walker Fredrick E., farmer
Wilson John C., farmer
Vance Wm., farmer
Vaughan Matthew, farmer
Vanderpool Harding, farmer

UNION.

Andress Harvy D., farmer
Atcheson John, farmer
Andress Orin, farmer
Armstrong George, farmer
Arnold Samuel B., farmer
Beedle John R., farmer
Brown James R., farmer
Burnett S. M., farmer
Brown Wm., farmer
Bird Anderson, farmer
Beedle A. C., farmer
Brown John D., farmer
Burgess A. B., farmer
Brown Thos, farmer
Blair Alexander, sr., farmer
Blair Alexander, jr., farmer
Baker John, farmer
Bird Butler, farmer
Brown James, farmer
Brown Wm. L., farmer
Brown John L., farmer
Barrow David, farmer
Barber H. P., farmer
Boyles P. M., farmer
Blair George, farmer
Burks N. W., farmer
Bird Wm., farmer
Bardrick Thomas, farmer
Blunk Amos J., farmer
Crawford W. P., farmer
Cooper R. D., farmer
Cox Eli, contractor
Cooper M. D., farmer
Cram Martin, farmer
Clearwaters John S., farmer
Clearwaters Levi, farmer
Cromwell G. W., farmer
Childers Benjamin, farmer
Campbell A. V., farmer
Childers John M., farmer
Cracraft Milton, farmer
Cracraft John, farmer
Duff William H., farmer
Duff James W., carpenter

Duff Louis M., farmer
Davis James R., farmer
Davis William, farmer
Etchison John, farmer
Ellis Martin, farmer
Edmondson, Wm. H., brickmaker
Fleming John, farmer
Farris James H., farmer
Farris Isaac F., farmer
Farris Charles, farmer
Farris James, farmer
Fry Jacob, farmer
Fuqua Charles, farmer
Farris William, farmer   .
Finch, S. T., lime burner
Freeborn Joseph, farmer
Fountain Henry, farmer
Faurote John, farmer
Guiberson N. W., farmer
Gordon Joel D., farmer
Guye George W., farmer
Guye James, farmer
Graham William, farmer
Gordon Samuel J., farmer
Gentry W. M., farmer
Gordon George W., teacher
Guiberson John S., farmer
Garrett William, farmer
Gilleland James H., farmer
Graham John W., farmer
Guye Samuel H., farmer
Guiberson William B., farmer
Goode John W., farmer
Gentry F. M., farmer
Graham Adam, doctor
Graham John, preacher
Grant Edward, farmer
Gidean Jacob M., farmer
Hildebrand Samuel, farmer
HOLLIDAY S. L., farmer, res on
    n w qr sec 30, tp 76, r 26
Hilton John, farmer
Holton John P., farmer
Hall James C., farmer

Higgs Altred, farmer
Housington A. J., farmer
Hollingsworth Z., farmer
Janes Harvy, farmer
Justice John J., farmer
Jessie William T., farmer
Lee Harvy, farmer
Lee E. B., wool-grower
Love T. S., farmer
Lull Alexander, farmer
Leckliter Henry, farmer
Lane J. S., farmer
Long J. H., farmer
McConkey William, farmer
Mercer Clinton T., farmer
McDaniel Henderson, farmer
Miller Henry, farmer
Miller E. T., farmer
Miller George, farmer
Madison Charles, farmer
McKinzie Aaron, farmer
Montgomery John, farmer
Matthews S. W., farmer
McGinnis Joseph, farmer
Mills E. S., farmer
Montgomery, E. K., farmer
Maggs J. C., farmer
Neal Robert, farmer
Nolan Patrick, blacksmith
Needs John, farmer
Orman John, farmer
Pitzer Wm. F., farmer
Pendleton T. H., plasterer
Porter H. D., farmer
Porter D. M., farmer
Porter Aaron, farmer
Pepper S. N., farmer
Palmer Daniel, farmer
Pettit Nathaniel, farmer
Phillips Levi, farmer
Quillen P. F., farmer
Robinson Thomas, farmer
Riner Peter, farmer
Rhodes Samuel, farmer
Ross Zachariah, teacher

Reigle Elias, farmer
Ralston Samuel, farmer
Renfro W. H. H., farmer
Rogers C. J. lime burner
Ruby John, farmer
Ritchie John, farmer
Shill John, farmer
Stocking Charles H., farmer
Seevers John, nurseryman
Stevens George W., farmer
Simpson George, farmer
Seevers Columbus, clerk
Sturman Wm., farmer
Stafford Elias, farmer
Stafford O. P., farmer
Stafford E. H., farmer
Sturman John J., farmer
Seevers Alfred, farmer
Spencer Isaac, wool-grower
Smith W. R., farmer
Simpson John S., farmer
Stingly Eli, farmer
Staufer Joseph, farmer
Sturman Thomas, farmer
Smith Levi, farmer
Shafer Wm., farmer
Smith Edward, farmer
Shafer John, farmer
Thornberry James M., farmer
Thornberry G. J., farmer
Thompson J. S., farmer
Winters Alfred, farmer
Weaver Henry K., farmer
Wiggins Van B., farmer
West James, farmer
Warl Woodward, farmer
Walker John H., farmer
Whitt Noah, farmer
Weaver Solomon, farmer
Wilkin J., W., sawyer
Wells Alonzo, farmer
Vanwy Henry, farmer
Vanwy G., W., farmer
Vandoren C., farmer
Young George W., farmer

CRAWFORD.

Atchison N., farmer
Bell George, farmer
Bell Enos, farmer
Blair Alexander W., farmer
Bell Abner Sr., farmer
Brown John W., farmer
Bell James, farmer
Bell Abner Jr., farmer
Brassfield John, farmer

Blosser George, farmer
Blosser C. H., farmer
Cason J. W., farmer
Cunningham John, farmer
Crosby John W , farmer
Carson James M., farmer
Cason Thomas T., farmer
Cassida Frank, farmer
Conner Stephen, farmer

Casey Mitchel, farmer
Davis George B., farmer
Donahue Michael, farmer
Doane Zachariah, farmer
Dorrence James H.,
Dorrence William S., farmer
Dillon Thomas, farmer
Doane William H., farmer
David Patrick, farmer
Esken John M., farmer
Eyerly George W., farmer
Fenton Thomas, farmer
Folwell Thomas, hotel keeper
Felton William H., farmer
Faid Frank, farmer
Grossman Valentine, farmer
Galagher James, farmer
Gallagher James Sr.,
Gamble Michael, farmer
Gillaspie James, farmer
Gamble Robert, farmer
Greeny John, farmer
Garvey Patrick C., farmer
Gill James, farmer
Gill Patrick, farmer
Gamble John, farmer
Holton, William, farmer
Hershey George, farmer
Handy James W., farmer
Hughlin J. M., miller
Henderson Thomas L., farmer
Howell Lanson, farmer
Hughart Campbell, preacher
Howell Aaron, farmer
Howell Nelson, farmer
Howell Patrick, farmer
Harrington Patrick, farmer
Jordan George W., farmer
Jordan James V., farmer
Kanard George H., farmer
Kanard Oliver E., farmer
Kinkanon Nathan, farmer
Kennedy William, farmer
Kirby William, farmer
Kirby James, farmer
Leyman D. M., farmer
Loftis Michael, farmer
Lee J. M., farmer
McLaughlin Thomas, farmer
McDowell Robert, farmer

Melwy Thomas, farmer
Marland John, farmer
McCarty H. L., farmer
McLeas Anderson, farmer
McDonald D., farmer
Morris Robert, farmer
McDonald Thomas, farmer
McDonald John, farmer
Morgan David, farmer
Madison Jerry, farmer
McGlown Michael, farmer
Narna Edward, farmer
O'Conner Andrew, farmer
O'Conner William, farmer
Potter John, farmer
Potter E. J., farmer
Pulfermaster Henry, farmer
Parks J. L., farmer
Riley Patrick, farmer
Potter William, farmer
Ryan John, farmer
Rees John R., farmer
Reed David, farmer
Rhinehart Isaac, farmer
Snyder Charles, farmer
Scott Milton, farmer
Smith Patrick, farmer
Stark Doane, farmer
Shannon Samuel E., farmer
Shreeves Jonah, farmer
Smith Bartholomew, farmer
Stout Elvis, farmer
Smith L. A., farmer
Turk William M., farmer
Trouth Jacob, farmer
Tool Thomas, farmer
Whitt Francis D., farmer
Washington George B., farmer
Weekly William, farmer
Wolf George, farmer
Witham James, farmer
Wiggins Luther, farmer
Williamson John L., farmer
White John, farmer
Weidman A., farmer
Wilkin Robert, farmer
Young Harmon, farmer
Wilson Silas, farmer
White Samuel, farmer

WEBSTER.

Bard Wm., farmer
Baugh John A., farmer
Bertholf James, farmer
Baily Silas, farmer

Baugh Wm. C., farmer
Brockman F. A., farmer
Cunningham P. R., farmer
Davis Henry C., farmer

Drake A. D., farmer
Dickinson James A., farmer
Davis Otho, merchant and farmer
Darnell John S., farmer
Evans Asbery, carpenter
Earl Henry, farmer
Ettien John, farmer
Ellsbury Wm. N., farmer
Gentry John, farmer
Graham Able, doctor
Hopkins Wm., farmer
Hart Andrew M., farmer
Hart Miles, farmer
Hooten John W., preacher
Hooten Levi, farmer
Hoadly A. G., farmer
Howard Dexter, farmer
Hart George, farmer
Johnson John W., farmer
Johnson A. S., farmer
Johnson Robert, farmer
Johnson Benjamin, farmer
Knowles W. B., farmer
Louden Edward, farmer
Lewis John, farmer
Lewis Joseph, farmer
Lotson Silas farmer
Monismith Tobias, preacher
Myer Thomas, farmer
McAferty James, stock dealer

Moore James F., farmer
Newman P. S., farmer
Oak John A., farmer
Pope Stephen, farmer
Pope Stephen, C., farmer
Propst S. S., farmer
Richmond Wm. S., farmer
Richmond Charles, farmer
Richmond George R., farmer
Richmond John, farmer
Richmond Wm., farmer
Richmond David, farmer
Schnellbocher John, preacher
Schnellbocher Peter, farmer
Schnellbocher Lewis, farmer
Scott Orange J., farmer
Silverthorn Joseph T., farmer
Smith Orice H., farmer
Smith Hiram C., farmer
Stone Thomas A., farmer
Tomblinson Elisha, farmer
Willette Geo W., farmer
Walker F. M., farmer
Wight James E., farmer
Wight Geo., farmer
Wight Theodore, farmer
Wight James M., farmer
Winkly Luther L., farmer
Zeering Henry, merchant

LINCOLN.

Alexander Elijah, farmer
Adkinson Alexander, farmer
Arnold Josiah, farmer
Anderson O. C., farmer
BROCK JONAS S., farmer resides
on the s e qr. of sec. 6, t 77, r 28
Betts Joseph, farmer
Brinson John, farmer
Bertholf, W. H., farmer
Banty Edward, farmer
Brinson Zebulon, farmer
Brinson John J., farmer
Bertholf A. M., farmer
Bertholf George T., farmer
Bradfield A. sr., farmer
Bradfield A. jr., farmer
Brinson Wm., farmer
Bertholf Andrew H., farmer
Bertholf John M., farmer
Brock George L., farmer
Beerbower George A., farmer
Conard Timothy, farmer
Clark Caleb, stonemason
Clark Rufus, stonemason

Crable, Isaac, farmer
Culverson James, farmer
Culverson James P., farmer
Cameron Wm. B., farmer
Carmichel, Moses A., farmer
Clemons Willis, farmer
Cook John H., farmer
Clark William L., farmer
Culverson John, farmer
Duncan William, farmer
Duncan John M., farmer
Duncan Samuel, farmer
Darnell Gideon H., farmer
Davis John, farmer
Dickerson Matthew, farmer
Elliott Asa, farmer
Epperson William, farmer
Evans James W., farmer
Evans William H., farmer
Fink Canada, horticulturist
Fisher Lewis L., farmer
Freeborn R. N., farmer
Garl Daniel H., farmer
Goodwin E. A., farmer

Genty Joshua, farmer
Genty J. H., farmer
Goodin William, farmer
Gordon Samuel A., farmer
Greenwood John, farmer
Gowin John, farmer
Hooton John, farmer
HOGLE ISAAC N., residence on the n w qr. of sec. 10, t 77. r 28
Hartsock William, farmer
Hooton Martin G., farmer
Harrell L. W., farmer
Howe L. T., wool carder
Hoff David, farmer
Hanks M. V., farmer
Holgarth David, farmer
Harmon William H., farmer
Hartenberger Frank, shoemaker
Hart Ezra C., farmer
Houston Sherwood, **farmer**
Huss James, farmer
Harmon John H., farmer
Huff C. W., farmer
Harmon Linville, farmer
James Nathan, farmer
James John, farmer
Jones Joshua H., farmer
Johnson Alexander, farmer
Kinney Alexander, farmer
Keith Jacob H., farmer
Keith James T., farmer
Kirkland John, farmer
Kirkland Thomas, farmer
Longnecker I. S., farmer
Leinard Jacob, farmer
Longnecker David W., **farmer**
Loehr N. W., farmer
Lorimore B. F., farmer
Leonard William L., county treasurer
Lorimore A. W., wool grower
Long Volney J., farmer
Lake Annon, farmer
Lake Calvin, farmer
Laidly Charles H., farmer
Leinard John W., farmer
Ludlow William O., farmer
Lawson Murphy, farmer
Lutton William, farmer
McBride John, farmer
Moore Anderson, farmer
Moore John H., **farmer**
Maston William H., **farmer**
Moore Ephraim, farmer
Moore Thomas L., farmer
Murphy John H., farmer
McKibbin Joseph, farmer

McKibbon John, farmer
McKibbon Josiah, farmer
Martin David G., farmer
Marley A., farmer
Macumber Alexander, farmer
Murphy James H., farmer
Macumber Henry, farmer
Miller Wm., farmer
Mackey John, cabinet maker
Macumber John, farmer
Newland Nathan, farmer
Newton Harrison, farmer
Norris John, farmer
Pendleton Leonidas, farmer
Payton James L., farmer
Porter James, farmer
Perkins Elijah, farmer
Pefford James W., farmer
Polloch Geo. R., farmer
Price Caleb, farmer
Perkins Isaac, farmer
Rodgers Wm., farmer
Rodgers James, farmer
Rodgers John, farmer
Robb Anderson, farmer
Rodgers Elther, lime-burner
Robb E. C., farmer
Roy Thos., farmer
Runnels Wm., farmer
Rippey Joseph C., farmer
Ragan Benj. F., farmer
Ruby Isaac, farmer
Rhodes **James** M., **farmer**
Russell Alex., farmer
Strong T. W., carpenter
Stewart J. W., farmer
Smith S. C., farmer
Strong Jefferson, plasterer
Snow Alvin, farmer
Smoot J. W., farmer
Shearer John, farmer
Shearer Jeremiah, farmer
Shupe Levi, farmer
Shaw Martin, farmer
Salisbury Cyrus, farmer
Shaw Geo. M., wool carder
Snow Darius, farmer
Stewart W. A., farmer
Thorp Jesse, farmer
Titcomb Benj., farmer
Tusha Andrew, farmer
Thornburgh Wm, farmer
Tarbell Wm., farmer
Tarbell W. H., farmer
Tarbell Phillip, farmer
Wellman David W., farmer
Wright John, farmer

Wright Wm., farmer
Wilkins Wm. F., miller
Whitworth Thos., farmer

Whitworth Robert, farmer
Vermillion, R. D., farmer

SCOTT.

Allen W. B., farmer
Armstrong John, farmer
Allen David, farmer
Allen Obadiah, farmer
Allcock L. W., farmer
Allcock W. C., farmer
Allen Whitley, farmer
Allen Isaac, farmer
Armstrong James, farmer
Akelson Wm., farmer
Bartenholtz John, carpenter
Banks John, farmer
Black James F., farmer
Bell Richard, farmer
Benge Alfred, shoemaker
Benge Joshua, farmer
Beam R. M., engineer
Beam M. W., farmer
Blair J. T., farmer
Brown E. W., farmer
Bell John, farmer
Breeding J. E., farmer
Bishop Jonathan, farmer
Brown M., farmer
Bowlsby B. F., farmer
Bell Edward, farmer
Bowlsby J. F., farmer
Bardrick Wm., farmer
Bishop A. J., farmer
Bird Q. C., farmer
Black Nathaniel, farmer
Banks Josiah, farmer
Breeding J. A., farmer
Breeding G. W., farmer
Beam Wm., farmer
Crawford F. M., farmer
Crawford J. M., farmer
Compton Joseph, farmer
Compton Granville, farmer
Close George, farmer
Compton David, farmer
Close M. G., farmer
Close G. R., farmer
Couch J. H., sawyer
Curtis A. M., sawyer
Compton Wm., miller
Cunningham B., farmer
Cox Manuel, farmer
Carter B. F., farmer

Cox Theodore, farmer
Crawford John, farmer
Dorrell Lemuel, farmer
Dawson H. C. farmer
Dawson Martin, farmer
Dawson Wm., farmer
Dawson B. F., farmer
Dorrell Charles, farmer
Dillett John, miller
Daniel Daniel, sawyer
Duel B. F., writing teacher
Daniel W. R., farmer
Debusk James, carpenter
Dowler Joseph, farmer
Dryden John, farmer
Dorrell W. G., farmer
Evans Henry, farmer
Eskew Alexander, farmer
Eskew John, farmer
Ellis Cyrus, farmer
Fuqua Charles, farmer
Fuqua John, farmer
Farraba Charles, farmer
Fuqua John H., farmer
Freestone Marquis, farmer
Finnimore Wm., farmer
Fleener David, farmer
Griffith Isaac, farmer
Gray D. S., farmer
Gettys James, sawyer
Gratner Henry, farmer
Gifford Joseph, farmer
Herrall C. D., farmer
Herrall E. W., farmer
Hamner George, farmer
Hamner James, farmer
Hickard A. A., farmer
Hamner Valentine, farmer
Harris Enoch, carpenter
Herrall E. L., farmer
Harris James, farmer
Hamner Solomon, farmer
Hamner John E., farmer
Hayden Nathan, farmer
Hinkle John, farmer
Hines Milton, farmer
Hinkle Sylvester, farmer
Hiatt Elam, farmer
Hamler Samuel, farmer

16

Holmes J. S., farmer
Hircock Wm., farmer
Hiatt Jesse, farmer
Hamner John, farmer
Hamner Wm., farmer
Holliwell G. W., farmer
Hollingsworth N. B., farmer
Hoover Israel, farmer
Hogg, Wm., farmer
Heas George, farmer
Jones John T.,
James Josiah, farmer
James Benjamin, farmer
Jones John T., farmer
James Ira, farmer
Jones Jacob, farmer
Jones Wm., farmer
Jones Morris L., farmer
Jones Wm. H., farmer
James John, farmer
James G. W., farmer
James Annon, farmer
Johns James W., shoemaker
Ilor George, farmer
Imes Wm., farmer
Kellogg Miles, farmer
Kale James, farmer
Kirk J. B. farmer
King Wm. M., farmer
Kirk, Joshua, farmer
King N. M. Sr., farmer
King N. M. jr., farmer
Landis Isaac, farmer
Little Henry, farmer
Lamb J. B., miller
Landers William, farmer
Landers John, farmer
Landers Felix, farmer
Landers Hiram, farmer
Leddy William, farmer
Landers Joseph, farmer
Lynch Wm., farmer
Larimore James, farmer
Larimore B. F., wool grower
Larimore Wm., farmer
Lynch P. S., carpenter
Leddy Patrick, farmer
Lake B. F., farmer
Landis Allen, farmer
Moore, Martin
Moore P. C., farmer
Mashon James, preacher
McKinza Thos., farmer
McConnelly James, farmer
Madison Jeremiah, farmer
Morgan J. P., farmer
Moore John, farmer
McBeth David, farmer

McConnelly A. J., farmer
McClellan W. H., farmer
Madison, J. F., farmer
Mattox W. R., farmer
McConnelly David, farmer
McConnelly Wm., farmer
McConnelly Arch., farmer
Moore Jesse, farmer
McClellan Wm., farmer
Moore Benj., farmer
McClellan J. L., farmer
Morgan R. M., farmer
Noble Wm., farmer
Naylor J. C., teacher
Ogburn Hartwell, farmer
Ogburn Merritt, farmer
Ogburn Milton, farmer
Oglesbee J., farmer
Odell Solomon, farmer
Ogburn Wm., farmer
Philby Enoch, farmer
Persinger Wm., farmer
Philby J. J., farmer
Porter George W., farmer
Philby J. M., farmer
Penton J. H., farmer
Price John W., farmer
Peach M. W., farmer
Philby Enoch, farmer
Pettitt Melancton, farmer
Ross S. A., farmer
Ralston A. J., farmer
Ross Cunningham, farmer
Rotherford W. H., farmer
Rutherford Elijah, farmer
Reed Benj., farmer
Robinson Mitchel, farmer
Rutherford S. T., farmer
Ray Isaac, farmer
Ralston Porter, farmer
Reed S. S., farmer
Rodgers Lewis, farmer
Robinson D. E., farmer
Rodgers John, farmer
Reed Thos., farmer
Rudeman Theodore, farmer
Smith Josiah, farmer
Stephens W. C., farmer
Scott James, farmer
Stith J. F., farmer
Smith Harry, farmer
Short James, farmer
Silliman J. R., stock dealer
Seymour Thos., farmer
Stevens Sullivan
Stephens Thomas, farmer
Schonover Hiram, farmer
Treut J. A., farmer

Thacker Wm., farmer
Travis James, farmer
Travis N. E., farmer
Trent W., farmer
Thornburg Lemuel, farmer

Ward J. S., farmer
Ward E. S., farmer
Wright Skelton, farmer
Wilkinson A. W., surveyor
Wilkinson W. S., teacher.

SOUTH.

Allcock W. S., farmer
Archer Asa, farmer
Anderson T. T., saddler
Allender James, farmer
Allcock James farmer
Archer O. H., farmer
Anderson W. H., doctor
Black W., farmer
Barton W. F., farmer
Bogardus John, shoe maker
Beam M. S., farmer
Beam H. T., farmer
Bradshaw W., farmer
Blair James, farmer
Blair Elza, farmer
Blair John H., farmer
Browne J. H., merchant and farmer
Blair George P., farmer
Branfield J., farmer
Black Abram, farmer
Brown W. L., merchant
Black George, farmer
Bell James, farmer
Blair Wm. E., farmer
Barton Wm., landlord
Betts J. W., miller
Carrothers L. W., farmer
Carpenter Wm. farmer
Collins Isaac, farmer
Carpenter P. V., teacher
Close F. B., farmer
Clanton Joel, farmer
Clanton M. E., farmer
Carter Peter, farmer
Caskey George, farmer
Carter Solomon, farmer
Caskey John, farmer
Collins James, farmer
Clanton Wm., farmer
Collins Henry, farmer
Conard Jackson, farmer
Collins R. M., farmer
Carter J. M., farmer
Cumings C. P., farmer
Cregmiles A.,
Cason W. P., farmer
Chadd Daniel, farmer
Clanton C. F., farmer

Deakins R. T., farmer
Deakins J. W., farmer
Dawns David, farmer
Dewitt James P., farmer
Debord M. C., farmer
Ellege Wm., farmer
Ergenbought W. A., miller
Fife Samuel, farmer
Foster Abram, farmer
Foster A. C., farmer
Fife Amos, farmer
Fenton John, farmer
Farney L. J., doctor
Garman John M., farmer
Guernsey M. A., farmer
Guilliams Wm., farmer
Guilliams sr. Wm., farmer
Garvey Duncan, farmer
Gulliam A. C., farmer
Hartman Alfred, farmer
Hartman John, farmer
Hadden A., farmer
Hattel George, farmer
Hugart Y. A., farmer
Hattel Francis, farmer
Huglin Joachim, farmer
Hartman George, farmer
Huglin J. G., farmer
Huff T. F., carpenter
Imes Ephraim, farmer
Imes G. W., farmer
Imes William, farmer
Johnson Alexander, farmer
James Thos. C., farmer
Keys T. H., farmer
Kephart A., farmer
Kimmer Joseph, farmer
Lynch Martin, farmer
Lovelace Samuel, farmer
Lathran John, farmer
Likins W. R., farmer
Levrich John R., blacksmith
Long E. A., merchant
Lepman G., farmer
Lawrence Wm., farmer
Mills Eli, farmer
McCandless John, shoe-maker
McCandless H. L., farmer
Morgan N. B., farmer

Mills James, farmer
Montgomery Robert, farmer
Mark Wm., farmer
Morgan jr. D. P., farmer
Morgan sr. D. P., farmer
Miller A. C., farmer
Moffitt Joseph, farmer
Mark Jacob, farmer
McLaughlin H. A., farmer
McLain Wm., farmer
Muster D. P., farmer
Morgan Oliver, farmer
Moser O. A., co. recorder
McClure Wm., merchant and miller
Nichel James, farmer
Nichol R. C., wagon-maker
Keeney J. M., farmer
Oglesbee John, farmer
Osborn S., farmer
Parker Archibald, farmer
Phipps James, farmer
Philby Green, farmer
Peak John W., farmer
Peak Solomon, farmer
Pomeroy N. P., farmer
Persinger M. D., farmer
Porter John, farmer
Peck Jesse, farmer
Peck G. H., farmer
Quinn James H., farmer
Queen Wm., farmer
Queen Hogan, farmer
Roberts Wesley, farmer
Robinett J., blacksmith
Rollins Pleasant, farmer
Rollins Caleb, farmer
Runkle John, farmer
Runkle Thos., farmer
Roach J. P., preacher
Reid A. B., farmer
Reid James, farmer
Ralston D. W., farmer
Scott Wm., farmer
Sweeny G. W., engineer
Steel Benj., grocer

Scribner Joseph, blacksmith
Smith G. W., farmer
Sanders Alfred, farmer
Steel George, farmer
Shutt Harrison, farmer
Steel Stephen, farmer
Smith A. B., doctor
Sherfey Joseph, farmer
Stewart sr. John, farmer
Stewart jr. John, farmer
Stiles Thos., farmer
Sharman Wm. H., farmer
Stickler Daniel, farmer
Shannon Thos. R., farmer
Small W. Y., sawyer
Schnellbocher G. W., contractor
Shelleberger J. W., farmer
Shannon J. W., farmer
Shannon J. M., farmer
Scott A. O., farmer
Shaffer Daniel, farmer
Shaffer George, farmer
Shaffer Nicholas, farmer
Stewart J. C., farmer
Tisdale R. D., farmer
Truster Jacob, farmer
Taylor J. S., farmer
Thompson L. P., merchant
Trotter James A., farmer
Walter Jonathan, farmer
Wilcox John, farmer
Wilderson John H., farmer
Wilderson Charles, cabinet maker
Walkup John A., farmer
Wheat Jefferson, farmer
Walkup J. H., teacher
Windship Matthew, farmer
Wheeler A. M., farmer
Wilcox A., farmer
Walkup V. A., farmer
Vance David, farmer,
Viney R. G., farmer
Young Geo. M., farmer
Young Wm., farmer
Young R. W., farmer

MONROE.

Akin Lewis, stock-dealer
Alexander Hugh, farmer
Blythe Benjamin, farmer
Berlin Joseph, farmer
Boling Ed., farmer
Bivin B. L., farmer
Boling Samuel H., farmer
Bullock John D., farmer
Bullock M., farmer

Bowman W. N., farmer
Bancroft John, farmer
Bowman S. T., farmer
Berry J. B., farmer
Berry J. Y., farmer
Berry J. H., farmer
Berry Joel, farmer
Berry Benj. H., farmer
Berry W. H., farmer

Bertholf Jack, farmer
Brinson James, farmer
Boling Charles, farmer
Cornelison John, jr., farmer
Cornelison John, sr., farmer
Cornelison Marsh, farmer
Clark Nathaniel, farmer
Calaway Abraham, farmer
Cummings Thos., farmer
Cummings Wm., farmer
Denny Eli, farmer
Ellege Jesse, farmer
Ferguson, D. A., farmer
Foster J. C., farmer
Foster Moses, farmer
Green Israel, farmer
Harris Harbert H., farmer
Husky Jacob, farmer
Hamblin Simeon, farmer
Hartsock Adam, farmer
Hartsock Benj., farmer
Hewitt Robert, farmer
Hamblin Josephus, farmer
Hamblin Seth, farmer
Harn W. T., farmer
Harris L. H., farmer
Johnston C. W., farmer
Kilgore H. H., farmer

Kilgore B. F., farmer
Klingsmith Samuel, farmer
Linton Geo. T., farmer
Linton B. L., farmer
Low W. W., farmer
Lewis John, farmer
Long Henry, farmer
Moore Wm., farmer
McClure R. T., farmer
Palmer Charles, farmer
Porter Ransom, farmer
Quinn Peter, farmer
Reasoner John, farmer
Roon J. P., farmer
Roby David, farmer
Ray Joseph, farmer
Sheldon M. R., farmer
Shiply W. P., farmer
Shiply Alexander, farmer
Stone J. J., farmer
Thompson E. B., sr., farmer
Thompson E. B., jr., farmer
Thompson John, farmer
Wilson Wesley, farmer
Weeks G. W., farmer
West Wm. H., farmer
Weeks C. P., farmer

WALNUT.

Abernathy John, farmer
Abernathy Wm., farmer
Abernathy S., farmer
Ackelson Thos., farmer
Allen Levi, farmer
Baker John H., farmer
Bird Thos. M., farmer
Brown D. F., farmer
Baker Samuel, farmer
Brown Jacob, farmer
Bird S. S., farmer
Blanchard Stephen, farmer
Blanchard O., farmer
Blanchard John N., farmer
Bird Isaac, farmer
Bishop W. H., farmer
Brown John M., farmer
Brown B. F., farmer
Beeler Fred., farmer
Calham S. J., farmer
Compton Abraham, farmer
Cornelison Wm., farmer
Cornelison A. J., farmer
Creger John H., preacher
Collis W. H. H., farmer
Drake Thos. R., farmer
Davis Wm. H., farmer

Duane Abram, farmer
Drake Daniel D. farmer
Delaplane Owen, farmer
Darnall C. C., farmer
Emerson James, farmer
Fivecoat Geo. W., farmer
Foster Thos. D., farmer
Foster N., farmer
Fivecoat Wm., farmer
Foresman James, farmer
Gilliam Richard, farmer
Gregory J. W., farmer
Gilbert R. H., farmer
Guthrie Wm. J., farmer
Gibbons J. W., farmer
Griffith Daniel, farmer
Guthrie John W. farmer
Guilliam Robt. J., farmer
Garrett Walter B., farmer
Gifford Benj., farmer
Hughes John R., farmer
Hogg John, farmer
Holeman Wm., farmer
Hiatt Aaron, farmer
Hann Hugh, farmer
Hillman John D., farmer
Holliwell David, farmer

Holeman Geo. W., farmer
Hughes Ellis, farmer
Hughes John R., farmer
Hindman Geo. W., farmer
Harper W., farmer
Hogg Geo. W., farmer
Hollingshead Henry, farmer
Hindman James, farmer
Hamilton J. C. W., farmer
Imes Jesse, farmer
Imes Michael, farmer,
Imes Geo. W., farmer
Jones E. B., farmer
Jones Geo. M., farmer
Kirk Daniel B., farmer
Kirk John, farmer
Kale Reuben, farmer
Kesler Stephen, farmer
Lake Ashford, farmer
Long A. L., farmer
Longshore Smith, farmer
Lake Johnson, farmer
Landis Saml. S., farmer
Lovelace Hiram, farmer
Landis Wm. T., farmer
Leasman Henry, farmer
Mayhew John, farmer
Marshal John, farmer
McLaughlin Wm. D., farmer
Moffitt Hiram, farmer
Marler Joseph A., farmer
McLeary W. S., farmer
Moak John, farmer
McClintick John, farmer
Moffitt Jacob, farmer
Means Lewis, farmer
McClure Allen, farmer
Mullen John, farmer
McCants Wm., farmer
Osborn James S., farmer
Osborn G. M., farmer
Osborn Judd, farmer

Power A. A., farmer
Pritchard Henry, farmer
Philpot B. F., farmer
Porter Isaac, farmer,
Porter John T., farmer
Porter James, farmer
Painton John T., farmer
Pierce Quinby, farmer
Rankin T. N., farmer
Rager Isaac, farmer
Rhyno Wm., farmer
Sawhill Alex., farmer
Smith J. J., farmer
Smith F. M., farmer
Smith I. N., farmer
Simpson Benj., farmer
Smith O. F., farmer
Smith Elijah T., farmer
Smith John T., farmer
Smith James W., farmer
Smith J. J., farmer
Smith Wm. farmer
Shoemaker Wm., farmer
Spurgeon Philip, farmer
Shipley John, farmer
Scott John, farmer
Simmons A. R., farmer
Spurgeon Wm., sawyer
Travis H. S., farmer
Travis M. B., blacksmith
Travis Sylvester, farmer
Trister James M., farmer
Thompson Geo. W., farmer
Vest H. S., farmer
Walker John G., farmer
Wilson H., farmer
Walker Saml. M., farmer
Weaver Ephraim, farmer
Wilson Joseph, farmer
Wright H. C., merchant
Young Lemuel R., farmer
Young Hamilton R., farmer

OHIO.

Arnold Eli, farmer
Anderson Wm., farmer
Arnold, Jacob, farmer
Brisben J. D., farmer
Bradshaw David, farmer
Bishop Noah, farmer
Bradshaw E., farmer
Bradshaw D. F., farmer
Bradshaw J. W., farmer
Borney Moses, farmer
Bithman Charles, farmer
Carver Caleb, farmer
Conn Simon, farmer

Clear Peter, farmer
Creger J. H., preacher
Creger Moffitt, farmer
Clifton Sylvester, farmer
Collins Elijah, farmer
Creger R. A., farmer
Clark James, farmer
Camfield M., farmer
Creger Samuel, farmer
Clavinger L. C., farmer
Clavinger G. W., farmer
Cooley F. J., farmer
Deardoff Wm., farmer

Dick John, farmer
Douglas James, farmer
Delong Fenton, farmer
Delong Ephraim, farmer
Deardoff Jacob, farmer
Deardoff Pleasant, farmer
Deardoff John, farmer
Davis Joseph, farmer
Delong Jessee, farmer
Ellis Calvin, farmer
Eyre Robert, farmer
Foresman G. W., farmer
Foster Thomas, farmer
Foresman Jacob, farmer
Foster R. J., farmer
Fleck J. P., farmer
Foresman George,
Farson J. H.. farmer
Fleck Nicholas, farmer
Fulton, Wm., farmer
Foresman J. H., farmer
Farson J. H., farmer
Gray J. S., farmer
Gearhart A., farmer
Garst Phillip, farmer
Garst Samuel, farmer
Gracy J. S., farmer
Gracy W. J., farmer
Gaust John, farmer
Hull John, farmer
Howlett J. D., farmer
Hart C., farmer
Hubbard Martin, farmer
Husted Thomas, farmer
Handy Henry, farmer
Huffman Thos., farmer
Holmes Isaac, farmer
Hartman J. D., farmer
Hoggett N. H., farmer
Hiatt E., farmer
Hogg Jackson, farmer
Holmes Wm., farmer
Hiatt Elam, farmer
Holmes A., farmer
Hecock, Samuel, farmer
Howlett, J. D., farmer
Jackson P., farmer

Kesler Elias, farmer
Long Solomon, farmer
Landis Peter, farmer
Landis J. C., farmer
Low Jonathan, farmer
Miller Van, farmer
McGuire Joseph, farmer
Moarman Brooks, farmer
Merchant A., farmer
McNeely Wm., farmer
McNeely James, farmer
Middleton James, farmer
McPherson J., farmer
Moffatt Thos., farmer
McGuire J. S., farmer
McNeely S. J., farmer
Phipps Thos., farmer
Phipps Jackson, farmer
Parker Ira, farmer
Peters Samuel, farmer
Renfro R., farmer
Reed Evans, farmer
Reager J., farmer
Risen Wm., farmer
Regle Henry, farmer
Roby Jonathan, farmer
Smith Thos. sr., farmer
Smith J. P. jr., farmer
Smith George, farmer
Shipley Abe, farmer
Simmerman David, farmer
Simmons John, farmer
Simmons Jonathan, farmer
Spence A. S., farmer
Shippy Robert, farmer
Shippy E. G., farmer
Sutton Ezra, farmer
Shutt F., farmer
Snider John, farmer
Stewart J. C., farmer
Sidenor J. E., farmer
White J. D., farmer
Wright W. W., farmer
Walker Thos., farmer
Young U., farmer
Young J. J., farmer

GRAND RIVER.

Arsmith A. W.,
Bonham David, farmer
Barker J. C., farmer
Barker O. W., farmer
Barker T. C., carpenter
Bice Josiah, farmer
Buchanan Jacob, farmer
Bonham A., farmer

Barker W. B., farmer
Badly H. H., preacher
Ballard S. T., farmer
Clark James C., farmer
Clark D. R., farmer
Craven J. D., farmer
Crawford F. A., farmer
Conway B. N., farmer

Cochran Wesley, farmer
Cochran John, farmer
Doty Samuel, farmer
Ellege James S., preacher
Granfield John C., farmer
Griswold Alvin, farmer
Gates A. L., farmer
Gilbert Elias, farmer
Gilbert Charles, farmer
Greer J. J., farmer
Griswold Martin, farmer
Griswold Richard T., farmer
Hartsock E., farmer
Hamlin John, farmer
Hillsberry John, farmer
Hillsberry Martin, farmer
Hasty A. J., farmer
Imes Laban, farmer
Imes Hugh, farmer
Imes Wm. C., farmer
Johnson H. F., farmer
Johnson J. F., farmer
Jessup Lewis, farmer
Jessup Martin, farmer
Johnson W. B., farmer
Knox Milton, farmer
Kivett Wm. M., farmer
Kerry Joseph, farmer
Long Joseph, farmer
Lowry G. W., farmer
Loomis A. H., farmer
Lane R. C., farmer
Lane John D., farmer

Lee Wm. O., farmer
McBee James, farmer
Martin A. C., farmer
Moon Ransom, farmer
Means Lewis F., farmer
Mobly Willis, farmer
Marley J. H., farmer
Mack J. H., doctor
Mobly Wm., farmer
Mobly Andrew, farmer
Pierce W. W., farmer
Pierce Hiram, farmer
Pierce E. J., farmer
Pierson J. M., farmer
Pierson T. J., farmer
Pierce J. C., farmer
Pierson J. B., farmer
Rawlings J. R., farmer
Rowe Martin, farmer
Robinson Sidney, farmer
Shearer Peter, farmer
Smith Lewis, farmer
Still Gabriel, farmer
Shoemaker W. W., farmer
Stewart E. C., farmer
Shoemaker F. M., farmer
Shultz Andrew, farmer
Shoemaker Wm., farmer
Satchel James W., farmer
Thomas John, farmer
Underwood Joseph, farmer
Wright Wm. C., farmer

INDEX.